HE GETS SOME RESPECT!

I stood and limped toward the after lounge. As I lifted a swollen ankle over the doorsill—

"Hail, O Mighty Gruenblum, puissant and indestructible!"

"Errrk!" My right hand clawed convulsively for a weapon.

"O Lord," there came an exceedingly reverent squeak, "Who endureth through great travail, wilt Thou guide Thy humble servants even as Thou did in days of yore?" The aliens had gathered in the after lounge. The talkative one swiveled an eyestalk at its companions: "Rejoice, ye people, for our Creator awaketh at last!"

"O Magnificence"—a second Yamaguchian rolled forward—"deignest Thou to speak unto Thy worshippers, revealing now Thy Holy purpose and design?"

"You guys seen anything of Cromney and his gang?"

"Lord, Thy servants hath immured the Evil Ones, with the victims of their late foul butchery, in the chambers beneath. Have we acted rightly?"

All three looked up at me with anxiety-filled optics.

What was I gonna say?...

THE NAGASAKI VECTOR

L. NEIL SMITH

A Del Rey Book

BALLANTINE BOOKS • NEW YORK

FOR ROGER OWEN
a bridge over troubled waters

Students of the history of the North American Confederacy may be interested to learn that the saddle-horn Telecoms encountered by Bernie Gruenblum were invented by that same admiral who figured so significantly in the overwhelming victory of Confederate naval forces at the Battle of the Bering Strait during the War Against the Czar (A.L. 180–184).

CONTENTS

The Temporal
Authorities

WE WERE IN OUR PRIVATE SUNLIT GROVE OF TREES
at the edge of endless meadows, the breezes fresh as they
stirred the knee-high grasses around us. We stood beneath
a spreading, ancient oak, my beloved and I, a songbird
warbling in the leafy branches overhead. She leaned against
the age-roughened bark, her warm, smooth hands in mine.
I gazed deeply into her—

The girl of my dreams *doesn't* have six hundred and
fifty-three pistachio-colored tentacles. *Nor* a ropy orange
neck slithering up to a single, glittering, faceted eye. And
I can tell you, right here and now, she *ain't* got a body like
a fluorescent-pink Army helmet.

So what in Contradiction was this Sterno-drinker's nightmare doing perched in the middle of my solar plexus, in-
terrupting a promisingly-prurient transmission from my
subconscious? I reached up and jerked off the DreamCap,
letting it dangle by the cable overhead, and remembered: it
was my turn to be God this week.

The alien shifted several dozen of its little legs politely
and tried peering into both of my perfectly ordinary optics
at the same time. Gimme a pain in the bridge of my nose.

"These printouts, Captain—" I *jumped* at the unexpected
voice whining through the bulkhead door behind me.
"—where should I put them?" Rand Heplar, the new Ap-
prentice/Observer the Powers-That-Be had saddled me with,
lugged a two-foot stack of computer-excretions, weighing
them down with his chin, onto the flight deck. Heplar was

a greasy little specimen, the sort you always suspected of having a secret collection of wingless flies in a bottle somewhere. Guess I'd told him sixty or a hundred times *never* to call me Captain.

I slid a dark-green uniform cuff back from my hairy wrist:

+ 15.9277	+ 22.8539
OCT 05	MAY 23
1630:42.9	0802:13.1

Display on the right face showed the century, month, and GMT back home—Ochskahrt Memorial Academy, Tsiolkovsky, Luna. Left side gave the date and local time. The watch? A graduation present. Finished sixteenth in a crowd of six-thousand-odd, *including* Spacers—the ones who *like* being called Captain—with their regulation-issue noblycleft chins and pansy powder-blue jumpsuits.

Fumbling in my coverall for a stogie, I happily contemplated telling the idiot *precisely* where he could put all that red tape, but settled on spurious civility to keep him off balance. "Dump 'em in the 'cycler, kid. I dunno why y'ran 'em off in the first place. *Georgie* memorizes everything important that comes in." The turtle-shaped alien shifted again, craning its leathery periscope at my nose. *"An' get this teratoid tortoise offa my torso!"*

Heplar gave a self-righteous gasp. "Why, *Captain!* You mustn't talk about the Yamaguchian Ambassador that way, and right in front of him, too!" He made little scandalized bustling noises as he fed the useless printouts into the recycler. Next time we saw 'em, they'd probably be tortilla chips.

"Tell y'what," I grunted. *"Show* me this overgrown barnacle's front, an' I'll stop talkin' about him at all!" Avoiding contact with his numberless miniature appendages, I lifted the Ambassador by the edges of his shell, swung off my pilot's recliner, set him gently on the deck—gentler than I felt, anyway—and lit my cigar, filling the cabin with aromatic blue-gray smoke.

"Him" and "his" were just a guess, anyway. Three of these . . . *things* underfoot aboard my ship, just perfect for tripping over when you were feeling too sure of yourself, and frigging lucky it wasn't the full complement of seventeen my bosses'd *wanted* to send along.

One of each sex, believe it or not.

"How about it, Your Ambassadorship? You give a fast flying fardle how I talk about you?" Not a centimeter over fifteen inches tall, it lifted an adoring eyeball toward me, emitting an ecstatic squeal, exactly like a kid's balloon when you stretch the nozzle and let the air shrill out. "Just what I need," I confided under my breath to its glittering optic. "A nervous, creepy assistant, three alien kid-glove VIPs, and a handful of greenhorn passengers down Earthside stumbling through an EVA that seven different risk-computers regarded as 'marginally lethal'!"

Heplar sniffed, a quizzical expression on his semipsychotic mug. "Did you say something, Captain?" He turned, eyeballed my *El Ropo* in full smolder, grimaced, and went back to work manufacturing confetti.

"Nothin', Igor, only talkin' to myself."

Talking to myself. Swell: a twenty-third century Norman Bates shuffling around behind me wearing the same Temporal Green livery which graced my own wiry frame; a trio of psychedelic pasties for the Gorgon Medusa who'd decided *I* was their Deity; and a flock of bulgy-domed academics whose only link to my vessel up here—and home—was the telemetric toilet paper I had Heplar paying back into the recyclers. Enough to give me gray hair, if I hadn't lost most of it already to this much-overrated profession. Why me? Why was it always——

Me? I'm Bernie . . . okay, make it *Captain* Bernard M. Gruenblum, ODF(T)532779-687659921-A, late of the Academy's Temporal Division, and master (putatively speaking) of *789 George Herbert*.

In short, a bus driver—if you happen to consider a time machine a bus.

That's how *Georgie* and I happened to be here at the moment, hovering invisibly, 30,000 feet above the site of

Hideyoshi's Tokyo in ancient Nippon of the 1590s A.D., waiting to pick up our paying customers.

Bright idea'd been to ferry out this load of eggheads—representing institutes of higher sinecure all over our beloved Solar Dominion—to find out just what made medieval Japanese society go back *en masse* to sharp, pointy, sweat-powered weapons and "give up the gun."

Lotta birdbrains *still* think it was some kinda Noble Experiment.

Rats, I coulda told 'em: ever see what newly-firearmed peasants do to the expensively-armored aristocrats whose ancestors have been "protecting" them out of everything they've got for centuries? Japan's Nobunaga gang, here, was merely quicker on the uptake (an' a *whole* lot fast-and-fancier-talking) than the feudal Tammany of Europe. Shucks, there ain't a political situation *anywhen* that couldn't be improved with a couple million Saturday Night Specials. Naturally, the self-appointed bigwigs *always* have a vested interest in a Sullivan Act of some kind.

But no one ever asks the bus-driver, me, who's seen more fresh history being made, carmine-hued and smoky in the morning chill, than anybody else. Instead, they send these pointy-heads out—all classroom theory and no pragmatics—after training 'em for months to look, act, talk, and *think* whatever way the locals do it. Speak the language, eat the food, pick your nose with the socially correct finger.

Some of this makes sense. We can't afford taking chances in this racket, for some pretty good reasons:

First, the past may be Prologue to you, but to us, it's *plastic*. One misplaced pebble on the Road to Mandalay, and the future we go back to *might* not be the present we took off from. No idea how much of a change it'd take, and we *never* wanna find out. Solipsistic suicide: everything gone up there but me and thee—an' *I* wouldn't care to be *thy* insurance agent.

Naturally, the Academy takes precautions. There's a pair of stationary time-field generators buried under Tsiolkovsky, concentricked one around the other, forming a sort of *reality-lock*. Inside, the great-granddaddy of all databanks contains every historical fact they can punch into a memory chip. Outside, an identical set-up constantly checks itself against the first, ensuring personkind's past—and the Academy's *present*—stays *put*.

Every now and again, one of my sloppier colleagues flubs it, generally by letting the yokels way-back-when glom an eyeful of his timebuggy. Easy to let happen: *Georgie*'s a ninety-foot discoid packing enough spare horsepower to make planetoids outa planets. Even with half her output diverted into protective fields, she'll leave big purple blotches on your retinas when she's wound up for a century-sized jump.

Some eras see our little mistakes as Holy Manifestations, others just as UFOs. On account of that *and* the color of our uniforms, those finger-waved cretins in SpaceDiv sneeringly call us "Little Green Men." In either case, such apparitions tend to get talked about—whole careers have been devoted to writing them up—and this alters what was "really" supposed to happen. The reality-inspectors under Tsiolkovsky notice things like that, and the Academy sees it as a General Court-Martial, usually meriting a pilgrimage by Shank's mare to the base of Spectacular Ochskahrt Memorial Pylon, over two miles tall, with a brightly-glowing beacon visible from the Asteroids on a clear night.

And out there, it's *always* a clear night.

It's merely a fifty-kilometer hike, a piece of cake in Luna's one-sixth gee. Trouble is, it's straight across the bottom of Spectacular Ochskahrt Memorial Crater. That's where Herr Professor Hirnschlag von Ochskahrt made his Great Discovery (time-travel and a faster-than light drive) and his Big Blooper, back in A.D. 2007. We still haven't figured out where he went wrong, but the crater's a couple thousand meters deep and so radioactive that the Asteroiders can damn near see *it* glowing, too. By the time the court-martialed victim makes it to the Pylon, his prognosis ain't so hot, but everything else is.

There followeth a decent lead-lined burial; the Academy humanely leaves *this* shit-detail to gorillas and chimpanzees with electronic control implants, elderly ones who've outlived their usefulness as janitors, factory assemblers—we even employ *genuine* grease-monkeys. Then the computers get cranked up to assess the risks of *un*doing whatever caused all the hoorah, and a flunky (yours truly, f'rinstance) gets sent back to counterbalance the original error. Sometimes it's pretty lame and off-the-cuff—like the twenty-three inconvenient witnesses in Dallas one November I recall or the phony government commission we set up to declare that flying saucers are "swamp gas"—the stories I could tell.

But mostly I just drive the bus, chauffering ivory-tower types: geologists, paleontologists, archaeologists, pret'near every kinda -ologist you can shake a stick at, not one with half the practical education I got in my left pinky.

Ignoring Heplar's scowl of disapproval, I stretched across the cabin toward the custom walltap I'd installed myself, pouring my first beer of the afternoon. A green light chose that instant to start winking, accompanied by an irritating *bleep-bleep-bleep*—clowns who design things like that oughta have to listen to 'em. 1645:00.0—'least this load of tenderfeet was punctual.

"There's Recall, kid. Mind y'strap down anything loose." I flopped the beer onto the console—it sloshed and gurgled invitingly at me—took a final nicotinic drag, and limbered up my button-pushing fingers like a pinball virtuoso going for another free game.

"Very well, Captain." Somehow the punk managed a sneer and a snivel at the same time. "Anything else, Captain?"

"Yeah, see to the Ambassador an' his fellow whatcha-macallits . . . and Heplar?"

He looked up from collecting aliens, eyebrows doing a little dance in and out of his hairline at the unaccustomed sweetness of my tone. "Yes, Captain?"

"DON'T CALL ME CAPTAIN!" I keyed the sequence; wasn't all that much to it, just a reminder to *Georgie* that I wanted her to follow a string of prepunched instructions. We vanished from our present location with a little blue

pop! while I dedicated all my professional expertise to sifting us gently back into existence 30,000 feet lower—decorative grove of trees just outside the city—practically phasing us in a single molecule at a time. Show me any Spacer who could accomplish *that* by the seat of his fancy azure ascot!

Gear down, *Georgie* ran out the boarding ladder. Didn't personally plan leaving the control deck this time, but from sheer reflexive precaution, I patted my left armpit, making sure that, underneath the overall, the hammer was locked back on my antique Gold Cup .45. The one the Academy and I pretend they don't know about. Hell, they understand: I won't mess history up 'less it tries messin' me up first. The pistol's a tad more'n four centuries obsolete, but unlike a laser or even its contemporary .357 Magnum, it'll stop a man dead without necessarily killing him—and make a sabertooth kitty *real* sick.

The big wraparound viewscreens were full of autumn leaves. Bet that clearing hadn't twenty centimeters more diameter than *Georgie* herself. Grass, late-blooming flowers, tiny skittering things in the branches. Lotsa birds. "Welcome our sightseers in, kid."

Heplar unstrapped himself, stepped over a Yamaguchian or two, and left the cabin with another "Very well, Captain" I coulda cheerfully strangled him for. Instead, I kept my eyes glued to the board, fingers hovering over the Emergency Drive button, just in case. It's a brutally simple mechanism, won't take you anywhen back or forth in time, just three or four hundred klicks away, in any old direction, *fast*.

Found my cigar in the ashtray and relit it, drawing smoke. Hafta think about transferring Heplar, this relationship of ours just wasn't working out. My other hand had started setting up a course for home: upward in space, forward in history, all in one clean four-dimensional curve, to where the Ochskahrt Memorial man-in-the-moon's supposed to show up, 'long about May of 2285. Took some concentration.

A belowdecks monitor in the vicinity of my left elbow gave me a view from back of the boarding hatch downstairs.

I could see the nape of Heplar's vulture neck as he waited for our EVA party. Seconds later, he was joined by Professors Merwin and Hulbert, two old ducks in yellow academic union-suits I'd plumb near forgotten about. Though too elderly for field work, they weren't aboard 'cause they were useless. Either one of 'em could flick the back edge of a samurai sword with his fingernail, listen to it ring, and tell you how many laminations in the blade. Ancient weapons experts—(however you wanna interpret that)—from the Academy's own museum.

Never quite figured out who was Merwin and who was Hulbert.

Naturally, the first one through the pressure-gasketing was Dr. Edna Janof, an extremely tempting little confection, very shapely, the effect spoiled by an oddly cruel expression which flickered across her otherwise kissable features whenever she didn't think she was being watched—kinda careless for an anthropologist. She shucked off her local disguise, as Heplar and the two professors jostled each other to hand her in, and turned to impress some vital philosophical observation upon her current flame, Dr. Denny Kent, a tall, postboyish sorta gink, neatly and semipermanently wrapped around Edna's long-nailed little finger.

Kent was in the econometrics biz, a MarxoFriedmanite Neo-Revisionist of the Old School, he'd informed me earlier as we were getting more acquainted than I'd wanted to. A little paunchy around his center of gravity, always grinning like he expected the girls t'swoon at the glimmer of his bicuspids blowin' in the breeze. None of 'em had for some while, but he was too good a sport to notice. A ne'er-do-well gone to seed, with a face like an overcooked pot roast.

Anyone for tennis?

Janof and Kent were followed by the Boffin-in-Charge, Dr. Ab Cromney (more Ph.D.s around here lately than a compost-heap), inches taller than Kent, but spindly and sparrow-chested, with a hank of hair like a shaving-brush, distinguished gray, but all of it straight up like he was taking high voltage. Political science, to abuse the latter word, was his game, but he had an annoying habit—abetted by Edna and Denny, who seemed to hang on his every phoneme—of making serious pronouncements obviously well outside his field of expertise.

Cromney'd initiated this oriental outing; applying through official channels it takes months—even years, sometimes—to navigate. Temporal, after all, makes up only the thinnest slice of the Ochskahrt Academy's Memorial interests. Most roads—and appropriations, it seems—lead to SpaceDiv and the Glorious Frontier they're out there ruining. Neglected as we are, our little green calendar gets pretty damned crowded.

But there's a lot more to it: each mission proposal burns up zillions of silicon-hours just making sure in advance that nobody jerks history out from under us like a cheap hallway carpet.

This time, however, the Academy shocked everybody by expediting Cromney's crackpot proposal in a scant five weeks, bumping worthier applicants and upsetting scheduling for years to come. I'd learned that Cromney took this as some kind of sign, but I knew the truth.

It was all for Little Old Me—or rather for my faithful worshippers, the Yamaguchians. Cromney and his people didn't figure in it at all.

One by one they divested themselves of pseudo-Nipponese habiliment, trotting off down the companionway and out of camera range. Professors Merwin and Hulbert were beside themselves (and each other) gathering up all the factory-fresh antique weaponry their colleagues had collected for them. Pushing half a ton of high-grade steel and low-grade technology on an antigravitic handcart, they made themselves scarce in the direction of the messroom. Heplar, being a good boy, dogged down the door when he and his little playmates were through with it; his mother woulda been proud of him.

Back upstairs where I keep the steering wheel, the Ambassador or one of his facsimiles, was making more nuisance of himself than usual, figure-eighting in and out between my feet like a housecat, as I continued with my temporagational arithmetic. He gave out high-pitched bleating noises at the upper limit of my hearing and temperament, swiveling his eyestalk around and around like a lawn sprinkler.

He stopped abruptly in his multilegged tracks, and I followed his stare to the after bulkhead where another of his kind was mountaineering clumsily over the doorsill. They met in the center of the cabin between a pair of jumpseats, skiddling into each other like a pair of friendly miniature Sherman tanks.

More rubbernecking and squealing. Thought I was gonna witness some impromptu alien illicitude—not that I'm interested in that sort of thing—but I had work to do. Instead, I turned back to the console, dialing another sack of beer to replace the one that'd gotten warm, and peered into the plotting tank, punching knobs and twisting buttons.

This business of finding the one-and-only correct line across *both* time and space can be tricky as all get-out.

I felt a tug: down between my Academy-green pantlegs, where they hang out over my old-fashioned lace-up parachute boots, were not just one, not merely two, but all *three* aliens, doing the Sonja Henie bit in and around my feet. I scored them a well-deserved 8.3 and generously resisted the urge to add a steel-lined toe-tip for artistic endeavor. "What's got into you little buggers, anyway?"

Another noise behind me, a scuff and shuffle of human feet. Keeping both eyes on the engine-status indicators as they hotted up, I reached for my beer-baggie. "Well, kid, our passengers all tucked away nice an' neat?"

A yellow light flickered on the board; the Yamaguchians seemed to be going crazy; I nudged a vernier microscopically, bringing *Georgie*'s highly-critical field-densities back into alignment, talking over my shoulder. "Take a gander at our VIPs here, kid. Don'tcha think they're acting kinda—"

WHAAAACK!!!

They're right, y'know, about seeing stars. Whatever it was collided with the side of my head just then, it started little teensy supernovas flashing on and off behind my eyes. And I couldn't find the right knob to adjust 'em.

It wasn't that I minded so much, but the pain. And I remember thinking: I'm never gonna get a beer this afternoon, am I?

Grounds for
Complaint

"GRUENBLUM, THIS COULD BE YOUR MOST IMPORTANT Mission Ever!" His fat face swam in and out of focus, changing colors every now and again.

Funny, I didn't remember it doing that the first time I'd had this conversation.

I did remember how much I'd always hated being addressed by my "naked patronymic"—almost as much as being called "Captain"—and the situation wasn't much improved by the fact that this hypercaloric moron was sullying his own name whenever he sullied mine.

Just to prove he knew what he was doing—and was doing it on purpose—he turned chartreuse, and posies blossomed from his ears.

Green-bloom, get it?

Things steadied down a little.

I'd thought about flicking half an inch of cheap cigar ash on his hand-imported carpet just to give him an idea of what was really what and who was really who. Unfortunately, I wasn't too sure about that myself, right now, "Cuthbert, I hate to spoil your fun just when you're getting warmed up, but this 'Most Important Mission' batbarf—that's what you *always* tell me!"

"Batbarf?" He blinked stupidly, then made an effort to regain his sense of inflated self-importance. "I'll trouble you to remember that it's *Colonel*, Gruenblum!"

"No, it's *Captain* Gruenblum, Cuthbert, and I oughta

know—I'm him. I mean, he. Least I was last time I looked
at the labels in my underwear."

I love to see a stuffed shirt splutter incoherently, especially when I'm the cause of it.

"Look, Cuthbert, do us both a favor and cut the crap.
I'm overdue for a date with this redhead over in Vonbraunsville, see? An' she's got the most terrific set of..."
I raised both hands by way of illustration. My cigar ash
was at least three-quarters of an inch long by now and none
too firmly attached. I looked around for an ashtray.

"Grandfather, will you *please* stick to the subject at hand?
This could be... well, it really *could* be your Most Important—"

I glared at him, and he shut up—a modest talent I cul-
tivate, which has its uses on occasion. More than anything
else, more than "Gruenblum," even more than "Captain,"
I *loathe* being called "Grandfather."

But, I sighed inwardly, it was true enough: this pompous,
cetacean-sized subsimian parked on the fifty yard line of
the desk in front of me—come on, *spit* it out, Bernie!—
was my very own darling grandson. One of them, anyway;
it's a cast of thousands.

What made it downright unconscionable was that Cuthbert was also my immediate superior: Lieutenant Colonel
Cuthbert M. Gruenblum, AdminTempDiv, OchsMemAcad,
SPCA, SPQR, and LS/MFT. Had the little family beauty-
spot on his blubbery jaw, and everything.

Shoulda had one of those vasectomies back when they
were offering two for the price of one.

Now he sat there, feeling hurt and pouting, something
he'd practiced faithfully since he was three but which looked
silly as a propeller beanie on a Lieutenant Colonel.

"Okay, Cuthbert, didn't mean to piss in your little red
wagon. Give it to me straight: *where* you gonna send me
this time, an' *what* am I supposed to do when I get there.

Low gravity's too good for some folks; seems to en-
courage subcutaneous superfluity. He rose from behind that
pretentious block of mahogany like the B. F. Goodrich blimp,

ran the back of a flabby hand under several of his chins,
and tried to pace back and forth. Doesn't work too well in
one-sixth gee, lacks dignity somehow, and the sound of
velcro shoesoles on the carpet gets on your nerves.

Rip, rip, rip!

"Well, you see, Grandfath—Cap—Gruen—"

Rip, RIP, rip, rip!

"Siddown, for Ochskahrt's sake, Cuthbert! An' try 'Bernie,' since you seem t'be havin' identity problems this morning."

I took another drag off my cigar and this time let the ash
fall—entirely accidentally, of course. There was a sudden
glitter at the baseboard; a tiny, rodent-shaped bundle of
chromium-plated machinery bulleted across the floor,
scooped up my oxidized detritus, chittered at me reprov-
ingly, and vanished into the wall again.

This seemed to throw poor Cuthbert off somehow. He
gazed at the bald, bespectacled portrait of Ochskahrt on the
wall behind his desk in prayerful appeal. "Where was I?
Oh, yes—it isn't so much the *particular* mission, cr, Bernie . . ."

Rip, rip, rip.

". . . it might have been almost any old mission at all . . ."

Rip, rip, rip, rip.

Was he *ever* gonna sit down again?

". . . so long as *you* are the pilot!"

He smiled brightly at this and plunked his behind into
the office-swiveler. Never felt so grateful for anything in
my life. Well, *practically* anything.

"How'd I get so lucky, Cuthbert?"

Curious now, I let a few more ashes dribble floorward,
they drifted slowly under the mild acceleration, and before
they lighted on the carpet, the electronic mouse was there
again, waiting for them.

"And *why* am I so lucky all of a sudden?"

"Because you're going to have some *company* on this
trip, Bernie. Besides your new A/O and whatever scientific
personnel it happens to involve, I mean." He gave me a

leer like an IRS agent writing up a seizure order for Tiny Tim's crutches on Christmas Eve. "You see, the Yamaguchian Legation, here in—"

"*Entropy and eggrolls!* Pylon take you, Cuthbert, I won't have *any* of those dagblasted little . . . just because I once . . . and anyway, it *isn't* 'Yamaguchian.' How many times do I have to *tell* you people, that's just some Earthie astronomer's monicker for their late, *un*lamented former star-system? If anything, they're Ganymedeans now, and . . ."

For the first time, almost in centuries, I couldn't think of anything else to say.

But I was thinking harder and faster than I'd ever done in my life.

All right, you can read the *official* report somewhere else if you're that type. And there's a popularized version circulating Earthside I don't even wanna *think* about.

But the plain and disgustingly simple truth is that the Yamaguchii or the Ganymedii—the "Freenies," actually—whatever you wanna call 'em, every single last one of the little misbegotten sons, daughters, and fifteen other what-have-yous-of-bitches . . . thinks *I'm* his God.

It all started innocently enough. But any mission which requires cooperating with the Spacers . . . well, I'd as lief spend a dirty weekend in Long Beach with a Marxo-Friedmanite Neo-Revisionist of the Old School.

Seems there was this splendidly normal main-sequence star, Yamaguchi 523 by the catalog, that suddenly went *kablomm!* one day. Only, by the time the news reached Luna, it'd happened several thousand years ago, light-waves being the notorious slow-pokes that they are.

Understandably, the telescope-johnies were mildly intrigued: if it could happen to a presumably well-behaved little hydrogen-burner like Yamaguchi 523, why not, then picking a star totally at random—to our very own dearly-beloved cosmic lightbulb, Sol?

Shucks, it'd make *every* day Ash Wednesday.

So they hawsered my precious *Georgie* up into a stinking Spacer's hold, warping yours truly, plus assorted slide-rule types, out to this former stellar system, now a rapidly expanding sphere of slowly cooling incandescent gas.

Then it was my turn. I took us all backward to a thousand years before the dust-up. We settled in on a revoltingly decorated ball of mud which I figured was gonna be well-off vaporized. Whole place looked like something you'd rub the dog's nose in and tell him t'do it on the paper next time.

The scientists scientized while I sat around counting rivets on the bulkheads, thinking wistfully about ordinary missions where I'd have the chance to savor local color—oughta see the way they dress the girls in ancient Crete! Sooner or later, I got bored enough to go out for a walk. *That's* how I ran into the Freenies, although they weren't in any condition to appreciate my godlike qualities then.

Y'see, they were *animals*.

No kidding, they weren't just primitives or savages. They didn't use tools. They didn't make fires. They didn't even follow the sports pages. They just hung around, well, being *animals*.

At the time, I thought (and never since) that they were kinda cute, in a stomach-turning sorta way. Same as they are now, of course: a foot-diameter hot-pink hemisphere, Ochskahrt knows how many wiggly little lime-green legs sticking out underneath, and this rubbery, wrinkled, turkey-neckish thing poking out the top, with a giant fly's eye nesting in the end.

Anyway, I started playing around with them, lacking anything more constructive t'do, building little traps and labyrinths t'see how bright they were, what they could be trained to do. For once, I could interfere all I wanted to with local events. This place—and the Freenies—didn't *have* any future history to screw up. Everything was scheduled to go up in subatomic particles at the stroke of the millennium.

Naturally, training required rewards. I tried all kindsa garbage, and it turned out they preferred percolator-leavings. Or old tea-bags. Even certain underhanded brands of artificially-processed orange-juice. In short, anything with caffeine in it. Hell, they even went for Midol.

Now it says here that caffeine measurably enhances human intelligence, and I believe it. Modern civilization'd be downright impossible without that first cup of coffee—what else could get a perfectly sane anthropoid up off his warm nest and out into the rat race every morning, day in and day out?

Notice that the "Age of Reason" didn't get into full swing until the little brown beans started getting imported and that the First Industrial Revolution cranked itself into gear on an island where everything comes to a screeching halt for the afternoon cuppa.

Thus it was, Freenie-wise, as well. They were bright little critters, as animals go, just teetering on the edge of whatever separates us from horses and kangaroos, and those well-used tea-bags of mine shoved 'em right over.

Our mission called for skipping ahead a few decades at a time, taking observations until the onboard whiz-kids figured out what'd made the sun go boom.

I'm telling you, before we left that planet, the Freenies (named by me, if y'want the ugly truth, for the sound of their voices) had bootstrapped themselves through a couple Industrial Revolutions of their own, begun using atomic power, and practiced a religion with me, Bernard M-for-Moron Gruenblum, as its Entity-in-Chief.

I've thought about *hara-kiri*, but I get woozy from a paper cut.

The Freenies hadn't *quite* invented starships, so after I made the mistake of opening my big fat face back at the Academy, we *rescued* 'em: huge fleets of starships, time-buggies in their cargo holds, ferried millions of the critters off their doomed planet, first to Luna, later to a Yamaguchiformed Ganymede.

The Red Cross served doughnuts and coffee.

I wish it'd been Sanka.

Cuthbert shifted nervously in his chair.

Afraid he'd take to pacing again, I essayed quickly, "What does all this have t'do with the price of fish-meal, anyway?

What does the Yamaguchian legation *really* want?" Experimentally, I let another cigar ash fall. Sure enough, the mechanical mousoid got to it before it actually hit the carpet.

Cuthbert blinked but stayed planted on his fundament. "Why simply to send a group out with you on your next full-dress assignment." He hesitated, and I began to get an awful feeling about what was coming. "It's a religious experience for them, Bernie, sort of a pilgrimage."

"A pilgrimage?" Yep, I'd figured right. Mentally, I started adding up my bank accounts, including the two in Switzerland and Hong Kong I didn't *think* the Academy was wise to—in this business you can collect a lotta highly salable antiques if y'know what you're doing.

"Why yes. As I'm sure you're aware, the Yama—Freenies possess the capability, far from unique throughout the zoological realm, to transfer individual experiences genetically, and—"

"How many?" I chomped my cigar, there being no bullet immediately available. His hands flopped on the desk like a midget hiding underneath had punched him in the groin. "Er . . ."

"Come off it, Cuthbert. We *both* know what I'm talking about: race memory. How many of the little . . . *darlings* do they wanna send with me, one of each sex?"

Considering the circumstances, you might say there was a pregnant pause. He looked at me almost apologetically, saying nothing. A highly eloquent nothing.

"I quit."

Punch Number Two. He spluttered, muttered, blustered, an' got flustered, all at the same time. Thought he was gonna have a hernia. "B-but Grandfa—Cap—Gruen—"

"That's *Bernie;* you're forgettin' yourself, Cuthbert. An' there ain't no way I'm gonna take *seventeen* of those creepy-crawlies along on a mission. *Nuts!* I'm only eighty-one years old; somewhere there's a job for me in what's left of the private sector: composing crossword puzzles; piloting a sanitation scow out in the Asteroids; my brother-in-law's gotta frog-fur farm out on Betelgeuse IX he's always wanted me to go halvsies on. I don't *need* you, Cuthbert, *or* your

Academy, an' I sure as shootin' don't need the grief."

"B-but Bernie..."

"I'm serious, Colonel."

"B-but Bernie..."

"You're repeatin' yourself, Cuthbert. Look, put *this* on your mirror an' snort it: you can get yourself another boy. An' the Freenies're gonna hafta get themselves another Deity—God ain't dead, he's just resigned!"

I rose, zipped the top two inches of my coverall for emphasis, and woulda jammed my hat on my head as a final gesture if they'd been in style this century.

The door was halfway dilated before my Leader regained his composure. "How many, then, *Major* Gruenblum?"

It's nice to be needed. "*Zero*, Cuthbert, an easy figure to remember, the ultimate Round Number—it's how many of you people in Administration have any brains!"

I started through the door.

Look at it his way: every kid an' all the telemedia in the Dominion may've thought the Freenies were cute as polka-dot suspenders; their rescue was the bleedin' heart story of the century. But, way down deep, the Academy—an' when you mention that institution, you're talkin' about all the government that counts in the Solar Dominion—the Academy was terrified by the little critters.

Think about it: a species which can pass on everything it's learned to future generations just by breeding; which had risen from leaf-hopping to atomic energy in a short ten centuries; and which now was scarfing up everything it could about our star-traversing, time-traveling civilization?

Come t'cogitate on it, it scared me, too!

"Grandfather..." I'll give this to Cuthbert; his gaze was suddenly cool and steady despite the sweat-beads crawling down his jowls in the fractional gravity, and I don't think I'd heard him more direct and businesslike before or since. "The Yamaguchians simply want the experience of Being-With-God, the opportunity to transmit it into their hereditary record. *That's* why they require an individual of each gender—"

"Yeah. All seventeen of 'em, clutterin' up my nice neat

ship." I sat down again. "Tell you what, Cuthbert. I'm feelin' generous this mornin': promote me two more grades—so I'll outrank *you*—let 'em pick out a *single* representative, an' I'll take him-her-it anywhere an' anywhen y'want. Bein'-With-God'll work its way into their race memory eventually. It'll just take longer, is all. An' the lucky winner'll have a lot more fun seein' it gets done right."

Cuthbert seemed to brighten noticeably. "Would you consider six, Bernie? Otherwise, the number of generations necessary, including fissionings and sporifications, to distribute data evenly among..."

I let him ramble for a while about genotypes, phenotypes, alleles, and "replicative verification densities." You know, dirty talk. Who knows, this all might turn out to my advantage, wangled right.

"Since when you been such an expert on Freenie genetics, Cuthbert? I woulda bet you took your advanced degree in polishing pants-seats."

He grinned sheepishly, opened a desk drawer, and tossed over a small bottle. Crimped metal band around the top, plastic stopper with a puncture-mark in the center. I brushed a thumb across the cue-dot on the label:

"Genetics and Information Theory/Yamaguchi 523: A Case-Study, by Robert H. Anson, Ph.D., Copyright 2285, Random-LaRoche Pharmcopublishers, Lagrange II, Earth. Protected in all provinces and territories under the Solar Dominion; reproduction in any organism or device, without express permission, strictly—"

RNA extracts—our own artificial race-memory.

Hardly ever touch th' stuff myself.

In the end, I didn't take those three promotions. Once you outrank something like Cuthbert, what've y'got? Instead, I let myself get dickered up to three Freenies in exchange for a very special RNA extraction from a certain Don Juan de Tenorio of Seventeenth-century Seville, collected surreptitiously by one of our more conscientious female bus drivers.

Peeling a fresh cigar, I started to discard the plastic wrapper in the Colonel's desk-disposal, then hesitated.

"Cuthbert, you know I've avoided gettin' too acquainted with the Freenies ever since the rescue effort, but an unsettlin' thought's just occurred t'me ..."

I tied the wrapper in a single overhand knot, held it above my head, and let it drop. It floated toward the floor with a graceful, rotating motion.

"What if the Freenies, once they really get t'know me, decide I ain't the kinda god they wanna be associated with? I mean, historically, deities get demoted pretty doggone violentlike!"

Spotting the wrapper, the housemouse dashed out from the baseboard—I *snatched* it from the air a foot before it hit the carpet—the little dickens ran around in confused circles, making noises like a teleprinter outa synch, bit the leg of my chair outa sheer frustration, and disappeared into the wall again. Probably never be the same.

All of a sudden, Cuthbert looked entirely too pleased, an' I didn't think it was because he'd come out ahead on our dealings. He steepled his fat fingers on his desk. "Well, Grandfather, just between you and me, I think people are greatly inclined to overlook *any* data which challenge their beliefs. Of course, *yours* may be the definitive case. I—"

"Yeah," I interrupted before he could get to the insulting part, "an' the Freenies're *people*, right enough. I'm the one who *made* 'em that way!"

Seemed like no time at all an' I was in the lovin' arms of my redheaded girlfriend over in Mare Fecunditatus. *Literally* no time, 'cause for some reason I couldn't seem to recall finally leaving Cuthbert's office or anything else in between.

But did it really matter? Somehow *we were in our private sunlit grove of trees at the edge of endless meadows, the breezes fresh as they stirred the knee-high grasses around us. We stood beneath a spreading, ancient oak, my beloved and I, a songbird warbling in the leafy branches overhead. She leaned against the age-roughened bark, her warm, smooth hands in mine. I gazed deeply into her bottomless azure eyes.*

The gentle wind caressed her pale blond hair. She smiled, shyly, glancing downward, dimples appearing magically in her satiny cheeks, lashes long and dark upon her milky skin. My heart began to pound, and I imagined I could see hers beating wildly as well in the breathtaking scallop of her sheer and lovely summer blouse. Her breasts were rounded and inviting. I bent to touch her, but she grinned, fumbling in an innocent, yet knowing way at the fastenings of my trousers.

Suddenly, my eager manhood—

"THAT'LL BE ENOUGH OF THAT, GRUENBLUM!"

I gasped like I'd been thrown outa bed into icy water. My private, sunlit glade had become *Georgie*'s control deck once again, and standing over me, while my eyes came slowly into focus, was Dr. Edna Janof, the DreamCap she'd torn so violently from my head—my ears'd be raw for a week—clutched in fingers trembling with anger.

That went well with the crazy look in her eyes. She hurled the DreamCap at me—its overhead cable kept it from connecting—turned on her heel, and stomped out of the cabin.

About that time, I discovered that I couldn't move.

There was a good reason for that. I'd been tied down to my pilot's couch with what looked like the decorative cording from a samurai sword. Running down my left sideburn was a sticky, warmish trickle, its source apparently the bowling-ball-sized knot of agony where something pretty hard had lately smacked me on the temple.

Bet I could guess the color of that trickle.

And I was probably staring at that "something pretty hard," right now: a Solar Dominion, Navy-Issue, X-ray laser pistol, one each, Dr. Ab Cromney's fingers wrapped securely around the grip, directing its grimly threatening muzzle at my battered forehead.

Inca
Dinka Doo

MY EARS HURT. FROM THE CORNER OF ONE EYE,
I could make out the big dual faces of my Academy-issue
watch:

+15.9277	+22.8539
OCT 05	MAY 23
1708:15.9	0802:13.1

But what did I care? I wasn't going anywhere.

"You must pardon our little Edna," Dr. Cromney offered
with incongruous cordiality, glancing distastefully toward
the bulkhead door where she had made her rapid, huffy exit.
"She has no small number of peculiar . . . sensitivities, and
this"—the heavy pistol wavered as he motioned with it at
the still-swinging DreamCap—"appears to be one of them."

That woulda been a swell time to jump him. I could feel
the sharp-cornered outline of my .45 still under the coverall.
But they never seem to tie down the stereodrama heroes
near as tight, somehow, as I found myself now. Doin' pretty
well, I reckoned, if there was any feeling left in my hands
and feet.

"Gotcha, Doc," I answered instead, givin' him my best
man-to-man wink. "'The secret fear that someone, somewhere, is happy.' Now *WHAT IN THE IRRADIATED NAME
OF HIRNSCHLAG VON OCHSKAHRT ARE YOU DOING
ON MY CONTROL DECK?*"

Heplar chose these words of mine to make his entrance on, nodded with illuminating familiarity toward Cromney, squeezed into the left-hand control position, and began deprograming *Georgie*. All that painstaking coursework I'd laid in, gone with a wipe of the erasing heads. It was gonna be a real pleasure putting a bullet into that mutinous skunk.

Cromney smiled indulgently. "For a fellow sufficiently erudite to quote Mencken, Captain, you possess remarkably little self-control." Now he wiggled his gun toward the co-pilot's seat. "Your assistant here—"

"My *former* assistant!" I hollered, abandoning a lifelong habit of keeping my emotions outa my work. "The creep's fired—*and* under arrest!"

Heplar looked up from his busywork. For the first time since I'd had the initial misfortune of layin' eyes on him, he *grinned*. I could see why he didn't make a regular practice of it: put me in minda Quasimodo's little buddies, hangin' off the eaves of Notre Dame Cathedral.

"As you will, Captain," Cromney continued, unperturbed. "In any event, with commendable hardiness, you began regaining consciousness earlier than suited our purposes. Young Heplar here made the uncharacteristically astute suggestion that the DreamCap might occupy your attentions until we were prepared to make use of you. However, ample indication arose"—he waved that Navy laser at the crotch of my uniform, and I aged ten years right on the spot—"at least in Edna's admittedly narrow view, that you were enjoying yourself altogether too much."

Tucking the pistol under his arm, he reached up to the overhead and snapped out the dream cassette, glancing at the label. "My, my, Captain, small wonder! She *is* a bit of a spoilsport where it comes to—well, I gather it's been Professor Kent's misfortune to discover that there has never been any woman born with more genuine feeling than a common bath sponge. He—"

"My heart *bleeds* for the twerp!" I squirmed, watching my fingers turning purple as the cordage cut into my wrists. "Cromney, I'm pretty well nailed down here. Why not put away that oversized flashlight an' tell me *what the hell is going on?*"

Cromney's hold on that Navy blaster didn't falter. I craned my neck, trying to see what Heplar was up to. He'd finished unpushing my buttons and begun ad-libbing a few of his own with what may have been the ghost of a chuckle.

It was echoed by Cromney. "How pitiably trite. This, I take it, is the point where I, as chief among the conspirators, am expected to Tell All so that you, the presumed protagonist, may then proceed to foil our dastardly plot and save the world." He shook his head with mock regret. "I'm inclined to *deny* you any such clarification, Captain; it would greatly please me doing so. And I assure you, there will be no opportunity for heroics on your part.

"However, it *is* necessary that I give you an indication of our intentions in order to enlist your cooperation, willing or—as I suspect will prove the case—otherwise."

He paused for several pulsebeats, as if waiting for a sarcastic comeback. But—remember the difference between a sadist and a masochist?—I didn't give him any. I *thought* of several, none worth being X-rayed to death by an ego-tripping crazy. I could feel a little warm pool of stickiness filling up the hollow of my collarbone—hoped it wouldn't get to my Colt. Nothing like blood for corroding steel.

Cromney was forced to resume awkwardly. "Very well, then, Captain. We are appropriating your vehicle, with the object of transporting ourselves to a milieu where its impressive and intimidating appearance should serve us well: Eleventh-Century Cuzco, five hundred years before the advent of the Spaniards to that subsequently unhappy land." He leaned back against the console, grinning smugly.

I groaned, despite myself. "Not another one of those! Teach-the-Incas-to-mop-up-on-Pizarro-creating-a-magnificent-Indian-civilization. Tell me, Doc, why not the Caribs? Why not the Aztecs? They were friendly, peace-lovin' folks, right after your own heart—with a ceremonial obsidian dagger!"

He waved the laser again, with a negligence that tied my stomach in a clove-hitch around my esophagus. "No, no, my dear fellow, nothing so naive as that. It could be *any* ancient culture, don't you see? Any gathering of savages with the requisite numbers and resources."

I groaned again, this time for effect. "The old *Connecticut Yankee* bit? Didn't they tell you the Academy lobotomizes a *hundred* would-be Sir Bosses, Jason dinAlts, and Lord Kalvans every year, each one with the same half-baked idea? Shucks, I understand, it was irresistible even *before* the invention of time-travel."

Like Colonel Cuthbert, Cromney had a problem: there wasn't enough room in the control cabin to pace back and forth, and it seemed to be getting to him. "But you've only the least important part of it, Captain!" He fidgeted. Was that a fanatic glint in his eye or just the lighting?

"Oh, I think I get it, Doc: with *Georgie* here, you an' your friends'll be gods in pre-Columbian Peru. Power, money, women..." I thought about those poor trusting Incas filling a room to the rafters with gold for Atahualpa's ransom. "You shoulda asked *me* what it's like bein' God— no fun at all. Why can't you nutsies ever think of somethin' original?"

"Be silent that you may do what is required of you!" Guess I'd sorta pinked him on that one. His fingers whitened on the pistol grip, veins stood out on his forehead, and the big glassy eye of the laser surged a foot nearer my battered face. Not exactly a net gain for Bernie, so I shut up.

Cromney expended visible effort reestablishin' control. "I'll not attempt to justify myself to you, Gruenblum, nor let you anger me further. You are a lackey of the entrenched powers, and what we aspire to *requires* no justification. Let it suffice that I and the others represent the Non-Ideological Re-Distributionist Society, who—"

"The NIRDS? That buncha quasi-leftist weirdos? Now I understand that MarxoFriedmanite routine of Kent's. He was feelin' around t'see if I'd throw in!"

Cromney smiled tolerantly, though he still looked a mite pale around the mouth. "The proper acronym is NRS, Captain. And you're correct: had you shown Professor Kent something other than the eternal sarcasm you display for all things in this universe, events might very well have ended differently for you."

Curiosity got the better of caution. "Then why're you keepin' me around? Why not just knock me off, get me outa the way?"

If I could get my right hand a little looser, maybe I could reach my .45—*if* my fingers'd work.

"Before you answer that, Doc, why don'tcha lemme have a smoke? I promise I'll be good, an' you can explain NIRD-ism to me again. Denny Kent ain't too articulate. Who knows, maybe I'll see the light—now how'd it go? Somethin' about '*thesis, antithesis,* an' *prosthesis*'?..."

Cromney did a number with his eyebrows. "Very clever, Captain, but of no avail. We will dispose of you in our own time, after you have served your purpose. Nor shall I loosen the *least* of your bonds. I am uncomfortably aware of the unarmed combat techniques taught by your reactionary masters." He shifted to a position against the console he musta felt was appropriately professorial.

Either that or he was afraid I'd karate-chop him with my earlobes an' was movin' back outa range.

"Finally, Captain, the NRS has nothing, in any explicit sense, to do with Marx or any of the ancient ideologues. You see, the classic advocates of Economic Democracy did all of their writing only *after* the First Industrial Revolution. By that time, of course, it was far too late for a suffering humanity. The new class of exploiters was established, the masses mindlessly enamored of consumption, and there was no *moral* revolution to equal the merely mechanical one. We shall *correct* that error of timing, return to an earlier era armed with rational, collective econometrics. Only when mankind is properly prepared, shall we permit advances in technology, and then only under the strictest, most humane..."

It was the usual. Go back in time, use a lotta fireworks an' high-tech to impress the natives, issue a few commandments. Then skip forward a few decades t'see how things'd worked out. Lay down the law again an' jump another generation or two, over an' over again, until your personal idea of Utopia's achieved an' you can put down roots as Philosopher-King an' resident Livin' Legend.

Kinda thing I'd done by *accident* with the Freenies.

I hadda hand it to Cromney an' his crew, though. T'my knowledge, nobody'd ever gotten this far with it before. Usually the real crazies never made it to the Moon, or at least to the Academy. Psych-exams weeded out potential problem-passengers well before they were okayed for a mission. An' usually the pilot didn't fall asleep on the job— could be our little Edna was *right* about the DreamCap.

On the other hand, the Academy's got lotsa secrets it doesn't share with bus drivers. Timeships just like *Georgie* are rumored to've disappeared before. Not many (I think), but enough t'make you wonder just how real history is, after all.

I had more immediate problems: Cromney, Kent, Janof, even Heplar—was *everybody* here a mutineer? What did they want from me? What did they intend *for* me afterward?

There was movement in the door behind us. Denny Kent had arrived from wherever he'd been keeping himself. Neither he nor Heplar, I noted with some amusement, was armed. So much for democracy. I turned my red, roughened, dishpan ears toward Cromney again:

"Naturally, it will be necessary at first to display ourselves in a manner to effectively enhance our credibility. In primitive cultures, this requires a show of force and wealth. But *only* for the sake of our eventual, benign goal, a truly egalitarian social order where such displays are unnecessary." He threw a glance at Kent, suppressing a shudder which he somehow managed t'transform into a broad, manly wink. "Yes, Captain," he said—more for the Professor's benefit than mine—"and despite the cynical manner in which you chose to express it, we shall have need of *many* local women. An unavoidable necessity in our show of power and riches."

He drew himself closer now, lettin' the laser muzzle drop a bit. "Moreover, I freely acknowledge that women have been oppressed, historically. Men, owing to their superior sensibilities, are more emotionally vulnerable. In any engagement of wills, the more ruthlessly destructive party always triumphs. And women, sir, recognize no bounds to ruthlessness. Like any dangerous animal, they must be controlled, as much for their own good as anyone else's."

Talk like that made me a mite uncomfortable. I wasn't prepared t'write the whole gender off, but thinkin' back, I couldn't recall *ever* meetin' a woman who had all her oars in the water. I'd often lamented m'self—usually over the seventh or eighth beer—what a shame it was they couldn't all be sensible, rational. Sorta like my *Georgie*.

He straightened again. "Also, as a practical matter, we have only one woman—"

"An' from what you tell me, she ain't much of a prize t'anyone, 'specially poor ol' Kent here, right?"

There was a feral growl. Before I could lift m'shoulders an' swivel m'head, Cromney an' Heplar'd both jumped up, pilin' themselves in fronta Kent t'keep him from doin' me an injury. My harpoon'd sunk home. They danced around awhile gettin' the Professor quieted down, but I had other concerns: by now my fingernails'd started turnin' black.

Wonderin' how all these loonies'd gotten assigned t'gether on a mission ticked off another point on m'worry list: I hadn't seen the Freenies since this nastiness'd begun. *They* were probably the reason the Academy'd been hasty an' careless settin' up this excursion. I'd been afraid t'ask after 'em in the faint hope the hijackers'd somehow overlooked 'em.

How do y'tie up a Freenie, anyway?

It was suddenly quiet again. Cromney—an' his pistol— rejoined me, his face livid, his hands shaking in fury. With nothing much to lose, I decided to risk pushing him further:

"Gotta question for you, Doc. What d'you think the Academy's gonna do while you're messin' around with their past—sit on their hands? Lemme tellya, the first misplaced virgin or purloined golden idol, an' there'll be ripples up an' down the continuum that'll have a fleet of planet-wreckers on your ugly neck so quick it'll—"

Alarmingly, Cromney threw back his bushy head and began to bray, his lesser cohorts essaying nervous chuckles behind him.

"By heaven, Captain, I've looked forward to telling you this for days! It's precisely where *you* come into the picture. You see, we *aren't* going back directly to Cuzco. Instead, we shall spend some little time patrolling the Fifteenth-Century Atlantic Ocean, destroying any exploratory European vessel which sails within a thousand kilometers of the New World. A few decades of disappearing ships and they'll go back to believing the world is flat!"

He turned to receive admiring glances from his underlings.

"*You* will direct that search and destruction, Captain, as I was severely limited in my choice of help"—he directed an angry look at my former assistant—"and young Heplar here confesses that his skills may not be up to it. In any event, only *then* will we sojourn to Peru—*by which time there will be no Academy to pursue us!*"

Yeah, that'd do it, all right. Sink Columbus on his first trip, scuttle John Cabot for good measure. You'll have wiped out *all* subsequent history in a couple of clean strokes, meaning no preliminary ripples to warn the Academy upstairs. The alarm bells on that fancy reality-lock could shrill forever—there'd be nobody left to hear 'em.

Could be we were doomed.

As if on cue, there was a blood-curdling scream from belowdecks. Heplar scrunched his head down between his shoulders even farther than usual. Kent blinked and turned white as a boiled cow's stomach.

The scream hadn't been female.

Cromney recovered first. "In answer to the question you've undoubtedly been asking yourself, Captain, there are, indeed, a pair of individuals aboard who are *not* a party to our . . . enterprise. Those two old fools from the museum."

"They had their, uh, chance, sir," interrupted Kent. "I practically, well, *begged* them to—"

"That will *do*, Denny. I believe that was one of the old gentlemen we heard just now, responding to our little Edna's tender ministrations. She is practicing, no doubt, the powers of persuasion she plans bringing to bear on you, Captain, should you remain uncooperative."

Another scream. This one shut off like a politician's smile when the polls close. I tried not to gulp visibly. "Oh, I convince real easy, Doc. Just try me."

Behind him, Kent nodded with dumb enthusiasm. Real class outfit I was dealing with here.

Cromney smiled sadly. "I rather doubt that, Captain. Be that as it may, young Heplar here will reprogram this vessel as far as 1492. You will be asked simply to inspect and confirm—or correct—his calculations. It is remotely possible, should you sincerely join the spirit of the occasion, that we may yet find a niche for you in our New Secular Order. Although, in honesty . . ."

He straightened, inhaled briskly. "No matter. For the nonce, we shall remand you to our little Edna's custody and let you think. Gentlemen?"

Silliest-lookin' strongarm men I ever laid eyes on; coupla wimps whose faces even Mr. Peepers coulda thrown sand in. But I wasn't quite myself that afternoon, an' they trussed me up some more, using side-cutters to detach me from my chair, picked me up bodily, and carted me outa the control cabin.

I banged a still-tender ear on the door-frame.

Across the after pilot's lounge, at the opening of the rear ladder-well, they simply tossed me down into the messroom.

It deserved its name.

I landed on my right side in a quarter-inch-deep, room-sized pool of blood, Edna Janof standing over me, a pair of glittering tiny manicure-scissors in her scarlet hand.

4

Harry's
Other Shoe

EDNA'S LOVELY VIOLET-COLORED EYES CON-
trasted nastily with the crimson running down her upraised
forearms. At the elbows, it dripped off onto my uniform.
Absently working the tiny scissors open and shut, she bent
over me, a little foamy spittle showing at the corners of her
mouth.

I was helpless to do anything but keep a wary eye on
her. Something had sprayed scarlet freckles all over her
face. One of those "somethings" lay crumpled along one
wall, its cruelly bound arms at unreal angles. A naked foot
stretched up across a lightweight plastic chair, wired in
place. Was it Merwin or Hulbert? Whoever it was, he didn't
seem to have toenails anymore.

Or any eyes.

She'd accomplished a whole lot more between those extremities. That's probably what started the screaming. I
know I'd have screamed. My coverall was soaked through
to the skin along the side I was lying on, and something
seemed to be dripping on my forehead. Despite myself, I
glanced up: an arm, ending in the tortured mockery of a
hand, hung limply off the edge of the dining table I'd skidded halfway under. I found myself wondering if anybody
was attached to it. Funny, the things you think of. It was
gonna take a total refit to clean *Georgie* up after this.

If there *was* an after this.

Another scarlet droplet from the table overhead caught
me squarely in the eye.

And *that* did it. Okay, Captain Bernie M-for-meathead Gruenblum, maybe you gotta take it lying down, but by Ochskahrt's Awful Accident, there's gonna be a pile of bastards horizontal with you!

I gathered my knees to my chin slowly, faking an abject terror I was trying pretty hard not to really feel. Edna leaned closer; the scissors nibbled the air in front of my eyes. Her own were whirling pools of insanity. I managed a little whimper.

She laughed.

I've heard it said you can drive somebody's nose-bone into their brain with an energetic, well-placed blow. Not being sure about that, I aimed the heels of my number nines right at the point of her cute little chin, figuring to fracture her neck.

And kicked!

I caught her on the lunge. She slipped on the blood-soaked carpet, taking my bone-crushing strike on her shoulder and flopped over hard. I stayed down, heels being my only advantage, and waited for Round Two.

It never came.

There was a curious thumping scuffle, a muffled female protest. I lurched up onto an elbow, sawing the cords painfully deeper into my flesh, and—

It was the Yamaguchian Ambassador—or one of his compatriots—plastered firmly over Edna's pretty little mug. She fought feebly, trying to tear him away, but the Freenie clung like an abalone. I felt something scrabbling at my wrists and looked down just in time to see another alien withdrawing a dangerous-looking crablike appendage back under his shell.

My hands were free!

I worked my stiffened fingers like a milkmaid practicing arpeggios. The cord was sheared through cleanly, the end of each filament like a tiny mirror. Nor did my miniature alien worshippers leave much doubt what they wanted their God to do now. It was thunderbolt time: Freenie Number Three had broken into my private locker and was skriddling his gory way toward me with my old Milt Sparks pistol belt tentacled high above his shell to avoid getting blood all over it. There were four spare clips in that combat rig, eight big fat cartridges apiece. I hoped I'd need 'em all.

Freenie Number Two unbound my legs, numb and practically useless. By now, Edna had stopped struggling and lay still, a sight that did my heart a lotta good. I dragged myself toward her, assisted Number One off her face, and felt for a carotid pulse. *Rats!* Still there—but just barely. I considered replacing His Ambassadorship, thought better of it, and then wondered why, finally evading difficult ethical questions by taking it out on my legs. I kneaded and punched them until it felt like my skin was carbonated, and took a fling at standing up.

Several attempts later, I was leaning shakily against a chair, trying to strap on the gunbelt. Levering the Colt out of its shoulder-holster (two spare magazines there, as well, under the off-armpit), I thumbed down the safety and gently pinched the slide back to check the chamber—dunno why I bother, it's *always* full of cartridge.

The slide shuffled forward again with that Cadillactic Gold Cup clank, but I left the safety off, resting my trigger-finger on the guard, and squished a path across the tiny messroom to the ladder. I took the treads slowly, quietly, and two at a time until my eyes were on a level with the deck above.

No one in the after lounge.

Up the remaining steps and onto dry carpet, leaving tracks Jack the Ripper would've envied. Heplar and Kent were still present on the flight deck, but Cromney was the one I worried about, with that heavy-duty Navy burner of his. Parked in my chair, he toyed absently with the DreamCap, not wearing it. The laser was out of sight.

"Gentlemen, it's just occurred to me that we might modify this vile device and use it to indoctrinate—"

While Cromney babbled, Heplar turned, glommed a horrified eyeful of me: soaked in blood, murder in my heart, and a cocked and loaded two-by-four-sized blue-steel automatic in my hand. The way his eyes widened, I thought he was gonna skin himself. His mouth started moving. I shot him.

—and connected with Denny Kent just as the idiot crossed the hatchway. He went down, half an ounce of lead buried in his adipose. I pivoted. The pistol belted my hand again, filling both rooms with its bellowing. Cromney clapped a hand to his ear—I'd been aiming for the bridge of his nose, but my fingers were still unmanageable—let the DreamCap fly, and snatched for his blaster. My old Colt bucked and roared a third time, and Cromney's fancy ray-gun burst in his hand, spraying components, meat and bone, all over the cabin. He screamed and lurched backward against Heplar, who stumbled against the console—

And the entire planet slammed down on top of me, grinding me into a million agonized fragments!

...I clambered back to consciousness, hurting all over from injuries of three or four distinct vintages. The .45 was still clutched in my hand. I flicked the safety up, not trusting my nerves, swapped for a full magazine, and stepped forward into the control room.

Georgie was in full flight.

'Course I'd realized that from the moment I'd awakened. There's no mistaking the feeling. And no confusing the distinct sensations of traveling in time with those of moving spacewise. We were doing both, and in a hell of a hurry.

The remainder of the cast was horizontal, draped at random over furniture, floor, and fixtures. Kent was still breathing. Thing about a .45 is, if you survive the first thirty seconds after being shot, you'll likely live out your normal span. Cromney lay unconscious and leaking—outa one ear and between what was left of his fingers. Made my whole goddamned day. I stepped over my former assistant, only treading on two of his ankles by unfortunate accident, and checked the board—

And looked up at the screens!

The numbers were reeling by too fast. An initial acceleration of eleven or twelve *G*'s had tripped *Georgie*'s overrides. The momentum we'd acquired was something pretty fierce. That numbskull Heplar had left *all* the arming-covers flipped open while he fumbled with the settings—a lazy kaydet's trick—and then had fallen against every go-button *Georgie*'s got.

But that wasn't what worried me now as I stabbed buttons, vainly trying to slow us down. See, you pass through time and space at the same time, on a complicated vector, passing over mountains and cities and rivers as you slip through history. Sometimes you gotta be *careful* what you pass over.

Georgie's shields are powerful, but even *they* have limits.

Heplar had plotted in an error so incredibly moronic, only flying over Krakatoa or Santorini on Boom Day could've compared. While I struggled helplessly, the dials whizzed around to the twentieth century, August 9, 1945. The map said Kyushu, the western fringe.

Nagasaki.

THERE WAS A WHITE LIGHT.

5

A Grizzly
Tale

SHHHWAAAP!

The eleven-thousandth picture-postcard pine-bough slapped me in the puss. Too played out even to feel particularly resentful about it, I finished putting my left foot down in front of me. Somewhere above the needle-carpeted floor, a goddamn bird was singing.

I ducked another branch. The Freenies waited impatiently on the trail a hundred yards ahead—there are advantages to being only fifteen inches tall. Clear of the trees at last, I ignored their minuscule intrepidity and picked out a nice, sun-dappled, lichen-encrusted parking place. Looked to be midmorning, though it'd been full light already when the pesky little critters rolled me out, and in this forest, I couldn't be sure. Couldn't be sure of *anything:* we were lost in a wilderness where there should have been a city.

Springtime in the Rockies. Fed by slowly melting patches of dirty snow, the aspen-lined creek paralleling our game-track gurgled cheerfully, mocking me. I leaned over and spat pink, from where the ten-thousand nine-hundred and ninety-ninth pinecone-laden tree-appendage had smacked me in the mouth.

I glanced at my wrist again, rewarded only with a hairy fishbelly strip where my Academy-issue Nukatron was missing, then spent a consoling moment dedicating unprintable free-verse to all but two of my former passengers. This was the third crummy, miserable day—not to mention two crummy, miserable nights—I'd spent wandering along what appeared to be the prehistoric Continental Divide. Trouble was, *Georgie*'s read-outs had been quivering at A.D. 1993 when I'd whispered my last reluctant good-bye.

I'd fingernailed my way up outa pole-axed disconnection from reality—it was getting to be a perversion with me—sprawled across the copilot's couch, pistol in hand, teeth in mouth, and confusion in what passed for mind. "Spectacles, testicles, vallet *und . . .*" Didn't seem to have many more contusions and abrasions than I'd already collected. Helluva tribute to *Georgie*'s defensive magnetogravitics.

Viewscreens coulda been an excerpt from *The Sound of Heidi:* a saddle-shaped stretch of breathing-space between the lofty cliché-capped peaks—the kinda flower-speckled meadow where they make beer commercials. Real scenic, it was: as close to 105°30′ West Longitude as'd matter to anybody but a stake-and-chain man; 40°30′ the other way. Call it a quarter past Wyoming, somewhere along the eastern slope of the Colorado Rockies. A large mustard-colored fly buzzed the outside pickups.

But, incredibly, *Georgie* was claiming it was 1993—half past teatime, April first, t'be exact. All Fools' Day, and for the moment, that seemed to include me. I *knew* this era better'n I wanted to. Shoulda been a countyful of subdivisions here, crackerbox houses row-by-row, semivandalproof public schools, nondenominational churches, shopping centers the size of Greater Mesopotamia, and about a million square klicks of bumper-to-bumper parking lot.

Yet it wasn't any weirder than what greeted my perplexed inspection of the interior of the timebuggy. Cromney, Heplar, and Kent had *vamoosed,* leaving some impressive bloodstains slowly fading into the housecleaning systems. My own uniform was dry and stiff with the stuff until I started moving around and it powdered off and fell away. This was turning out to be a messy assignment.

I checked the Gold Cup, filling the gunbelt's vacant clippouch from the shoulder rig, which I unzipped my coverall to shrug out of. Ain't the most comfortable way to haul a piece around, anyway—but highly concealable. Looked like the big autopistol'd carry three small oval etchings from now on, where my bloody fingertips had rested while I was dozing. Honorable battle-scars. We all got a few.

Okay, one mystery at a time.

If my would-be hijackers had recovered already, why had they left *me* armed and on the loose? Or still alive, for that matter?

I verticalized myself and limped toward the after lounge, discovering not one muscle, joint, or sizable surface anywhere that didn't inspire a groan when I moved it. Surprisingly enough, I was hungry, which probably meant I was gonna live. I lifted a swollen ankle over the doorsill—

"Hail, O Mighty Gruenblum, puissant and indestructible!"

"Errrk!" My right hand clawed convulsively for the armpit where my pistol *wasn't*, anymore—a gesture appropriate to shock-induced coronaries, as well.

"O Lord"—there came a high-pitched but exceedingly reverent squeak—"who endureth through great travail, wilt Thou guide Thy humble servants even as Ye did in days of yore?" All three Freenies had gathered in the after lounge, which was otherwise devoid of inhabitants. The suddenly-talkative individual among them swiveled an eyestalk at its companions: "Rejoice, ye people, for our Creator awaketh at last!"

"O Magnificence," uttered a second Yamaguchian, rolling forward as if he were on ball-bearings. His legs wiggled like cheap rubber special effects. "Deignest Thou to speak unto Thy worshippers, revealing now Thy Holy purpose and design?"

"C'mon, guys, knock off the Charleton Heston crap, willya? My head hurtol" Which was true, all of a sudden, bringing me to a state of anatomical unanimity. My hand brushed idly along the steel and black rubber of my pistol grip. "Seen anything of Cromney and the rest of his bug collection?" I pulled a cigar from its waterproof—and bloodproof, it appeared—pocket case.

The third alien piped up, just like the others, Mickey Mouse breathing helium. "Lord, Thy servants hath immured the Evil Ones, with the victims of their late foul butchery, in the chambers beneath Thy locomotive extremities." It pointed its turkey-neck toward the after stair-well. "Have we acted rightly?"

All three looked up at me with anxiety-filled optics.

What was I gonna say? The little farts'd saved my life—twice, now—and, thinking back on it, had tried to warn me even *before* the fireworks started. Shucks, standing there it took *me* several seconds to figure out that we were in even worse trouble than before. So why take it out on the Freenies?

Y'see, *omnia* Georgia *in partes tres divisa est*, to wit: the uppermost deck where we presently found ourselves; a larger middle deck for the paying customers—staterooms, dining area, etc., and, grandest of all, the lowest level, reserved for the engines, cargo, and maintenance supplies...

And Auxiliary Control. *That* was the cockroach in my enchilada: up here on the control deck were two separate hatches, one aft between the pilot's lounge and the bunkie where I'd hang my hat if I had one. That led to the passenger level and nowhere else.

But amidships was a second ladder-well, theoretically accessible only to the crew, which dropped directly to the lowest deck, the idea being to keep curious amateur fingers outa the bright pretty machinery. If things worked out as spiffily in practice as they do in theory, my tiny worshippers woulda had the badguys boxed and locked.

However.

On the tubular outer surface of the 'midships ladderway, as it passed through passenger-country, was a four-foot curving plate bolted on, clearly labeled in bright orange letters six inches high:

EMERGENCY ENGINE-ROOM ACCESS
AUXILIARY CONTROL
AUTHORIZED PERSONNEL ONLY

Somehow, even without Rand Heplar's contribution to this farce, I had the feeling Cromney was gonna figure things out and consider himself authorized. After all, y'can't make a New Secular Order without breaking regs.

In the couple of seconds it took all of this to whip past my little gray cells, I practically teleported back through to the console, quick-twisted two pairs of thumbscrews, and slammed up the panel they held down. In the recess underneath was a fist-sized module amongst all the spaghetti and shirt-buttons. I pushed it down a quarter-inch, turned it to the left. It popped out into my hand as half a hundred dashboard lights went yellow. I crammed it into a pocket with a long, grateful sigh of relief.

The frammis in question was *Georgie*'s field-density equalizer. Without it, she was grounded as thoroughly as if I'd yanked her powerplant. Here she'd stay until I could figure out what to do about the miscreants below. Replacing the panel, I rejoined Truth, Justice, and the Yamaguchian Way, who were still waiting for an answer from me like puppies at Alpo time.

"Tell y'what, fellas, y'done okay, all things considered. Hell, I coulda woke up dead, couldn't I?"

They'd screwed the after hatch down good and solid. Musta dragged my sleeping time-pirates and pitched 'em over the coaming, then somehow dropped the heavy lid without making freenieburgers of themselves in the process. I gave the wheel a gentle experimental turn, with no more luck than I'd expected. Appeared the prisoners had locked us out sometime after the Freenies had locked them in.

"Seems only fair," I mumbled.

"I beg Your pardon, Lord?" one of the Freenies squeaked.

"Hunh? Oh, yeah. Look, guys, I been thinkin'. . ." The forward hatch is always down, lock wheel dogged tight. Auxiliary Control ain't so much for flying *Georgie* from. Any disaster that takes out the control deck's gonna make scrap-metal of the rest of the ship. Mainly it's for the convenience of the overhaul mechanics—somethin' I'm *that* glad the Academy doesn't trust to its radiocontrolled gorillas. Yet. Now the 'midships wheel wouldn't turn, either. That meant the hijackers'd unshipped the access panel downstairs. I headed back to the control room, Freenies squiggle-marching right behind me.

"Like I said, I owe you fellas—first for Edna. She was gonna set me up in the tincup an' pencil business. Also for roundin' up the whole menagerie while I was, er, incapacitated."

I paused, rockered a gang of switches. Sure enough, the belowdecks monitors focused on a pair of gleaming half-meter vise-grips clamped through both lower hatch wheels, freezing 'em solid. Corridors were empty. Camera by camera, I tracked my prey to the messroom, then switched off real quicklike before someone noticed the monitor light.

I turned back to the Freenies. "Your 'Evil Ones' are down there, right enough, lickin' their wounds. Looks like Cromney's gonna be mashin' his peas left-handed from now on." I trickled to an awkward halt, mildly embarrassed at what I hadda say next, an' surprised to be. "Listen, guys, what I was gettin' at earlier is . . . well, I seem to've underestimated you all a mite. I . . . shucks, t'be perfectly honest, I can't even tell you apart. Whyn'tcha start by givin' me your names? Mebbe I can . . ."

There followed some kinda noisy chirping an' warbling contest that didn't do my headache any good. While the aliens were confabbing, I concentrated on the image of the lower airlock. The one everybody'd used back in Tokyo. Long as it was operating, Cromney and company weren't really all that confined.

Grinning, I punched a phony collision alarm into *Georgie*'s systems, suppressing the accompanying klaxons, and laughed out loud when I heard, even through her normally soundproof structure, the 'tween-compartments pressure doors thudding shut. Oughta keep those varmints where they were for the time bein'!

I was startin' to enjoy this. Cackling like a fool, I electrified all the doorknobs and flooded the corridors with vomit-gas—two standard Academy preventatives against anachronistic intruders. No time-traveler relishes gettin' boarded by Neanderthals, medieval sword-swingers, or twenty-first century Freedom Police.

I pulled a Command Override Key—only one aboard,

thank Ochskahrt—outa my breast pocket. It'd gotten kinda quiet, and I gathered the Freenies were done with their conference. "Well?"

Careful to avoid getting fried, I overrode the lounge door, heading for a locker starboard of the after stair-well. The Freenies were right behind me.

"'Well' what, Lord?"

"Well, what did you people decide?" In the locker there'd be a plastic suit allowing me to traipse through vomit-gas totally unregurgitated.

"Decide, Lord?"

A moment of exasperation: "You gonna tell me your names, or what?" Make that *double* exasperation: unexpectedly, the locker was on the intruder circuit and hadda be overidden. Inserting the insulated Key, I cursed every overcautious bureaucratic safety-fetishist who ever—

"But Lord, those *were* our names."

"Oh."

Nonetheless, by the time I got the closet open, I was chuckling gleefully over the fact that, like the Command Key, there was only *one* antigas outfit aboard ship. To the Freenies: "All righty, why don't I just think of somethin' t'call you that us mere mortal gods can pron—*smoldering slothdung!*"

Instead of a nice shiny plastic Yves St. Laurent, there hung a large manila-colored tag from an Academy inspection crew:

OBSOLETE EQUIPMENT
REPLACE AT NEXT OVERHAUL

"An I.O.U. for a pressure-suit? Goddamn form-fillers think the paperwork's as good as the real—"

"Which one of us, Lord?" One of the aliens tugged at my pants cuff with a greenish tentacle. It clashed with my uniform.

"Howzat again?"

There was a hint of disappointment in his little voice. "Which of us is to be named 'Smoldering Slothdung'?"

I turned from Ma Hubbard's cupboard to face my turtle-shaped worshipper. "Listen, let's not get into an Abbott and Costello routine here. From now on you're . . . Color."

"'Color', Lord?" I swear his compound eye almost blinked in astonished delight. Now where the hell had I left my cigar?

"Sure, sport. An' this one over here—hey you, eatin' that maintenance tag! You're Charm. That suit you, kiddo?" The second alien sorta quivered all over and *hooted!*, which— together with a missing p-suit and the sudden depressing realization that I'd rendered my ship impassable to *myself*— seemed to give my headache new lease on life.

With an option to purchase.

"I take it this meets with your approval?"

"O, indeed, Lord, a calling personally bestowed by the One True—"

"Just don't get effusive, okay? That leaves the one over there in the corner, lookin' for the sandbox. How 'bout Spin for a monicker? And t'round things off, let's make a . . . well, in the spirit of the occasion, call it a Covenant. Hereafter, you three are officially entitled t'call me Bernie and put a stop to all this conversational theology."

Silence. Limp necks. Lackluster eyeballs. Maybe I'd left my cigar on the monitor panel.

"All right, make that a *Commandment*. Bernie is a religious name, y'know, from the ancient, um, Urdu, meaning' . . . Bearer of Precious Ambrosia. Not caffeine, but brandy—close enough for Holy Work. Any of you guys got a cigar?"

In the end, I'd collected a whole handful of cigars, plus assorted lightweight survival gear, including my nifty combination lockback foldknife and thermolighter. Absorbs body-heat all day an' gives it back in stogie-sized doses. Pretty fair penlight, too.

Escape & Evasion wasn't exactly the course I woulda chosen for myself, but it started with *Georgie* screamin' at me from the control cabin.

"What in Ochskahrt's Rosy Red? . . ." Indicators said

there was a fire, small but very, very hot. General vicinity of the messroom. I slapped the intertalkie.

"Cromney, whatcha think you're doin' t'my ship, you brassbound bastard?"

A loud hissing I knew altogether too well almost drowned out the answering voice. "Denny Kent here, Capt—er, Gruenblum." Apparently, my .45 hadn't made the impression on him I'd hoped for. "We're cutting our way *out* of here, *that's* what we're—"

"Get away from that pickup, you cretin!" Cromney interrupted. "Captain, make things easy on yourself while you still have a chance. You're not going anywhere. Before too very long, we'll be coming up to get you!"

The hissing continued.

He was right. Without any accurate idea of where and when we were, I couldn't plot a course home that'd make any sense. I let it ride and keyed the video. They'd blinded it.

"Outa curiosity, Cromney, how'd you get the welding torch? I thought I'd closed off all the——"

There was a considerable pause. "Let us say only that there was a sizable, er, obstruction in the path of the starboard workroom door. Professor Kent now possesses a fractured humerus to add to his initial grievances against you and is operating presently under the influence of powerful stimulants—with a correlative satisfaction of once more having sacrificed himself to the Cause."

I shut my mike down instantly. This wasn't the time to let 'em hear me laughing hysterically. And to top it off, neoamphetamines were accumulative murder on the nervous system. Kent hadn't any surplus of brains to offer Cromney's Cause in the first place. Edna'd be tyin' his suit-boots an' helpin' him go pee-pee when the drugs wore off.

I turned to my faithful alien companions. "How about it, boys, should we tell 'em about the vomit-gas?"

"With all respect...*Bernie*." Charm was the one I'd always thought of as the Ambassador. "You had better begin considering what to do once they break through the door and recover from it."

I snorted. "My only fear is that they'll knock out the corridor cameras before I get t'see 'em pukin' their guts out. Wanna watch with me? I'll buy the popcorn."

Perched on one arm of my chair, Charm shook its eye from side to side. "Lord—Bernie—is it not the case that your perfidious assistant possesses the same knowledge of this vessel as yourself?"

"Not the same at all—RNA-drippings! Hadda get *my* education the hard way. Six miles t'school every day through blinding snowdrifts, an'—"

"Your pardon, Bernie." Color offered unwanted opinions from the cabin floor. "It snows neither upon Luna nor, if I am informed correctly, in your native southwest Texas." Spin was probably still looking for the kitty box. "However, may we not ask what recourse *you* might take in their position? Upon such contemplations may you formulate your own—"

"*Sweet Mudder of Citation!*" Cromney was a tricky hairpin. Could be he'd mentioned attacking me merely as a feint. Into my mind leaped an image of Auxiliary Control, including a big red lever curiously labeled FAILSAFE AUTODESTRUCT. *Surely* they wouldn't... But then I remembered that crack about sacrificing oneself to the Cause. Never *did* trust an unselfish sonofabitch.

"Vomit-gas or no vomit-gas, I gotta get down there before they do! Outa my way!" I checked my automatic and sprinted to the flight-deck airlock. I could Key my way back through the lock downstairs and...

Then I trudged back into the control room feeling like an idiot. The monitor agreed with me: they'd jammed their airlock, just as they'd done the 'tween-decks hatches. They were locked in, I was locked out. Bad design. Made a note t'complain if I ever got back home.

"*Great God in ARRRGHHH!*" said the intercom suddenly. I sniggered to myself. They'd finally holed through into the corridor to the tune of wretching, coughing, and the soft splashing of semiliquids in four-part harmony.

I hiked up the companionway air pressure, making sure they got a real dose, and felt for the reassuring bulge of the field-integrating frammis in my coverall pocket. There weren't any spares aboard, thanks to some unknown paranoid genius at the Academy.

"Hey, creeps," I shouted into the 'talkie, "when you're through turnin' yourselves inside-out, just file out the starboard lock, stark naked with your fingers interlaced on top your heads! Anybody tries t'get cute, there's a .45 slug waitin' for him—or *her!*" I added, torn between the vision of Edna Janof in the altogether or Edna Janof fulla bullet holes. I didn't get an answer from below; dry heaves tend t'preoccupy you.

I punched up some specifications. *Georgie*'s lethal explosive radius was a startlingly modest five kilometers, 99.999 percent of her energies being directed upward in a pillar of fire'd make C. B. DeMille turn twenty-three shades of envious chartreuse. I closed my mind savagely to the thought of my best girl endin' up like that; time Bernie an' his little friends made like pea-soup.

Somehow, when I wasn't looking, it'd gotten black as pitch outside. What I needed was a local hilltop, something with a nice cliff backside t'drop over if and when I saw the flare. Another heat-alarm winked on the board—*Georgie*'s way of tellin' me Cromney an' his cronies were workin' on the engine-room hatch. I gathered up my worshippers and left the flight deck. Pistol in hand, I cracked the lock.

Thunder split the air!

By the time I unglued myself from the overhead, gratified that the Gold Cup's safety was in good condition, a solid wall of high-country rain filled the darkened meadow. I glanced at my—

Those sons of bitches! Somewhere in the past few crowded hours, they'd managed t'smash my graduation watch! Dunno why I hadn't noticed before. I unstrapped it hastily, wondering what the microfission instrument might've leaked all over me already. Firming my conviction, I stepped outside, letting my left wrist take a good rain-soaking. The Freenies were right behind me.

Lightning flashed!

And three hours later, I was as lost as I ever have been.

In hopes of later recovery and repair, I'd buried my fractured Nukatron near *Georgie*'s landing ramp, given her titanium flank a fond final pat, and made for the sheltering pines. They're overrated. Dunno if you've ever tried using a tree t'get outa the rain. Wasn't long before I was wet clean through an' crinklin' up around the edges. The Freenies chittered happily, their carapaces shedding precipitation like greased Teflon. Intermittent lightning strokes ruined my night vision; the downpour itself was blinding. I kept looking for a cave, the bole of a big tree—anyplace where it was drier'n I was.

Next time I turned around, I couldn't tell which direction *Georgie* was.

The rain finally faded away, leaving the goddamn trees t'dribble down my neck another couple hours. Darkest night I ever did see. I spent most of it looking for my ship. And all the next day. The hills were lousy with vacant, flower-filled meadows. Goddamn scenery, anyway. I did stumble across the skeleton of an elk, which cheered me up no end. If *he* couldn't make it out here in the boonies where he belonged, what chance did Mister First Nighter of Greater Oklahoma City stand?

Says here in the survival manual, "When in doubt, go downhill"—especially if you're following a creek, few of which flow the other way. "Eventually, you'll come to civilization." That's how I spent the second day and mosta the third, following a creek. It led me to another creek.

Nights I endured with my suit turned up as high as it would go (not high enough), hunched over a cautious little teacup-sized fire. Second morning, I woke up covered with frost. Warmed through by a vigorous fit of coughing, I ate the last of my concentrates, sharing powdered instant coffee with the Freenies, who seemed otherwise content to forage.

The principal disadvantage to nature-in-the-raw *isn't* that it's uncomfortable. It's boring. One authentically rustic tree or boulder looks pretty much like another, and half a million acres of 'em tends t'pall. Nothin' to listen to except the squishing of your muddy shoes. Gimme a junkyard or a roadside holoboard *any* time—idiots who like gawkin' at the Great Outdoors never hadda measure it one exhausted footstep at a time, using moldy leaves for toilet paper an' not knowin' if they were ever gonna make it back t'beer-on-tap an' that redhead in Vonbraunsville.

It was the third night, now. As before, I shaved a couple twigs an' touched 'em to the lighter in the handle of my knife. They smoldered agreeably; I only sneezed once. Setting them carefully on a bed of rust-brown needles and other twigs, I blew them into a tiny, sputtering fire and rested till I wasn't dizzy anymore.

It was dark again, as seems t'happen with some regularity. The fire flickered as I fed it, baking myself on the front side while my back froze, then turning to bake my back as I stared, flame-blinded, into the fathomless night.

I'd given up on Color, Charm, and Spin for intelligent conversation. Dirty jokes involving seventeen sexes hafta be spelled out for unfortunates with only two. Likewise, they didn't get "The Sleeve Job," even *after* I'd explained it, and considered "The Green Horse" just plain dumb. All they could blabber about was how Gruenblum had invented coffee-nerves, thus saving Yamaguchikind from destruction. I'd heard the story before.

It was more diverting just observing the little critters—reminding myself sourly that's how I'd gotten stuck with 'em in the first place. Now they had names, seemed I could tell 'em apart more reliably. English was their only language, cribbed offa cornflake boxes an' suchlike I'd had in my garbage along with the teabags and coffee grounds. Among themselves they revved it up to 78 RPM.

That eye of theirs could focus telescopically, I discovered; each of them could see a thousand stars in the Seven Sisters and insisted on naming every one of 'em, until I put a stop to it. At the opposite end of the scale, they were fascinated at the minute protozoans t'be found under every leaf and in the rain-filled hollows, even as they munched 'em down and swallowed. They were dismayed when it turned out, in the gathering twilight, that I could only see in the narrow spectral band that they called ultrared to infraviolet.

Some kinda god *I* was turnin' out t'be!

So here I sat before my tiny, ineffectual fire, weary and bored, shivering and soaking wet as usual (never seemed t'get dry in those woods), listening to the local coyotes praying to the moon, and my own minuscule worshippers debating the question: since Gruenblum is Omniscient, Omnipotent, and Benevolent, how come were we lost?

Simple: I was Stupid, too.

Suddenly, all conversation stopped. Three straining eyestalks pointed toward a wild thrashing in the bushes that defined our little clearing. Blinded by firelight, I drew my Colt, seeking a target in the leafy gloom. Over the tromping and crashing, which grew louder, came a clamor like a Canada goose being molested by a set of bagpipes.

I thumbed the hammer back. Adding a shaky left hand to the shaky right hand on the pistol grip, I pointed its garbage-can snout in the direction of the disturbance. Mountain lions, sabertooth tigers, black bears, grizzlies—only Ochskahrt knew, and he was dead—*this* animal was *real* sick, maybe rabid.

The Freenies stretched their necks, peering into the darkness.

Abruptly, two huge hairy paws thrust through a house-sized raspberry bush not ten feet away. I placed my front sight right between them, waiting tensely to see more. Something cylindrical and queerly flexible swung between the claws.

The racket ceased. Over a moist, fur-covered ebony muzzle, a pair of savage eyes blinked at me. I blinked back, wetting my lips. Each massive shoulder of the gigantic ursine monster bore a brightly-colored stripe—connected to a day-glo yellow knapsack! At the ponderous, blackly-furred waist lay a broad leather belt; at the right hip, carried diagonally forward in the "appendix" position, hung an automatic hand-cannon that made my pistol suddenly feel like a bracelet charm.

The creature's gaze calmly took in the palsied quivering of my .45, the little fire-camp I'd built, the three funny-looking organisms presently crowding each other behind my back.

It opened its cavernous mouth, revealing hideously gleaming fangs.

"Please don't shoot me, Mister," the gorilla said. "I'm the President's only niece, and he wouldn't like it."

6

The Jape of
the Ape

SO IT'S 123 B.C.—THAT'S 630 A.U.C. TO US CITI-zens—an' I'm decked out in my snazziest gabardine toga, swappin' conversational Latin at a lie-down dinner for two with this left-wing Tribune, Caius Sempronius Gracchus, I ran into at the corner of Vth and Esquiline, playin' bocci in an S&M bar.

In the second-century Republic, they're all S&M bars.

This Gracchus puts me in minda Denny Kent. We're arguin' sword-control; he says the Senate oughta decree anything shorter'n a cubit—'specially those cheap bronze Saturnalia Specials—gotta be confiscated, melted down, an' cast into the memorial likeness of his martyred brother, Tiberius.

The Tribune's scheme'd do away with 99 percent of all the gladii an' spathae in the Eternal City. I wonder what he'd make of good ol' Bernardus Semiticus here, with a .45 caliber ballista tucked under his left armpit. I allow as how certain Greeks mighta thought well of his idea, an' look how they finished up: servin' us candied pheasant bladders.

He gets sore, throws a buncha grapes at me, I jump up t' flatten his nose, an' one of the slaves hollers "Bucketeers!" Nobody punches out a Tribune, says the night-court Quaestor. I wind up playin' seventh paddle in a trireme headed for the Cornish tin-mines and doubling on chains.

—I woke up shivering and sweaty, trying to remember where I was. *Brrrr!* Been a long time since I had *that* one.

Bernie's Roman Holiday. Gotta take things slower; this havin' seventeen adventures in thirty-six hours is for the young guys.

I turned over in bed, reaching for the light-switch before I recalled that where I was now, all y'gotta do is ask: *"Fiat lux!"* I whispered, still in the mood of my nightmare. And behold, there *was* Italian sportscar soap. Little section of the wall pretending to be a digital clock at the moment said it was 4:07 A.M.

I thought back over the past several highly-perplexing hours.

A rising moon had silvered the meadow; mingled hints of columbine and evergreen drifted on the breeze. The gorilla with the knapsack and pistol winked at me, squashing her concertina back together with a reedy moan and hooking its tiny brass latches. Suited me fine: "Lady of Spain" was never parta *my* Top 40. She put it on a rock, set paws on her hips, and regarded me and my three cowardly companions with critical amusement.

"Well, aren't you going to invite me to sit down? And I'd appreciate it if you'd tuck that little gun away before one of us gets hurt." Not waiting for the invitation, she plunked herself on the ground—'bout Richter Force 5, I estimated—beside the fire.

I holstered the three-pound wedge of carbon steel I was *used* to thinking of as Jove's Thunderbolt. "Beg your pardon, er, Miss. Bernard M. Gruenblum at your service." I glared at the three miniature aliens concealing their pusillanimous selves behind me: "An' these are my familiars, Color, Charm, and Chickenshit." Charm peeked timidly around one of my knees, his eye twinkling in the firelight.

"I'm Koko Featherstone-Haugh," the gorilla answered with a seated curtsy. She pronounced the last name "Fanshaw," spelling it for me. "In case you're interested, this is my Uncle Olongo's ranch you're trespassing on. Got anything to cook over that fire? I'm *famished!*"

For the first time since I'd landed here, the night-time

sky was clear. Flames threw Koko's dancing shadow across the clearing. I sorted dully through the pine needles and gravel that'd accumulated in my pockets.

"Instant coffee, but nothin' t'torture it in. We been kinda nibblin' at it, the way a kid does Kool-Aid." I shivered in the gathering mountain chill and turned my suit up another notch. "Tastes terrible."

"I can imagine!" The ape grinned, a fearsome sight if ever I witnessed one. She hadn't really been talking all this time, I suddenly noticed. Her voice seemed to issue from an instrument strapped around her left wrist. "I've got a little pan here somewhere," she offered pleasantly, shrugging out of her knapsack, "and even some more coffee. Also instant, I'm afraid. You say your little friends like it, too?"

Now *here* was a scenario they hadn't prepared us for in time-travel school: *kaffeeklatsching* politely with an affable, English-speaking female simian in the midst of a pine-scented jungle where there shoulda been a ticky-tacky metropolis of several million purely human folk. Gorillas of my acquaintance were little more than hairy robots, servants in a chronically labor-short economy, with electronic implants on their cortices, controlled just like a model airplane. Like the Yamaguchii when you take away their Folgers, they were liable to lapse back into sullen, unresponsive animalhood when the current was switched off.

Somethin' surpassing strange was goin' on here.

Koko probably agreed. I followed her significant glance toward the Freenies, looked back at her, and wiggled my eyebrows sheepishly. "Guess I sorta misplaced my flyin' saucer, Ma'am."

"Mr. Gruenblum," she observed absently, levering an enormous metal skillet outa the pack and unfolding its handle with a *clunk!*, "If you're going to miss the point when I'm trying to be subtle—*who in Lysander's name* are *you people, and what are you doing on my uncle's ranch?*" She hadn't *quite* gone for her bazooka; when you're her size, it'd be gildin' the lily.

"Uh, I'm gonna answer that question, Miss Featherstone-Haugh, but before I do, wouldya mind tellin' me . . . what *year* this is?"

When travelin' in the past, you're ordinarily ill-advised t'tell the truth about yourself. The Academy frowns on it. Severely.

But I was up against something new here. From my pointa view, this was pret'near three hundred years ago. History is one thing I'm supposed t'*know* about—the backa my hand's an unexplored frontier by comparison. But if this was 1993, it wasn't any 1993 that *I* remembered.

She looked me over as if seeing me for the first time, gave the Freenies another inspection, then back t'me again, and my little green coverall. "Why it's 217 A.L., of course."

I took out m'last cigar, watched her unfold the pan's collapsing legs, fill it from the nearby creek, and return to the fire. I added a few more twigs and branches, enjoyin' the natural incense of sage an' soft pine—but not much else that was happening.

What the hell did "A.L." stand for? And who in *Ochskahrt*'s name was this Lysander? Only one I knew about was a Bronze Age channel swimmer. Her grouping *me* with the Freenies—". . . you people . . ."—had sent a quiver down my spine. Could be she'd never *seen* a human bein' before, an' I was just as alien to her as they were.

What had she meant, her uncle was the President? President of what?

Wasn't sure I wanted t'find out.

By now the water was boiling. Koko began sprinklin' powdered pseudojava into it, the aroma filling my nostrils an' makin' the Freenies perk up suddenly. I found I'd forgotten to light my cigar.

"Uh, Miss Featherstone-Haugh—Koko—I really wasn't kidding about losing my flying saucer. I know it's gonna be hard t'believe, but, well: *I'm from the Moon.* The little guys, here, are from Ganymede."

I helped her share out the coffee into small metallic nesting cups and set those for Color, Charm, and Spin out in a row beside the fire. As usual, each critter settled himself over his container, covering it completely. When they arose again, I knew, the coffee'd be gone. Kinda disgustin' to the uninitiated. Put me in mind of a Yoga demonstration I'd been forced t'watch one time.

"The Moon?" Nothin' seemed t'rattle Koko. She sipped her coffee, squinting at me through the steam and wrinkling her nose. "Do you know Admiral Mitchell?"

"Admiral who?" Again I reminded myself to light my cigar.

"William Lendrum Mitchell, Confederate Navy—retired, of course. He's actually a friend of Uncle Olongo's, but the only person I've ever met who lives up there." She gazed out at the frozen stars, a dreamy inner focus to her big brown eyes. "Funny, I've been clear to the Asteroids—Ceres—with my uncle, when I was little. But never to the Moon."

Precisely at that moment, something gigantic and ellipsoid drifted overhead, deadly silent, 'bout a mile long, an' movin' poleward several hundred klicks an hour. Its sleek form was defined by rows on rows of brightly-colored windows.

"The dirigible *San Francisco Palace*"—Koko answered my wild stare—"bound for Calgary, Anchorage, and points north. Used to stop in Gallatinopolis, too, before they quit having Congress. Uncle Olongo says she was the first catalytic fusion airship ever—imagine *that*, and still in service after all these years!"

Somethin' was definitely screwy here. Catalytic fusion hadn't been commercially perfected till the middle of the twenty-first century—an' dirigibles'd blasted themselves outa fashion in the 1930s. It was like watchin' a New England whaler powered by a nuclear reactor.

Quit havin' Congress?

I took a big gulpa coffee, gears whirlin' around inside my head—an' burnt the hell outa my tongue.

Never did summon up the moxie t'ask what a 114-year-old court-martialed Signal Corps general was doin' retired from the *Navy* an' livin' on the Moon. Instead, I let Koko explain how she was really a city girl, gettin' the most out of a welcome break from school.

"Recess was always my favorite subject, too," I told her, pouring myself another cup. The Yamaguchians were back for seconds, too, each with his little container clutched greedily in a pair of slender green tentacles. I let Koko be mother an' scratched around for a twig t'light my much-neglected cigar from. "I'm just passin' through, m'self."

She sighed tornadically, stirring coals. The flames leaped a foot higher and receded. "Dirty bad old school—it's such a waste of time! I'd *so* much rather be here . . . or out *there*." She pointed skyward to an extra star I'd noticed where there shoulda been an empty orbital position. "But Uncle Olongo insists—"

"Yeah," I commiserated. "The Powers-That-Be have a way of doin' that." I thrust the twig into the flames, moistening the end of my cigar in anticipation. There was silence for a while.

"Bernie?" Firelight danced in Koko's eyes.

The end of the twig bubbled and began to char. "Yeah, kid?"

"Are you going to get into much trouble? I mean, for losing your flying saucer?"

It was a swell question. I almost felt guilty for havin' brushed her off with half an explanation, but the Academy's rules defend the existence of an entire universe, an' they can't be bent, even for a nice young lady—of whatever species—sincerely concerned about my hide. Hell, for all I knew, this situation I was in might justa been *caused* by such a breach!

"Well, *my* particular Powers-That-Be have some rough-mannered ways of handlin' lapses of discipline. 'Bout the *best* I can expect is that they'll dock my pay for the next coupla eons. The worst . . ." Visions of the Ochskahrt Memorial Pylon rose before my bleary inner eye. "Kid, I don't think y'wanna hear about it."

She hesitated, building up her courage. "You can tell *me*, Bernie. You see, I already *know*."

I frowned, confused. "Well, as some wiseacre once said,

'T'know what y'know—an' t'know what y'don't know—
is t'*know*." I lifted the burning twig toward the end of my
cigar. "Know *what*, kid?"

"That you're a Time-Traveler."

"*WHAT?*" I dropped the twig an' spent a few undignified
moments hoppin' around slappin' at my lap. Even the Freenies swiveled their eyestalks an' pointed on the young gorilla
like a pack of huntin' dogs.

Recovering the twig, I started to rev up my cigar again.

"Sure, Bernie. You've given yourself away a dozen times,
you and your little friends. I may be just a kid, but I'm not
stupid. I haven't been to Ganymede, either, but I've got
friends who have. There certainly aren't any 'Freenies' there.
Besides, *everybody* knows about Admiral Billy Mitchell,
the Air Navy hero who helped us win The-War-Against-
The-Czar."

"OWCH! Sonofa—" While I'd been reelin' in my jaw
from where it'd fallen on the ground, the twig'd finally
burned down to my fingers, givin' me a broiled thumb
t'match my parboiled tongue. Groucho, Harpo, an' Karl
trundled to me with affectionate concern, one of 'em spillin'
his coffee on my foot in the process.

I hardly noticed it.

"Look, Koko, what I do for a livin's s'posed t'be a secret.
Even if I survived the punishment for lettin' on, all my
descendants'd be born with—"

I'd *almost* said, ". . . three balls and a purple goatee . . ."
but thought better of it under the circumstances.

"—two heads an' a permanent case of mange."

"Some secret!" Koko snorted. "What possible explanation *could* there have been? But don't worry, Bernie. *I*
certainly won't tell anybody—and neither will Uncle
Olongo." She hunched closer toward me, conspiratorial delight written all over her furry face. "Now that we've taken
care of *that*, why don't you tell me how you and your cute
little friends managed to get stranded here. Maybe I can
help!"

Charm emitted a delighted *peep!* and skittled around the
fire to rub against her legs. The traitor.

Could loose lips get me *back* my ship? All I seemed t'be accomplishin' by myself was incubatin' a pneumonia culture. Somethin' about this hairy, muscle-bound school-girl seemed to inspire more confidence than I'd ever felt in any *human* bein'. Maybe it was the ponderous delicacy with which she carried her 400-kilo self. Maybe it was the kindly way she treated my tiny worshippers. Maybe it was the fact she'd already guessed all the "burn-before-reading" parts by herself, an' the only way I was ever gonna get outa this predicament—or even find out where I was—was t'let her have the whole soap opera, Academy or not.

I'd like t'think that was the case: hardnosed decision-making in the face of insurmountable realities—an' not that I was wet, cold, an' hungry. Us Gruenblums was always made of sterner stuff. Whatever the reason, I sang like a bird.

Koko oohed and aahed in all the right places, grimacing over the murders of Merwin and his elderly colleague. She was interested in *Georgie*, fascinated with sixteenth century Japan.

". . . Cromney's invented a new form of fascism, an' he can't wait t'try it out." I extracted the field-density equalizer, brushed off the mud and pocket vegetation, and held it up in the firelight. "But he ain't goin' *anywhere* without this!"

She shook her head sadly. "Hamiltonians—Professor Cromney and his followers, I mean. That's what they sound like. We've had a few like that, even here in the Confederacy. Don't worry, Bernie. Uncle Olongo and the boys will help you find *Georgie* first thing in the morning."

She yawned—a sight that woulda made Elmo Lincoln himself high-tail it for the tall pineys—an' consulted the multipurpose thingummy on her wrist. "You know, it's almost two o'clock in the morning!"

"Yaaahh," I answered through a wide-open yawn of my own, "we want an early start tomorrow. Didn't happen t'bring an extra bindle, didya?" I glanced at her King Kong-sized rucksack; damn thing woulda done for a sleeping bag itself.

She blinked. "Why, no. I brought one for myself, just

in case, and you're perfectly welcome to it, if you really insist, because—"

"No, no, wouldn't wanna inconvenience—"

"*Because,* unless you actually enjoy freezing to death and having bugs crawl all over you..."

She stood, grasped me by the wrist, and before I knew it, I was standing on my feet. Half dragging me across the clearing and up a little rise at the end, she pointed a proprietary digit down the hill.

There in the valley under the moonglow and the Milky Way, not five hundred lousy meters from my damp, dark, miserable campsite, Uncle Olongo's Cabin lay in a broad, warm pool of buttery electric light.

7

Zootier
than Thou

OLONGO FEATHERSTONE-HAUGH, AMERICA'S twenty-fifth President (not countin' Gallatin's final term an' "None-of-the-Above"), was an Everest of flesh in an avalanche of reddish-black shag carpet. Only it *wasn't* the United States, but the "North American Confederacy"—and the list of former Chief Execs included four women, two Indians, a black guy, an' a French-Canadian Chinese.

But I'm gettin' aheada myself.

Havin' seen my little fire extinguished carefully, Koko shepherded us aliens down to a rambling three-story mansion she honestly regarded as a modest working ranch-house. A whitewashed timber fence separated lawn from pasture; the usual moron'd lined up head-sized rocks along the graveled pathway an' painted 'em—incandescent pink. Freenies musta thought it was a ticket queue.

Maybe it only *seemed* like a three-mile hike around back. Even this late, somebody was stirrin' in the hangarous kitchen, a graying female Koko addressed as "Grandma Goldilocks," who plied us all with fresh hot biscuits, more butter'n I'd ever seen collected outside a USDA warehouse, scrambled eggs, an' heaps of tiny, oddly-flavored, thin-sliced steaklets. My companions appreciated the gallons of steaming coffee. So did I. Never keeps me awake when I don't want it to—I can take a cup t'bed with me like warm milk.

Before very long, I was seein' double; too much food, too little sleep. My fuzzy hostesses frog-marched me, the

seemingly tireless Freenies taggin' along, to a guest-room
down a half-kilometer of corridor. Kept thinkin' about the
Yankee who fell into a Texas swimmin' pool an' went down
hollerin', "Don't flush it!" Exceptin' for that Roman REM
extravaganza 'bout an hour later, I hit the pillow an' didn't
return to the land of the livin' until three o'clock next afternoon—naked as a jaybird.

Well, if it hadn't embarrassed the simiennes, it wasn't
gonna embarrass me.

The fat quilted coverlet was gaily printed with cattle
brands an' cactuses. The bed-frame, constructed outa Co-
nestoga wagon wheels, matched another one hung horizontal from the ceiling mounting half a dozen chimneyed lamps.
The walls were spongy, weathered mesquite, an' the throw-
rug on the floor mighta once been a gorilla itself, except
for the baling-hook claws at its corners an' a nasty *Ursus
horribilis* snarl I damn near shoved my foot into gettin' outa
bed.

Found my clothing, crisp an' spotless, in a mock saloon-
doored closet, courteously left open. A momentary panic
subsided when I noticed the field-density frammis lying with
my other pocketry on a beer-barrel dresser, in a lamp rigged
out t'look like a tiny hand-pumped horse-trough. Without
thinkin', I began climbing back into Academy greens, but
somethin' rebellious started me riffling through the other
outfits left for me t'choose from.

Trousers here were sturdy, baggy, flared, with extra-
wide belt-loops, as if everybody lifted weights in their off-
hours an' needed kidney support. There were tunics of a
military cut (overlookin' the almost Yamaguchian patterns
and colors), a sorta Nehru-necked sportscoat the Shah of
Egypt mighta liked, whose bottom edging swept the terra-
cotta floor, an' right beside it, three regular no-foolin' kilts,
complete with sporran, two of 'em honest plaid—an' one
paisley, for Ochskahrt's sake! Also a couple hooded numbers halfway between a cape and a *serape*.

I kept my Airborne Rangers in preference to the pointy-
toed monstrosities at the bottom of the closet, selecting a
pair of pleated orange pants—the most conservative at

hand—and an epauleted robin's-egg blouse. I was prepared t'get laughed at for what I was throwin' together—after all, nobody trained Mrs. Gruenblum's little boy for *this* mission—an' make corrections later. Under one of those cloak-things, silver-gray an' tossed back rakishly, I strapped my blood-stained pistol rig; made me feel better in unknown territory, an' last night I'd noticed even Grandma Goldilocks was heeled—a semitrusive four-barreled derringer of about .60 caliber, which, with a locket on a golden chain, had constituted her entire wardrobe.

"When in Rome," I shuddered, recalling the dream, "say hello to the table."

It was lightly overcast an' drizzlin' outside, the sun an anemic brassy disc. The window opened out on a meadow edged with evergreen almost black in the fine mist. At the limit of vision grazed several dozen quadrupedal blobs, supervised by a hazy figure on horseback.

Checking my pistol chamber, I took a final gander in the portion of the wall adjusted to nonreversing mirrorhood, turned one way, then the other, an' waggled my eyebrows. "Reet!"

When the door got outa my way politely, I discovered Color waiting for me, sucking on a tea-bag. "The trousers are properly worn tucked into the boot-tops, O Lord." Hopping on one leg while making adjustments to the other, I followed this fifteen-inch fluorescent arbiter-of-fashion as he trundled down the hall—the string an' tag of the tea-bag trailing out from underneath his shell.

They were gathered in the living room, and I'd guessed right about the gunbelt, at least. Olongo Featherstone-Haugh couldn't tuck his trousers in; the pair of denim Bermuda shorts he was wearing, complete with leather tag and copper rivets, missed the scallops of his sixteen-inch red, white, and gold-eagled mule-ears by a mile. The Tony Lamas matched a heavy leather pistol rig. The shorts matched a monogrammed vest with copper buttons. Parked across the room on the back of a massive roll-top desk was enough pearl-gray Stetson to hold revival-meetings in. Koko sat beside him in a squaw-dress with a concho belt and thirty pounds of turquoise jewelry. The President looked just like a giant furry Dallas Cowboy cheerleader.

It wouldn'ta been *too* crazy t'start lookin' for *Georgie* right here in this room. Plenty of space between its leather-paneled walls. Both gorillas occupied a two-tone calfskin sofa only slightly smaller than the *San Francisco Palace*, Koko with a cup of coffee on her knee, Olongo with a cooler in his hand that put me in minda that Texican swimmin' pool again. He waved me to a similar settee across an acre of slab-rock coffee table, little trilobites an' petrified seaweed peekin' up through plate-glass. Lunch was steaming in the middle, plus a stand of Cuban cigars. Badly torn, I evaded the issue by takin' a better look around.

First thing when I woke up that mornin', I'd triggered memory-cues I had on twentieth century history—data implanted during Academy days, supplemented regularly since, via DreamCap. Wasn't sure what good it'd do in this instance: just sittin' in this room generated dissonances enough t'send me to the migraine ward.

It was like the bedroom, piled higher and deeper: brick-tile floor; black iron chandelier and wall-sconces, both with pseudokerosene fixtures; more wagon wheels an' empty grizzly bears; deer, elk, an' moose-antennae everywhere y'looked. The couch I sat on was draped with a cougar hide.

In one corner, a glassed-in case displayed three dozen deadly-looking hand-weapons, most of which, by rights, shouldn'ta been invented yet. Perhaps oddest of all, over the arched adobe walk-in fireplace hung a portrait of the 1900's most-respected flatto idol, John Wayne, enigmatically inscribed: *"To Olongo, warmest re-gards, Mike."*

"My dear Captain Gruenblum!" The west-of-the-Pecos ambience suffered immediately for Olongo's Oxford accent. "Do please make yourself comfortable, old man. It isn't often we've the pleasure to entertain a certifiably Mysterious Stranger."

He gestured with a broad hand toward the soup an' sandwiches a modestly-attired Goldilocks was arranging on the table, filled his own gigantic glass halfway with tomato juice, and upended a plastic can of beer into it. It fizzed.

I looked at Koko, wondering how much she'd told him. "Don't mind if I do, Your Presidency. I see m'friends're taken care of; if introductions're still in order, say hello t'Color, Charm, an' Spin." The aliens bobbed their eyes politely.

"I suppose," the President observed, "that we all have our little quarks."

The Yamaguchians perched on a divan upholstered with an Indian blanket an' pulled up to the table. Coffee an' salad were the order of the day for the essentially vegetarian critters. I followed their example, adding a square foot of sirloin, thought about the beer—got vetoed by my stomach—an' settled back.

"And this grim-visaged fellow"—my host nodded toward a figure standing by the floor-to-cciling picture-window—"is Austin Clintwood, my foreman. Koko leads me to understand his services may be of some use to you."

Clintwood was tall for his height, dressed in faded blue-jeans, leather chaps an' vest, a brightly colored shirt that clashed with his bandanna, and the ubiquitous broad gunbelt, well-used. His feet were bare. At his hip an age-grayed automatic hung, and from a pocket of his vest, the tag-end of a Bull-Durham sack. Hat and spurs he held politely in one hand, but he seemed impatient t'be out an' doin' whatever cowboys go out an' do. A shame, 'cause he was the first Confederate I'd met who wasn't a gorilla.

He was a chimpanzee.

His William S. Hart get-up was spoiled just a mite by the banana he was munchin' on, but the voice slipped outa his wrist-talker low an' steady, almost a whisper. "Howdy." He was an ape of few words, strong and silent.

"Howdy yerself," I answered. "Seen any spaceships lately? 'Bout twenty-five meters, round an' shiny?" I gestured with my hands.

Clintwood gave his boss a sour look, as if t'say *this* is what you dragged me in here for?

"I assure you, Austin, the gentleman's quite serious." Olongo gestured toward the Freenies. "And truthful, if these little fellows are any—great Albert's ghost, how very condescending! For all I know, the three of you could be...sincerest apologies, dear friends, I—"

"My fault, Mr. President," I cut in when Olongo finished arguin' with himself. I nodded toward the chimpanzee. "Don't blame your ramrod none, either, for bein' skeptical." I fought down the depressing mental image of Ochskahrt's pylon. "Guess I'm gonna hafta tell the whole blamed story over again. How much do they know, Koko?"

I stretched for one of the Havanas on the table.

She sipped her coffee delicately. "Only that I found you wandering around out there, looking for your 'flying saucer'." She winked. "And that the Freenies are from Ganymede."

"You didn't mention I'm a—"

"Gosh, Bernie, I didn't think you wanted me to!"

"Discretion. If I weighed another three hundred kilos"—I looked down, grinning at my skinny frame—"think I'd askya t'marry me, Miss Featherstone-Haugh. Olongo, Austin, Grandma Goldilocks, you're lookin' at a Man-from-the-Future..."

Never trust a Gruenblum t'make a long story short. Every scrap of food vanished from the coffee table, bite by bite; we clear-cut Olongo's grove of cigars; he had t'send out for liquid reinforcements.

Mumbling indistinct obscenities about the past week's constant drizzle, Clintwood had his pistol disassembled, parts scattered all over the tabletop, an' was cleanin' it. Fella *never* left off workin'. Only when the thing was dry, spotless, an' back together in his holster did he obey his boss's direct order to relax, aided by a brace of double bourbons.

Somethin' labeled Old Lysander. Smelled just like the solvent he'd used t'clean his autopistol, t'me

I had a tough time gettin' the story past Nagasaki.

"Did I hear you correctly, young man?" Grandma Goldilocks thumbed up the volume on her hearing-aid. She'd turned out t'be Koko's real grandmother; the young gorilla had "divorced" her parents—Cinderella and B'wana—

Olongo's brother. Never did get it straight whether Goldilocks was Cinderella's mom or Olongo's.

"Yeah," came Clintwood's sibilant voice, "I don't savvy why they dropped the *first* uranium bomb on the Nipponese, let alone the second."

"Plutonium, Austin. An' y'got me, friend. Always thought they shoulda *demonstrated* the damn thing to the Japs— woulda scared 'em right outa their kimonos, an' they was on their last legs, anyway.

"The second bomb? That was just plain downright meanness. I hear tell it was originally intended for Berlin. Story is that Roosevelt made a deal with the Russians—you followin' this?—not t'keep a spare bomb around, so the Truman Administration hadda find a way t'use it up."

"And several tens of thousands of sapient beings with it—after which they prosecuted the *Germans* for mass murder! This is beginning to sound distressingly familiar, Bernie," the President shuddered. "Pray finish as quickly as you can."

I didn't stop t'wonder, then, how Olongo knew about World War II. I simply brought everbody up t'where I'd almost taken his niece for a grizzly an' put her concertina outa its obvious misery.

"So y'see, it ain't just gettin' back t'2285. Find *Georgie*, that'll take care of itself. Trouble is, I ain't sure what *kinda* twenty-third century's up there waitin' for us. That'll due respect, you folks ain't parta any continuity I recognize."

"Oh dear!" cried Koko, a stunned look on her fur-fringed puss. "And I thought I had everything figured out! Uncle Olongo, what's going *on* here?"

The President stared out at the gathering darkness, puffing his cigar. "Captain Gruenblum—"

"Bernie."

"Very well, Bernie: what you've told us is exactly *perpendicular* to any referential frame we're prepared to deal with. Journeys into the past and future? There are imaginative stories . . . what's that writer's name—Proxmire, something like that. However, Koko's surmises related to a phenomenon, albeit not a whit less fantastic, yet demonstrably real: accidental transposition across the lines of probability."

I stared at my host. "How's that again?"

"Bernie, the universe is broader than *anyone* might have suspected only a decade ago. There are... 'places' where, for terrible example, George Washington and Alexander Hamilton *won* the Whiskey Rebellion, or—"

"Hold your horses!" I muttered eighteenth century memory-cues; data popped into place on my cortex: "But they *did* win, Olongo! Washington started collectin' taxes like he wanted, an' Aaron Burr shot Hamilton in a duel."

"Burr?" Olongo mused. "Don't recall hearing that name before; I'll make inquiries. But this is precisely my point, sir: you may be from the distant future, but you're also from an alternative reality, and if that *was* a military uniform I saw Goldilocks processing for you this morning—difficult to tell when there's only one of the things around—then I believe I know *which* alternative reality."

My head hurt. I didn't understand all this "alternative reality" jazz—ideas like that are dangerous, quietly but savagely suppressed by the Academy. But I'd figured out what was wrong now. Somebody—Cromney an' his gang or even another set of temporal tinkerers on a different mission—somebody'd finally messed things up catastrophically. A significant historic event somewhen had been altered, through carelessness or malice, destroying subsequent history as I knew it, an' substituting this *Planet of the Apes* thing that was goin' on.

There *wasn't* any more Academy, nor any west-Texican Oklahoma City suburbs where I usta hang my nonexistent hat. Findin' *Georgie* wouldn't do me—or the Freenies— a licka good. There *wasn't* any future t'go home to.

It was full dark once again; the rain hadn't let up for a minute. Discussion didn't end there, but my contributions to it got unaccountably less frequent as I succumbed to a sudden, paralyzing fatigue. Guess I'd been through a lot lately. Mebbe it was the marguerita Goldilocks provided that finished me off. As the Freenies tucked me in—least that's how I remember it—my thoughts were whirlin' round in circles down the drain.

If we were well an' truly stranded here, recoverin' *Georgie* was still my number-one priority. I missed her worse'n any *livin'* creature, an' she was an incalculably valuable survival asset.

Besides, there was the possibility I could take her backward in time, find the rupture, an' repair it—hold on, *there* was an ethical snarl! Restorin' my own time-line'd be at the certain funereal expense of these kindly generous simians I'd met here. Gorillas an' chimpanzees'd go back t'bein' drawers of wood an' hewers of water.

Don't think I *ever* cared much for that.

Destroyin' the North American Confederacy seemed just as rotten as whatever had destroyed my world. One thing for sure: Cromney, Kent, an' Janof'd gotten me into this—in their case, catastrophic destruction, for preference courtesy of my Colt .45, seemed like a *swell* idea.

I fell asleep reflectin' that I shoulda followed Aus Clintwood's example an' tidied up my piece. Just hadn't... seemed...polite...at...the...

8

Boots 'n' Saddlesores

"YIPPEE!!"

The normally laconic Austin Clintwood hollered through a wind-battered grin, slapping his bucking steed with a wide-brim hat. His ornate saddle creaked as stresses shifted from stirrup to stirrup. His mount veered in circles, pitching, rolling, but he hung on gamely to the shouted satisfaction of the simian cow-punchers gathered on Olongo's front lawn.

"Ride 'em, Aus!"

"Ride 'em, cowboy!"

"Wahoo!"

Clintwood made a final pass, leaned t'starboard, an', graceful as a prairie hawk, spiraled upward a hundred meters, the dual electrostatic impellers of his chrome-plated sky-scooter rising an octave. He wiped a forearm across his brow, grinned self-consciously, jammed on his *sombrero,* an' vanished over the pine-covered hogback behind the ranch-house, no doubt already his old no-nonsense self again.

A pale an' shamefaced sun was makin' its debut through the drizzle at the opposite end of the valley.

Olongo leaned back in his massive front-porch rocker, finishing his first cigar of the morning, our breakfast— steak an' eggs—already a glorious memory. Koko perched up on the rail, anxious t'get on with things. I was sitting on an empty nail-keg, dreadin' the ordeal t'come.

It wasn't just the liquid nastiness drippin' from the eaves, though I didn't look forward t'gettin' this mornin's borrowed cowboy-suit all soggy. The job hadda be done. Drove me plumb crazy wonderin' what Cromney an' his pals'd

been up to all this time. It's just that I've never gotten along
that well with horse-flesh.

The President stopped rocking, stubbed out his cigar on
the side of his boot-heel. "Well, sir, I suppose we must be
off. That was, after all, our purpose in arising at such a
shocking hour."

Olongo figgered there wasn't any reason a gentleman
rancher oughta keep the same ungodly time-table medieval
peasants had before electric lights an' late-late-shows got
invented. Today was an unwelcome exception; we had miles
t'make, no surplus of daylight t'do it in.

Koko jumped up, nearly knockin' me over. The three of
us, followed closely by Color, Charm, an' Spin, crossed
the broad graveled yard to the horse-barn. No chrome-plated
cayuses for us. Matching Clydesdales were already saddled
up for the gorillas. A brace of Shetland ponies waited for
the chimps who'd go along. Standin' there in the not-too-
unpleasant-smellin' gloom, I sized up the midsized mare
they'd picked out for yours truly, while she did the same
t'me.

We weren't gonna like each other.

I'd been checked out on horses at the Academy; main
problem at one-sixth gee's stayin' velcroed to the saddle. I
walked around to the big gray's port gunwhale, keepin' a
respectful distance from her iron-shod torpedo-tubes.

"What are you doing, Bernie?"

"What's it look like, Koko? Gettin' on m'horse."

"Well, there's really no need to mount from the left. Our
animals are brought up ambidextrous!" T'make the point,
she hopped up on the right side of her fringe-footed beer-
dragger. "See?"

So much for my equestrian expertise. I shoved a reluctant
foot into the stirrup. They'd bullied me into a paira gaudy
Justin winkle-pickers, after all. Somethin' gruesome about
gettin' thrown an' *dragged*. Just when I was nicely off-
balance there was that old familiar tuggin' at my pants leg.

"Bernie, are you *quite* certain you're up to this?"

I looked back over my shoulder. "Ambassador, your
heartfelt concern's duly logged, an' I appreciate y'wadin'

through all this *caballo* exhaust just t'do my hypochondri-ackin' for me. But I'm feelin' fine—now leggo my leg!"

Charm shook his eyestalk, sharing a look of pessimism with the other two Freenies behind him. "You weren't feeling fine last night, Bernie. There was more to your fainting-spell than simple fatigue or a small volume of alcohol, I'm certain of it."

Now he mentioned it, I'd thought it was a little strange, myself. One minute I'd been chewin' the fat with the Feath-erstone-Haughs, an' the next, a Yamaguchian was rollin' that Nudie's bedspread up under my chin.

"I'm tellin' you, I *didn't* faint!" I wrapped both hands around the saddle-horn. "I passed out—there's a differ-ence!"

"Bernie, my fellows and I have been thinking about this and are deeply concerned about your health. Haven't you noticed yourself how your attention wanders, even lapsing into somnolence, whenever—"

"Charm, you an' your little buddies better leave the thinkin' t'me. That's the whole point t'religion, ain't it? An' when'd you ever heara *God* gettin' the punies? Now get outa my—*unh!*"

I heaved a leg over the leather, clingin' to the pommel for dear life. The Ambassador an' friends scooted hastily clear of the hoofs. The saddle creaked an' canted—I dunno, they never seem t'screw 'em on tight enough. Meanwhile, the reins'd gotten outa hand somehow, the ends droppin' on the ground. I leaned forward, stretchin' painfully to retrieve 'em as the mare gave me a sardonic look.

"Okay, dog-food, so I *don't* know what I'm doin'. Let's see *you* drive a time-machine!" I shook my head t'clear out the cobwebs.

She snorted, dropped her nose into a clump of hay at the back of the stall, nearly pullin' me off over her neck.

Koko pranced her stallion up to tower over this four-legged practical joker an' me. "Don't let her do that, Bernie. Show her who's boss!"

I jerked up on the reins without effect. "I think she knows!"

By some special dispensation from Mr. Murphy, I finally got the animal moving, backed up, turned around, an' followed Koko an' Olongo out into the drizzle, chimpanzees providin' a rear-guard. As we crunched an' clopped our way across the graveled yard, three little forlorn Army helmets, incandescent pink, dwindled gradually in the distance, wavin' their periscopes in sad farewell.

One thing about travelin' by mare's-shanks: it's *slow*.

Seemed like a quarter past forever before we were across that valley, startin' up into the trees. One of the chimps galloped around me t'confer with Olongo, then rode on ahead. I was busy unrollin' the yellow plastic slicker from my saddle cantle, precipitation creepin' down the backa my neck. I'd *refused* t'wear one of those ten-gallon pizzas like everybody else. But the Confederacy'd solved another age-old problem: didn't get hot an' sweaty under the raincoat; somehow it breathed *and* kept me reasonably dry at the same time. I looked down at the mare, water sluicin' over her forelocks, an' sneered.

Turned out her name was Bella, an' from the unhappy moment we laid eyes on each other, it was all-out war. Every sprig of vegetation was her cafeteria. Damn near sprained both arms each time she dipped her head t'grab a snack. She sidled just close enough t'trees an' boulders t'not *quite* scrape me off an' took delight in lashin' me with her rain-soaked rear-end flyswatter.

I've known *Spacers* smarter an' more cooperative than horses.

I did discover that not everybody who hangs around four-legged motorcycles is uncritically batty about 'em. The remainin' dogie-puncher ridin' behind me advised—between ineptly stifled bouts of snickerin'—not takin' any nonsense from Bella. Told me t'get downright *rough* about it, in a manner he surprised me by demonstration' an' which I expected any moment was gonna call the wrath of the Confederate SPCA down on my skinny little shoulders.

I was startin' my fourth cigar when Olongo waved at me t'join him. The mare broke into a trot, just about givin' me an inertial appendectomy, until I kicked her an' she shifted gears.

"Tallyho, old anthropoid! We cut 'em off at the pass yet?" Once started, Bella was tough t'stop. I overshot an' hadda circle back.

"We'll see directly," answered the boss ape. He reached down to his saddlehorn an' flipped the top away. "Go ahead, Austin."

A tiny, tiny voice replied. Olongo gestured; I flipped my own pommel open. Musta been a lotta transistors inside the hollow titanium saddle-tree; a miniature 3D screen was deliverin' an aerial travelogue.

"—be sure, but there's somethin' there. Mebbe eighty, ninety feet, an' circular. It's the lower pasture where you shot that five-pointer last fall." Clintwood shifted the viewpoint to himself, pulled out his little bag of makin's, rolled a coffin-nail one-handed, struck a kitchen match off his upper right canine, an' lit up. Behind him, the mist-blurred horizon tilted crazily as he kneed the scooter into a long, lazy bank. "I'll give ya another look!"

Wasn't too informative. The screen was small; the weather obscured the meadow several hundred feet below. Clintwood wanted t'set down but got vetoed. One well-soaked branch through those kilovolt impellers, fore an' aft, Olongo cautioned, an' there'd be fireworks from here to the Dakotas. Even after sophisticated image-enhancement at both ends, the circularity on the ground was just barely visible, Georgie's size, an' darker'n her surroundings. I was surprised t'feel my heart flutterin'. Musta been the altitude.

"That's the girl, Your Prexyship! How soon can we get up there?"

"Austin?"

"Boss, your party's about three and a half miles due east b'southeast. I'll flip back an' guide you in."

"Nonsense. Get back to the house and dry off, old sod. This isn't decent flying weather. See what damage you can do the case of Kingsley's that came in this morning—and Austin?"

"Yeah, boss?" The camera soared from meadow, up

through foothills an' ghostly peaks, across an eggshell-colored sky an' down t'landscape at the opposite compass point.

"The Escadrille lost its greatest pilot when you were born too late for the Prussian War. Out." He snapped his saddle-horn shut. "Well, old fellow, not much longer now."

"Yep," I answered, strong an' silent, checkin' the chamber of my Colt.

The mare twisted around an' bit me on the knee.

Wasn't anything about this meadow t'distinguish it from any of the other ten I'd stumbled through my first nights here. Thanks to the constant drizzle, y'couldn't see from one end to the other. We cleared the pines, navigatin' foot-by-foot from Clintwood's coordinates.

I rubbed my injured knee, grudgingly thankful for the nearly-indestructible fabric I was wearin'. Just inside the pasture, we pulled up behind a little copse of aspen theoretically between us an' the timebuggy.

"What now, O Commander-in-Chief?"

Olongo smiled, a ritual learned from humans. Among his own people, baring the choppers meant serious—an' terminal—social intercourse. "You know, the last Confederate President to bear that title in earnest was Sequoyah Guess, killed leading American volunteers in the Mexican War."

"Sounds good t'me. Be a lot fewer dust-ups if the guys't started 'em hadda go an' get shot at."

"Indeed. That was the idea." He opened his saddle-horn again, made a few surprisingly minute adjustments with those giant hands of his. "Well, my boy, you were well advised burying that damaged timepiece of yours. You see the blip, here? That's where you'll find it, and, by extension, your ship as well."

Standin' on legs made shaky an' unreliable by three hours in the saddle, I rooted around in the saddlebags while Bella made things interesting by tryin' t'step on my foot. The inseams of my jeans felt like they were on fire. Horsepersonship—you can have it!

Bravely: "I'm ready for all contingencies, Olongo. Think this is enough lead foil? I'd hate t'give up that watch. An' speakin' of gettin' shot at—*stand still, Bella!*—I wanna point out that this is my flight now. Don't want any of you nice folks hurt on my account."

I loosened up my war-Colt in its scabbard.

"Why *Bernie!*" uttered a scandalized Koko. She swung off her Clydesdale, shaking the ground. The chimps'd ridden out on the flanks a few yards, triangulatin' on my violated Nukatron warranty, an' were comin' back now.

"Quite right, my dear. Captain Gruenblum, we would be remiss in the extreme abandoning you at this juncture. There are certain *standards* in the Confederacy, particularly regarding courtesy to guests." He dismounted with surprising grace.

Wasn't anything I could say. Lefty, Olongo's point-man, kneed his pony up beside me, showing fangs in a manner hardly meant t'convey amusement.

"Ever now an' agin, Cap'n, we get some grief from Hamiltonians." He pulled a heavy Dardick-style pistol from his holster, testing both magazine an' cylinder t'make sure they were fulla ivory-colored triangular plastic cartridges. "Don't see as it makes no nevermind whether they're domestic or imported, right, Dex?"

The other chimpanzee, Dexter, reached back to his saddlebags for a telescoping shoulder-stock which he slid into the backstrap of his Mauser automatic, substituting an enormous drum for the smaller box magazine. He pulled the bolt back a fraction of an inch, assuring himself there was a thumb-sized cartridge in the chamber, let it clack forward again, an' grinned savagely.

"Dex's daddy fought in Uganda," supplied Lefty, thinking that explained everything. The other cowboy never said a word, but simply rested that long-barreled pistol-carbine across his leather-clad leg an' showed his teeth.

"Bernie, you know the tactical situation better than we." The President carried something called a Webley Electric— .17 caliber, ultrahigh velocity. Inside, a nylon rotor lifted wire projectiles from the hundred-round magazine to the acceleration coils. I'd seen him test it this mornin' on a cottonwood stump. The sawdust'd *steamed* for twenty minutes afterward.

Koko carried the .11-caliber version, two-hundred to the clip.

"Right," I answered, thinkin' hard. "Far's I know, I ruined Cromney's only real weapon, but *Georgie*'s got facilities for fabricatin' practically anything, an' some pretty scary talents all her own. Theoretically, no offensive armament, but meteor-defense, force-fields..." I yawned an' blinked, tired, I figgered, from the trail. "Best we sneak aboard 'fore we get spotted in the open."

There was a pleasant damp an' woody smell t'my new vantage-point—nose four inches above the turf. I could see a hundred varieties of tiny wild blossoms, none more'n a quarter inch across, takin' advantage of the temporarily tropical moisture. Come cactus-weather, things'd be different.

The drizzle'd finally let up, but fog clamped down in its place. Even if I'd stood—targetin' myself immediately to *Georgie*'s multispectral senses—I couldn'ta seen more'n two meters. Instead, I crawled along through soaking weeds, tryin' t'keep my rump down, hopin' the liquid sunshine'd blanket my IR signature.

We'd agreed t'spread out, gorillas an' chimps circlin' through the trees so's to approach the landin' site from all directions. I'd waited in the aspens for Olongo, Lefty, Koko, an' Dexter t'get into position.

There'd been a squabble 'bout the kid.

"...and you, my girl, may remain and keep our mounts togeth—"

"But Uncle Olongo, that's not fair!"

"My dear, the *universe* isn't fair—it's simply lawful. Besides, your grandmother would never forgive—"

"Leave her out of this and speak for yourself! I'm three times Dex or Lefty's size, twice Bernie's, and a better shoi than *you* in my sleep! And I've practically memorized this part of the ranch. Ask Austin!"

He waggled a broad finger at her. "Argument from authority, Koko. Austin isn't here any more than Goldilocks. And Dex and Lefty are grownups, whereas you're merely—"

"What's *age* got to do with it? It's a Free System! I'm a sapient individual with *rights*, one of which is helping Bernie, if I want!"

Sheepishly, her uncle admitted he'd held the same position on children's rights next-t'last time Congress'd met. He gimme a helpless look.

"Leave me outa this! I'm justa guilty by-stander!"

Meantime, the chimps were tyin' their ponies to a branch—either they were sidin' with the kid or knew her better'n I did. In the end, they had the situation pegged: she fanned out with the rest of us, an' providin' things were runnin' t'schedule, she'd be pantomimin' a peanut race this minute, just like me.

Couldn't be much farther. I watched for *Georgie*'s bulk t'loom up outa the pea-soup, listenin' t'dew-drops drippin' offa sagebrush, my own raggedy chicken-hearted breathin', not much else.

Oughta be *somewhere* 'round here.

I wondered how old Koko really was.

A standup gunfight'd be a relief. Better'n scrabblin' around in wet landscapin'. Pistol in hand, I crawled another soggy yard.

A piddlin' little breeze parted the ground-clutter suddenly, an' there she was, a big gray metal dome, some Eskimo's idea of a high-rise, three, mebbe four meters away an' lookin' just gorgeous t'me. Cromney an' his minions musta been plumb loco, gettin' snuck up on thisaway—less'n they figgered t'drygulch us.

I shook my head—goddamned Louis L'Amour atmosphere was gettin' to me. Tryin' t'dig a slit-trench with m'belt buckle, I crept toward the saucer. This was gonna be iffy.

She was sealed up tight. Hafta hope her recog patterns hadn't been tampered with. Once she saw m'face, she'd let me in. I'd skedaddle to the engine-room, turnin' the thermonuclear tables: be amusin' t'see how *they* liked bein' threatened with Failsafe Autodestruct.

I could practically feel the big red lever in m'hand.

Georgie ain't a perfect hemisphere; she slants in underneath a ways. I ducked under, got m'fingers on the rain-slippery lip of her circumference, inchin' into the view-field of one of her outboard monitors.

SWOOOOOSH!!

Ever been in the middle of a twister? One second I had aholda my ship, the next I was lyin' all tangled up in a heapa furry arms an' legs, gunbelts, chaps, an' Stetson hats, in the center of the ninety-foot circle where there *wasn't* any *Georgie* anymore.

By some miracle, m'eardrums'd survived the implosion. Barely.

"But Bernie!" complained Koko, extractin' her left foot outa her uncle's armpit. "What about that . . . *thing* you've been carrying around in your pocket? I thought that was supposed to—"

"This frammis?" I removed Dexter's elbow from my eye while he pulled the muzzle of Lefty's gun outa his ear. I took the object in question, turned it over in my hand, feelin' stupid. Could be the Freenies were right about my mental processes lately.

"Oh, Cromney an' his crew're still around, somewhere within a few hundred klicks. But y'don't need a field-density equalizer for the Emergency Escape Drive."

Sunlight broke through the fog, fillin' the pasture with rainbows an' diamonds.

They helped me dig m'wristwatch up, cleanin' their knives in the wet grass an' checkin' 'em afterward against Olongo's educated saddle-horn. I smoothed down the radiation-proof foil.

Bella wasn't very glad t'see me. We'd thought we were ridda each other. First time I turned m'back, untanglin' her reins from the bush I'd tied her to, she bit me on the shoulder-blade.

All of us were more tired an' discouraged than our exertions accounted for. My friends sorted out their mounts from the vegetation, climbed into the saddle, an' we started the long trip back.

All I had t'occupy my consciousness was failure—an' the agony which painted itself along the insides of my legs from knee t'crotch.

Halfway there, Aus Clintwood dropped in from the sky, freshly-polished chrome gleamin' in the sunshine, to deliver a thermos of coffee an' a bottle of somethin' labeled "Kinglsey's Pennsylvania Whiskey—The Drink That Makes You Drunk!"

Even Koko had a swig, without a noise of complaint from Olongo. She deserved it. I wished it'd been morphine.

We rode on.

It was supposed t'be too cold so far this year. It was supposed t'be a couple thousand feet too high. But somehow, not a half-hour from the bunk-house, Bella managed t'step right in the middle of somethin' fanged an' scaly.

The diamondback hissed an' rattled. Bella screamed an' reared. Snatching at the saddle-horn too late, I catapulted over her neck, crashing not an arm's length from the coiled infuriated snake. With no consciousness of drawing it, my .45 was in my hand, sights lined up, just as the reptile struck.

click

9

Green Blooms
the Gumshoe

Zzzzap!

The kewpie-doll belonged t'Koko. Her snap shot took the rattler's head off, leavin' the resta the critter twistin' an' writhin' in the freshly dampened lap of a badly shaken time-traveler. My own hammer'd fallen without effect; the old reliable Gold Cup National Match, the rod an' staff that'd comforted me for decades, lay inert an' useless in my tremblin' hand.

"Bernie! Are you all right?" The President and Koko echoed one another, fightin' t'get their horses back under control.

"I'll live." I glanced at my own mount, flailin' on her side an' makin' horrible noises. "Better look t'Bella, though."

"Uncle Olongo!" Koko cried. "You've got to *do* something!"

The good news was the mare'd broken her leg.

The bad news was that, no, they *don't* shoot horses. The Confederacy's got some sorta electromagnetic band-aid; knits bones together ten times faster'n they'll heal on their own. Della'd be up an' around in a week, makin' some other dude's life miserable.

I hoped she'd blow a fuse.

"But you've fed me, put me up, put up *with* me, an' saved m'life! I can't let you do this!"

Olongo leaned on the fender—make that "skirt"—of the

metallic-blue Tucker ground-effect machine, lookin' at me through the opened plastic bubble. "Balderdash, dear boy. I simply won't hear any further objections."

He handed in a pistol, a "loaner" t'pinch-hit for the useless .45 folded into its gunbelt on my lap. It was a .375 high-pressure Magnum, manufactured by a Browning Company in Nauvoo, Illinois.

Funny, the way I remembered it; the Browning family'd gotten burned out with the resta the Midwest Mormons an' moved t'Utah.

Weren't any front or rear sights on the .375. Underneath the muzzle-crown, doin' double duty as a recoil-spring plunger, was a minuscule tubular laser. Haul up on the trigger-slack, it'd put a bright red dot where bullets'd follow if you kept on tightenin' your finger.

I'd field-stripped my .45 immediately on the trail. The firing-pin an' its little spring were rusted in their tunnel through the slide as solid as if they'd been welded. Blood had started the process, back aboard *Georgie,* an' the steady rain'd done the rest. What I couldn't figger was why I hadn't thought t'clean it before the damage was done.

Mormons still in Illinois? I yawned, a sudden unaccountable fatigue settlin' over me, an' shoved the Browning in a pocket of my coveralls where it *clinked.* Olongo's hospitality hadn't stopped at loanin' me a gun. Keepin' company with the pistol was enough gold coinage t'get me arrested for profiteerin', smugglin', hoardin', tamperin' with the currency, or any other euphemism for seekin' independence from government counterfeitin' in practically any culture I'd ever visited.

I was gonna *need* that gold. So far, I'd met chimpanzees, gorillas, an' one horse more'n I'd ever wanted to. Earlier this afternoon, I'd even met a herda unicorns.

You ever hearda unicorns?

Now I was gonna meet a real, live Bear.

I'd been sittin' on a fence, talkin' to the Featherstone-Haughs, gawkin' at a flock of critters who aren't s'posed to exist, an' tryin' t'forget the numerous aches, pains, scars.

an' bruises Bella'd inflicted on me that mornin'. A siesta the Freenies'd insisted I take seemed to've ironed all the injuries in permanently.

"What do you think of my uncle's new corral, Bernie?"

"It's okay." I took a drag of my cigar t'kill my sense of smell.

"That's exactly what Wyatt Earp said!" She started gigglin'.

"'Earp' is the correct expression." Olongo groaned, changin' the subject. "Really, old man, I can't imagine why I didn't hit on this scheme straightaway." He drew on his own cigar, lettin' blue smoke trickle around his fangs.

Koko nodded, unrepentant. "He's a good man, Bernie. Olongo's told me so many stories, I—"

"Look, friends, *nothin's* simple about any parta this." I pointed into the paddock where forty or fifty four-legged office-spindles were millin' around, decidin' who was gonna be bull of the woods. "Who'da believed even *this?*"

In popular mythology, a unicorn's a *horse*—probably a snow-white Arabian—with this one little difference. But it ain't so. Check any medieval tapestry. They're smaller, meaner, a *whole* lot smellier, basically goats, with chin-whiskers an' catty-corner pupils. I'd been wonderin' what in Ochskahrt's name they were good for.

"By Jefferson's quill, what d'you think you've been eating since you arrived? Steak, sausage, milk, cheese, all with the distinctive inimitable flavor my genetic engineers predicted. I daresay they'll be a Confederate mainstay within a decade."

"Kinda luck *I* been havin', I'll be around t'see it, Olongo, y'got any idea how humilliatin' this notion of yours strikes an Academy man?" I chewed my cigar an' sulked.

"But *Bernie*—" Koko hopped down, took a step an' grimaced, then slid a seven-inch knife from her belt an' scraped the bare soles of her feet in disgust.

"Listen to her, clumsy though she be." Olongo dodged a wadda unicorn extrusions flipped off the end of his niece's baby bowie. "You've a valuable item stolen, and, I daresay, more unseemly acts committed in the process than we've witnessed in the last five years."

I directed m'gaze at the hogleg on his hip. "Didn't exactly figger muggin' t'be *too* profitable, this necka the woods. But *a private detective?* Whatcha think this is, a paperback novel?

Givin' the livestock a last proprietary nod, the President turned. *"This* detective, sir, is singularly qualified: unassailable integrity, an unquenchable passion for problem-solving. There was the curious matter of the libertine librarian, for example, or that peculiar 'telephone clone' debacle. But in any case, he'll appreciate the spot you're in. You see, he's from *your* world, Bernie."

Olongo stumped around the hovercraft to the driver's side. Leanin' in, he shook tentacles with the Yamaguchii lined up in the back, gimme a clasp that bulged m'fingertips, flipped some dashboard toggles, an' stood back.

"Bon voyage, my friends! The car'll come back on its own—as I trust you'll do someday yourselves!" He blew his nose on a blanket-sized kerchief.

Impellers roarin', Koko hadda shout: "I'll be in town day after tomorrow!" She waved; the Freenies answered with their eyestalks. The canopy slid shut, steerin' wheel beside me tiltin' of its own accord. The vehicle rose, trundled forward. I turned an' waved as we whipped around a corner of the barn, drifted through a graveled curve, an' *boomed!* through Olongo's front gate.

The speedometer said 190, an' it wasn't in kilometers.

"Road Service!"

"Errrk!" This place was gonna be the deatha me yet. Before me, a translucent white panel'd suddenly become a brilliantly colored screen, displayin' the animated image of a pretty girl. She wore a canvas duster an', atop her nineteenth-century hair-do, a drivin' cap an' goggles.

"Oh, dear!" Her cartoon eyebrows knitted cutely. "I didn't mean to startle you! Your Laporte ETA is perfect for a movie this afternoon. Would you like to see one?"

"Say, who's drivin' this thing?" I glanced trepidaciously at the movin' pedals on the floor. Groundspeed was up t'300!

She smiled, special effects twinklin' in her eyes. "Well, er . . ."

"Bernie."

"Bernie. Both your route-program *and* myself are generated by a Hodgson 66F computer in the Confederation Boulevard/Tomtinker Lane Intersective. I'd *love* to answer more questions, but there wouldn't be time for the movie. Won't you call me back"—she winked—"any old time?"

I cleared my throat. "I, er . . ."

Her image faded, replaced by an enormous pistol pivotin' slowly till its 3D muzzle pointed at the bridge of my nose. Didn't fool *me*. I settled back.

Minutes later, with excited aliens watchin' a rear-seat repeater, Mike Morrison, playin' "Nasty Jim" Brannigan—security investigator for San Francisco's Emperor Norton University—had singlehandedly stopped a "dataheist" on Montgomery Street. Still chewin' the barbecued bagel he'd been havin' for lunch, he leveled the biggest automatic I've ever seen at a slimy villain cowerin' on the slidewalk amidst a heap of ill-gotten microcassettes.

"Listen up . . . Herbert. This here's a .760 Kolibri, th' System's most powerful handgun, an' it could blow yer head . . . . right off."

A powerful surge of *deja vu*. Funny, why did Morrison's shabby tweed *serape* bring *orangutans* t'mind? Hadn't met even *one* of them, so far.

He thumbed down the cocking-lever: "T'tell th' . . , truth, Herbert, in all . . . this excitement, I kinda fergot whether I fired twelve shots or . . . thirteen."

The weasel-faced inside-man squirmed, glancing desperately around at the carnage already wreaked by that gigantic weapon.

"Tell me . . . Herbert," Morrison's cold, almost asiatic eyes narrowed as he put pressure on the trigger, "Do ya feel . . . lucky?"

As the film drew to a climax, Nasty Jim heavin' his business-cards into the bay, our hovercraft rolled up t'626 Genêt Place, residence an' office of a real, live detective.

Edward William "Win" Bear was squat an' heavy-set. Somethin' like the grizzly Koko'd turned out not t'be. Big hands, no neck t'speak of, close-cropped hair, an' ears the size of taxi-cab doors. Gray suit, brown shoes, white socks— "cop" written all over his ugly kisser.

I liked him.

He greeted me on the rubber-covered drive curvin' up t'what coulda been a Swiss chalet designed by Frank Lloyd Wright. Most of the ground level was garage, but after introductions all around, we went upstairs half a floor, an' while the investigator measured scotch for me, Kahlua for the Freenies, I stared out the wall-sized front window. This was s'posed t'be a densely populated neighborhood. *Looked* like a city park, the only other house in sight a big Spanish fortress replica, far away across a crabgrass-covered thoroughfare, adobe an' wrought iron, just a touch smaller'n Versailles.

Bear handed me a drink. "I understand you've got a special problem, Captain. Olongo 'commed while you were on the road." He mixed his own with milk. Yechh.

"That's Bernie"—I peeled a cigar—"an' 'special' ain't the word. He tell you where I'm from?"

The detective motioned me to a couch backin' on the window, took a seat across from me. His cloak, already wrinkled, caught on the grip of his heavy old-fashioned revolver. "Goddamn it, I'm *never* going to get the hang of—yeah, he told me. Not sure if I believe it, though. Life's complicated enough already. There's lots of 'ordinary' immigration these days. Hell, they've taken to calling this neighborhood the 'U.S. of C.' But a man from the future? Stretching things a little."

Yawning slightly, I pointed to the Freenies, sittin' on their highballs.

Bear grinned, shaking his head ruefully. "Okay, I'll tell you what. My wife's, well, out of circulation for a while.

And crime isn't exactly a growth industry in Laporte, anyway. Olongo vouches for you. I'll see what I can do."

Out of circulation? Sounded ominous. Bear widened his Wallace Beery grin. "Sorry! I should remember how it felt when *I* first got here. Therapeutic electronarcosis—every year we take a two-week nap. It's supposed to double life-expectancy, prevent cancer, and so on. I had *my* beauty-rest last month—been trying to work into phase with Clarissa—but it'll be another cycle at least before we're matched up. Meantime, I'm a carefree bachelor again—bored out of my fucking mind!"

I nodded, relieved. The Academy has lotsa life-extension techniques, some they even share with the public. But this was a new one on me, an' tryin' t'square bein' three centuries into a past many ways ahead of my own era technologically . . .

I shook my head t'clear it. "Well, I appreciate y'goin' to the trouble. Say, is the President moonlightin' as your press-agent, or do you really have 'unassailable integrity'? Don't think I ever run into one of them before."

He scrutinized me closely. "In its most virulent form." He sighed. "It's a gift from God, and you know how *those* always turn out."

"Well, I won't hold it against you. What've I gotta do t'get started?"

Bear rose, both hands in his pockets bunchin' up the cape behind him, an' chomped down on the hawser he was smokin'. "The whole story, first, from the beginning. The object's to recover your ship, maybe do something about the crooks who took it. I'll ask nosy questions, over and over, until you're sick of it. Need that drink freshened?"

Somethin' disgraceful was happenin' t'my capacity here. I declined, hand over glass. "Okay, you're the detective: three years ago, the Academy tapped me for an archaeoastronomical mission t'Yamaguchi 523, that's a G0-class star in—"

"Hold it! *What* academy? Also, was this three years ago, meaning 1990, or three years previous to 2285? And what, in heaven's name, is archaeoastronomy?"

I fought down a gargantuan yawn. By fits an' starts, he finally heard it all, listenin' as he mushed back an' forth around the livin' room. Only really *good* pacer I'd run into so far.

While I struggled t'stay awake, he nodded, grunted, screwed up his forehead from time t'time, an' stopped me for an occasional clarification.

By the time we were through, I was exhausted.

"Well," he said at long last, "I guess that'll do it for now. Bernie, do you realize how many Top Secrets you've told me? How's your Academy going to feel about that?"

I fought t'keep my eyes open. "I reckon what they don't know ain't gonna hurt me."

Bear grinned, wider an' wider, till I thought he was gonna tear his head apart from the inside. He busted out laughin' uncontrollably.

Shucks, I hadn't thought it was *that* funny.

Then his face turned green, an' posies blossomed from his ears.

10

Outa
Condition

IN THE SIXTIETH YEAR OF THE COMMUNIST REFOR-
*mation, a young disciple sat at the feet of his guru, a jour-
neyman of the Erisian tradition, and asked, "What, then,
Master, is the seemly manner for society to organize itself?"*

*Like the rest of the little coeducational band taking mo-
mentary refuge in a rubble-filled cellar, both wore Army
field-greens, the Red Star picked away and replaced with
a hand-fashioned Eye-of-Horus. They cleaned and oiled
their captured Kalashnikovs, blued steel and plastic glinting
in the candlelight which flickered at the mouth of an empty
vodka bottle.*

*"Consider a flock of sheep . . ." replied their squad-leader,
tucking his heels into the lotus position on the packing-crate
where he sat. He'd just finished dismissing socialism, fascism, and democracy as things equal to one another.
". . . submissive, brainless, needing to be watched every
minute, against predators, natural disaster, and its own
stupidity, by the shepherd and his noble canine."*

*The student-soldiers nodded, murmuring. Most were
newly arrived from agricultural regions and understood. I
squatted back against a crumblin' wall, gettin' it all down
on a fingernail recorder. This was my eighteenth subjective
week surveyin' a crucial stretcha history, an' I was lookin'
forward to the flesh-pots of decadent twenty-second century
Oxnard when this was over.*

*"How much better-off the herd would be," continued the
teacher, "did it consist of creatures like the estimable guard-*

dog: fierce, bright, capable of caring for itself without *such 'help'.*"

"But Master," protested the young questioner, "of what possible use would such a flock be to the shepherd?"

Fastening the flap of his holster and rising, the sergeant smiled. "I see, young chela, *that you have grasped the lesson."*

And in Moskva the following year, there was *no hundredth anniversary of the Revolution.*

"*Bernie?*"

"Nnnghmm?"

"Bernie, *please* wake up!"

Opening the eyes some sneak'd glued shut when I wasn't lookin', I saw Spin an' Color still sittin' with Bear, Charm on the floor, tuggin' at m'pants leg. He swiveled his attention toward the detective.

"You see how it is with him, sir. It now becomes imperative that we . . ."

The little dickens hesitated, rolled six inches closer to the investigator, then back.

"Mr. Bear, Bernie seems never to have taken in the . . . well, the *actuality* of our present whereabouts. In *him,* this is greatly disturbing."

"*Now jushta doggone shecond!*" Hell, even *I* heard the slur in my voice. I jumped up, an', abruptly dizzy, hadda sit right down again. That was when I noticed I'd spilled my drink some time ago. Two whiskeys, or was it only one? An' *already* I was under th' proverbial!

Bear, startled: "Mr. Ambassador, what, precisely, are you talking about?"

Charm assumed a professorial tone: "Kindly observe— forgive me, Lord— how some . . . *thing* seems to impair Bernie's cognitive faculties whenever certain topics are approached . . ."

The detective volunteered no reply. Charm continued from the floor, tryin' his own purely figurative hand at pacin' the carpet.

"Bernie," he squeaked, an octave too high for the gravity

of the subject-matter, "Lord, I realize it is presumptuous of me to speak thus—"

"I know, Charm, but I was too polite t'mention—"

"—Yet, all three of us have noticed that whenever the, er, practicalities of time-travel are discussed, you . . . *Bernie?*"

"Zzzzzt—whazzat?" I shook my head groggily. "Ochs-kahrt's orchids! Musta dozed off there, Your Ambassador-ation. What were you sayin'?"

If a Freenie coulda shrugged, Charm woulda. "A case in point, Mr. Bear. It appears to be some variety of psy-chological tampering. I fear that this is the source of many of our recent brushes with disaster, including Bernie's near-fatal failure to maintenance his side-arm."

"Well, that can be taken care of this afternoon." Bear peered closely at me. I didn't like it much. *"Conditioning,* is that what you're thinking, Charm? Some kind of hyp-nosis?"

The Ambassador gave another of his shrugs-by-impli-cation. "It is difficult to say, sir. The phenomenon does not exist among our species. Bernie, would you agree that . . . *Bernie!"*

"Zzz—unk! Only restin' my eyes, fellas! I'm, cr . . . hypnosis?" Through the haze I began t'see his point. "I don't seem t'be hittin' on all sixteen cylinders, lately, an' that's the pitiful truth. But what's it got t'do with time-trav . . . zzzzz . . . ."

"Bernie!"

"Okay! Okay!" I got up, fightin' disorientation, stomped m'feet for circulation, an' started pacin' back an' forth m'self, justa stay awake. "Keep talkin', while I'm still conscious t'hear it!"

"You've been conditioned," Charm continued, "not to speak of t . . . you-know-what, especially with, as you often put it yourself, 'the locals'."

"Yeah? Well, then it ain't workin' very good. I've blown m'cover t'Koko, her Uncle Olongo, half his roughnecks, an' now Sherlock here, an' the worst that's happened is I tend t'zonk off every now an' again."

"Right," Bear answered sarcastically, "and occasionally

set yourself up for suicide. Let me see that pistol of yours a minute."

With reflexive reluctance, I recovered the Milt Sparks rig from where I'd tossed it on the end of the couch, slid the Gold Cup out of its scabbard, cleared both chamber an' magazine well, an' handed it over.

Bear grunted. "First G.I. .45 I've handled in half a dozen years." He jacked the slide. "You make a habit of handing people loaded guns?" He held a big brass cartridge between his thumb an' index finger.

I plopped onto the couch, shocked to the bone. Of course! I'd emptied the chamber first—the classical dumb boot's trick—neatly shuffling the first round from the magazine in behind the ejected cartridge!

"All right! I believe everything you've said, Charm! I believe it!" I could feel my ears redden, but Bear, bless him, went on's if nothin'd happened.

"This is the fancy target model, isn't it? What's the trouble with it?"

Overcoming embarrassment, I told him about the firing pin. Hirnschlag von Ochskahrt alone knew what else was amiss, both with the .45 an' me—an' I hoped he wouldn't tell.

"Well, it should be fairly simple, then." The detective reached for what appeared t'be a thick, white, legal-sized clipboard on the coffee table, its upper half consistin' of the same translucent pseudoporcelain as the video unit in Olongo's car. The lower half was keyboard, which he used.

"Will?" A pause, then: "Oh, hello, Mary-Beth. How are you?"

From this angle, all I could make out was a colored image an' a voice too small t'be overheard.

"No, she's still electrosleeping, be another week . . . Why thanks, I *am* pretty tired of punching my own kitchen-buttons. Maybe tomorrow night, if that's convenient."

He looked up at me, then to the Freenies.

"I might bring a guest or two along, if that wouldn't be imposing. Which reminds me why I called. When Will gets back from his militia meeting, tell him I've got a job for him, if you would. Fairly urgent—the customer's carrying a borrowed life-preserver." Another pause. "Okay, fine. Love to Fran. Bye."

Bear set the educated clipboard down, nodding out the window behind me toward the Alamo replica across the street. "Will Sanders," he explained, "a good neighbor, the best goddamned gunsmith in Greater Laporte, and also an immigrant American, like you and me. That was one of his wives I was—"

"Mormon?" I thought about the Browning in my coverall pocket.

"No"—the detective grinned—"just greedy. *What?*"

The Ambassador was pullin' at his pants cuff. Glad t'see it happen t'somebody else for once.

"Your pardon, Mr. Bear, but we were discussing the matter of Bernie's, er, delicate—"

"So we were. I . . . say, why don't you guys call me Win?"

"Yeah," I echoed. "Us gods are all alike. Informal. Listen, fellow sapients, could I get a word in here? I don't much care t'be talked about in third person!" I stoked up a cigar—another gift from the Galloping Gorilla. "Main thing is—always assumin' you're right about this conditioning thing—what're we gonna *do* about it?"

Charm: "It would appear, Lord, that the condition is relatively specific. For example, you're permitted to discuss er, you-know-what with individuals of your own calling. It should be greatly inconvenient, otherwise."

"*Permitted?*" I squeaked, almost soundin' like a Freenie.

"Yes, Bernie. I believe a direct breach of the inhibition might render you completely comatose, perhaps even kill you. However, Koko freed you from a portion of the compulsion by telling you that she knew what you are."

"And yet," Color offered from the couch, speaking for the first time, "her conception of you-know-what seems sufficiently disparate from yours, Bernie, that the prohibition generates uncontrollable drowsiness and lethal carelessness."

The former of which I was beginnin' t'feel again. I got

up t'pace. My legs felt like columns of lead. I sat down in a comfortable chair by the fireplace instead. It all seemed too much trouble t'think about.

Abruptly, Spin's eyestalk straightened. He skittered closer t'Bear, persuadin' the detective t'bend down to him. There was a whispered conference.

I yawned.

"That's it!" Bear exclaimed. "Bernie, look at me closely!"

I tried, but the haze was thickenin'.

"Bernie, I don't know exactly what Olongo told you about me or if you've thought about it much, but—...—...—..."

Suddenly, I couldn't hear him. His mouth kept makin' words, but it was like tryin' t'read in a dream. The whole room seemed dark an' gettin' darker. By the time he'd risen an' crossed over t'me, he was a blur in little better focus than his surroundings. I couldn'ta told him from Koko or the Man In The...

"—...—...—" Somethin' seized me by the shoulders, shook me. "...—...!" Bear's face swam into momentary sharpness but insisted on turnin' round an' round like a slow-motion pinwheel. I tried t'move.

"...—carefully, Bernie! Listen to me! I'm telling you that *I'm a time-traveler myself!*"

I pitched over onto the floor, the pain inside my head like a draft-dodger's eardrums at the moment of truth. I was conscious of my elbow an' forehead hittin' the carpet, of convulsions fit t'break every bone in m'scrawny carcass, then a feelin' of *release!*, blood gushin' from my nose.

An' suddenly it was over with.

My vision cleared. Hearing returned. The haze inside my skull evaporated as if somebody'd jerked a dishrag through one ear an' out the other. The air seemed fulla oxygen again.

I sat up, sneered contemptuously at the whiskey in Bear's outthrust hand, an' dashed it down. Even through the cow-juice, it burned nicely, but that was its only effect. Meanwhile, data seemed t'be fallin' into place in my noggin like punch-cards in a sorter.

"God's wounds!" I said briskly. "Also gosharootie, holy shit, an' twenty-three skidoo! But you're a *sidewise* time-traveler—across alternate universes—*not* lengthwise, like me, right?"

"Right!" shouted Bear an' Charm an' Spin' an' Color, all at the same time. Sounded like a calliope in rut.

"Right—you came from a . . . *dimension* separate from the Confederacy, where history turned out different, branched off at some critical choice-point an' developed independently after that. Prob'ly the Whiskey Rebellion, since Olongo saw fit t'mention it."

Bear was nodding violently, grinnin' from ear t'ear. I watched those appendages closely, expectin' flowers t'start blossomin' from 'em any moment.

I said, "An' I'm from the future of *your* universe, not this one!"

There was a huge collective sigh of relief. "Welcome back to reality, Bernie," Bear said, "whatever *that* is."

"Why those unexpurgated slime-mold-suckin' sneaky misbegotten sons of—who'da thought even a bastard like Cromney'd do a thing like this t'me? Musta been when I had the DreamCap on, an'—"

"Oh Lord!" Charm exclaimed, an' for the first time, I wasn't sure how he meant it. "You still don't see it, do you? It was that Academy of yours, not Cromney! Doubtless all the time you were in training as a youth."

Now he'd said it, it was obvious. An' entirely consistent. I felt around for incipient signs of drowsiness, but even the nosebleed'd stopped.

I rose. "Awful sorry 'bout the carpet, Win."

"It'll have cleaned itself by morning." He smiled, giving me a hand. "How do you feel?"

"Aside from innumerable internal injuries—mostly to m'pride—just like somebody'd screwed all my sparkplugs back in place. Thanks. Pylon take those bureaucrats, I'm gonna file complaints in *googolicate* when I get back—'less I *nuke* th' mother-humpers first!"

I took the fresh drink he offered, retrieved my cigar, an' noticed that the burned spot on the carpet was already healin' itself. Back home, a metal mousoid woulda come out an' pissed on it.

"Okay," I said to my fellow time-traveler, "you gonna tell me about it?"

He chuckled. "I arrived in the North American Confederacy seven years ago—and about as explosively as you did—while investigating the political murder of a theoretical physicist."

He'd been a *public* eye in those days. Homicide Lieutenant Edward Bear—"Win" because of A. A. Milne—had run afoul of SecPol, predecessors of the twenty-first century Freedom Police, and very nearly been eighty-sixed himself.

The physicist in question had been contacted by Confederate scientists by means of a "probability broach" whose inventors'd originally been plumbing for a way around the lightspeed barrier.

Shades of Herr Professor von Ochskahrt!

But things'd turned out differently, an' the U.S. government's nastiest covert branch took a dim view of unauthorized communications from the Twilight Zone. They'd machine-gunned the uncooperative American scientist an' chased Win through his experimental hardware, straight into anarchist heaven.

While fendin' off badguys an' foilin' their plot t'import nuclear weapons—considered gauche in the Confederacy, an' consequently never brought to the full flower of development exhibited elsewhere—Win'd had t'make adjustments to a society without laws, police, armies, any government at all—which nonetheless seemed t'operate just swell, thank you.

Even the trains ran on time.

"It's the first *adult* society in history, Bernie," Win finished. "Politically, *legally,* you're entirely on your own, to operate a business, shove opiates in your arm, break your neck sky-diving, buy or sell sex—or anything else—invent new things or enjoy the oldest ones, like dirty movies and books. It's up to you to profit from your successes and suffer the full responsibility for your mistakes."

I laughed. "Y'think humanity's up to it? Whatcha do here, euthanize th' crooks an' dummies?"

"Bernie"—he shook his head—"a culture like this, despite possible appearances, *doesn't* run on good will *or* rationality. Those are just *results*. It runs on *greed*—self-interest, if you prefer. You know, somebody—was it Korzybski or Donald Duck?—once pointed out how we get stymied by certain words and phrases that cause us to give up on things before we really try."

"Yeah," I answered, "like 'impossible' or 'it'll never fly' or 'we'd hafta get a supplemental appropriation'." I sipped my drink.

Win grinned at me. "That last one never seemed to stop anybody for long. But in this case, the operant verbal roadblock is 'the perfectability of Man'—or rather the notion, absolutely correct, that such perfection is impossible. It keeps us from inquiring why people have to be perfect in order to be free."

"Or how come workin' for the bureaucracy makes you *perfecter* than civilians!"

"Right!" He laughed. "Sure, running your own life can be a little uncomfortable at times, especially for those of us who grew up in a system where success was punished—*fined*—so failure can be rewarded through the welfare system. Hell of it is, I've found that by respecting everybody's sovereignty, you liberate them to cooperate far more cordially than when they're *forced* to get along. What finally convinced me, about the second year I was here, was a strike; the host-mothers' unions wanted shorter pregnancies and were picketing their chief customers, the commercial orphanages—baby-brokerages, to you. The orphanages had picket-lines around the union headquarters in retaliation. Secondary boycott, sauce for the goose. And nobody thought a thing about it. People *have* to play fair in the Confederacy; there isn't any other choice.

"Good god, I'm starting to preach! I need another drink!"

He rose t'accomplish that, while I jingled the coins in m'pocket, considerin' Confederate kindness an' generosity. "Mebbe I understand now why Koko insisted on helpin' me. How old is she, anyway?"

The ice clinked in his scotch an' milk. "The President's niece? I seem to recall Olongo mentioning . . . eleven or twelve, perhaps. I know: you're thinking about the lethal hardware she probably carries. Everybody does, regardless of age, and *that* took me longer to get used to than anything else. But Confederates believe—and'll lecture anyone who'll stand still long enough—that you can't teach individual responsibility by denying the pupil the chance to practice it. Besides, if you make exceptions where rights are concerned, for anyone or any reason, you've established a deadly precedent for doing it eventually to everybody else."

"An' *that*," I nodded ruefully, "would likely be an unhealthy exercise t'advocate in these parts. All the same, there are folks as hold that makin' kids act like grownups is bad for their little psyches. Take the fourteenth century—"

"*You* take it. I read *A Distant Mirror*, too, and that's one place where Tuchman had it wrong. It wasn't a matter of kids growing up too fast but of adults who never *did* grow up. And it got worse, after that, not better. Look at the Crack in the Moon."

"The *what?*"

"You know, back in the 80s, when the Russians decided to 'teach the Chinese a lesson'—*oh no! 'George Herbert'*—for Wells, the novelist? Your time machine's christened for H. G. Wells?"

"Whoo! When you change the subject, Sherlock, you don't mess around. An' it's *G. H.* Wells, not—holy steaming batshit!"

He looked at me grimly. "We thought we had it all figured out, didn't we?"

I looked right back. "We did at that, but we were wrong, weren't we?"

"There *isn't*," he said carefully between gritted teeth, "a crack in the moon where you come from, is there? And Wells' first name was—"

"I'd *hate* referrin' t'my best girlfriend as *'Herbie'*."

"How do you feel, Bernie? Any dizziness? Nausea?"

"No. You plannin' t'sprout flowers from your ears or anything?"

"What?"

I looked up toward Heaven. "Where the fuck *am* I, anyway?"

Heaven remained noncommittal.

11

Stone Walls
Do Not

"WASHINGTON, ADAMS, JEFFERSON, MADISON, Monroe, *John Quincy* Adams, *Andrew* Jackson, Van Buren, *William Henry* Harrison, and Tyler." Win Bear ticked 'em off until he ran outa fingers.

So it was my turn: "Polk, Taylor, good ol' Millard Fillmore, Pierce, Buchanan, Lincoln, *Andy* Johnson, Grant, an' Hayes, an' Garfield."

Win continued. "Arthur, Cleveland, *Benjamin* Harrison, Cleveland again, McKinley, *Teddy* Roosevelt, Taft, Wilson, Harding, and Coolidge."

"Hoover," I shot back. "Roosevelt II, Truman, Eisenhower, Kennedy—"

"*Kennedy?*" The detective blinked with surprise. "You don't mean—"

"John Fitzgerald Kennedy," I answered, cuein' data in place inside m'skull, "1960 through '63, when he got himself ventilated—"

"Whatever happened"—Bear took a stiff drink of his neighbor's whiskey—"to Richard Milhous Nixon?"

"Nixon? Nothin' more'n he deserved—but we ain't got t' that yet."

"Sure you have—in 1960. Two terms. Followed in '68 by Henry Cabot Lodge. Then Hubert Humphrey, Jerry Brown, and finally Henry Jackson, who was President in '87, when I came to the Confederacy."

"*Whew!* We *are* from different time-lines! Way I heard it, it was Eisenhower in '52, Kennedy, *Lyndon* Johnson—

109

then Nixon—followed by Ford, Carter, Reagan, an'—"

"Hold on there!" Captain Will Sanders looked up from the gun-parts scattered on the table-cloth, a big guy, broad-shouldered with curly blondish hair of a highly unmilitary cut, heavily-muscled forearms, an' a surgeon's hands. There was a mildly Slavic look to the set of his eyes; he was clean-shaven, wore cowboy boots, jeans, a short-sleeved bush-jacket. "Much as it pains me to admit it, I'm confused!"

He wiped his oily hands on a rag and extracted a gnarled, full-bent briar from a jacket pocket. "Win, I'd always assumed we were from the same history-line: the bad-guys won the Whiskey Rebellion; Scoop Jackson wound up President. I bugged out in '88—that's 212 A.L., locally, Bernie. *'Anno Liberatis,'* dating from the Revolution, in case nobody's thought to tell you. But *your* list of recent American Presidents is closer to mine than Win's is: Kennedy assassinated in '63; Johnson abdicating over Viet Nam; Nixon over Watergate . . ."

He looked t'me for confirmation, then continued: "In my history, Nixon was succeeded by Nelson Rockefeller, who died in office—'in the saddle,' you might say, and quite a coverup *that* was! Then Gerald Ford, then Henry Jackson. Hell, *none* of us are from the same place at all!"

Win'd gotten his free dinner twenty-four hours earlier than expected. Apparently, when Sanders'd returned that evenin' from his meetin' of the Greater Laporte Volunteer Militia an' Mountain Rescue, he'd insisted we come over for barbecue—an' overhauled firin' pin. The idea of a non-functionin' weapon plain drove him nuts.

"He's an odd character, all right," Win'd told me earlier as he set his answerin' machine, turned on the burglar-rejectors, an' switched the lights out—all from his lap with a Telecom pad, that fancy electronic clipboard thingie he'd used t'make his phone calls. "You recognize the alias, of course: 'Sanders,' as in 'living-under-the-name-of—' Same goddamn A. A. Milne that got me stuck with 'Win.' Also, I think, 'T. W.,' presumably for 'Trespassers W—' Consequently, everybody calls him 'Will.'"

"On th' lam, hunh?" I folded up my nonfunctioning .45

in its tackle, made sure the .375 in my pocket wasn't pointin'
at anything I wasn't willin' t'lose, an' ushered the Freenies
out the front door, Win lockin' up behind us.

"I'm not sure," he said. "I get the feeling somehow that
he might have been in politics, except that he feels like an
excop, and I should recognize the symptoms. Something
really horrible seems to have happened to him back in the
States, and he won't talk much about his past. Mysterious."

I snorted. "After *this*, I ain't gonna talk about *my* past
anymore. Nobody back home'd believe it—say, where we
goin'?"

We'd walked along the springy-surfaced driveway to the
street. I was about t'step down onto its golf-green paving
when Win did an abrupt left-face, grabbin' me by the sleeve,
makin' me stumble over the Freenies.

"You *don't* want to go out there," said the detective.

I pointed helplessly toward the *hacienda* directly across
from us. "Why in Ochskahrt's name not?"

MMMMMmmmmm!

Somethin' vaguely mechanical blurred past at about two
hundred klicks an hour, another comin' along the other way
the very next instant.

I *think* they were hovercraft.

"I get th' point!" I told him, tryin' t'stop shakin' as I
followed along the rubber sidewalk toward the corner.

"Nobody *quite* believes Will Sanders, either." Win continued our previous conversation. "He stayed with Clarissa
and me the first couple weeks he was here, and one night,
in his cups—he was in pretty rough condition at the time—
he claimed to be the only person ever to make it to the
Confederacy without benefit of the Probability Broach."

"Besides me."

"Besides *nobody*—this 'spatiotemporal displacement,'
you say it's accompanied by a bluish flash?" I nodded,
following him into what looked for all the world like a
roadside bus-stop. We rode an escalator down. "Obviously,
a variation on the P'wheet-Thorens Broach. But Will's story
is that he became so miserable Stateside, he began day-
dreaming, visualizing a society personally ideal to him until

it became more real, in every detail, than the world he lived in—*and he was here!*" The investigator shook his close-cropped head. "For all he knows, his body's still over there, curled up in the corner of a padded cell, sucking its thumb."

The stairs carried us into a brightly-lit arcade lined with shops an' stands, past yet another flight leadin' further downward. There was scaffoldin' an' big sheetsa hangin' polyethylene. "They buildin' a subway down there or some-thin'?"

We both looked over a little kiosk in the middle of the mall—roach-clips, hash-pipes, cokespoons, cigarette light-ers, an' snuff-boxes. "Or *something*—they're digging below the subway for the new Interworld Terminal. Somebody there'll be regular commercial traffic between here and the States."

Glancin' at the display, I said, "Gonna be a helluva surprise t'Phyllis Schlafley an' the DEA!" I could see it now: some kinda floodlighted archway with the legend *"Abandon Sanity, All Ye Who Enter."*

Win bought a bottle from a vending machine. The Freen-ies an' I rode with him across the underground shoppin' center an' up to the other side of the street. I'd been thinkin': "Naturally," I said t'Win's broad back as we exited at ground level, "Sanders' pipe-dreams included a paira beautiful chicks t'make life interestin'."

He turned. "Those women *are* his life, Bernie. Like Bronco Billy of yore, he's who he wants to be, and whatever that is, he's certainly paid the price."

A brief hike found us at a twelve-foot hole in an adobe fortress with enormous oaken doors. 623 Genêt Place. The passageway opened on a jungled courtyard. Mary-Elizabeth Sanders met us by the pool.

"Win!" She grabbed the gumshoe by his prominent ears an' kissed him on the nose. Easy t'do, since she was a couple inches taller'n he was.

He reddened. "Awww..."

Mary-Beth was *somethin'*. Smooooooth, about thirty, shoulder-length curly hair that mighta been describable as "mousey-brown" on anybody else. She was slender, long-legged, with slim, capable hands an' sea-green eyes. She wore a clingy, coppery little somethin' that went down to her ankles an' seemed t'evaporate here an' there just for effect—that, an' a perpetual kinda secret smile.

I shook her hand, blood suddenly poundin' in m'veins, watched her get acquainted with Larry, Moe, an' Curly, then straighten back t'five-foot-nine an' park us at the table, askin' about drinks.

Win remembered the wine. "August," he offered, "a very good month."

She crinkled prettily around the eyes an' went for a corkscrew. Win peeled back the foil an' started on the wirin'. "Shit!" He shook his hand.

"Trouble?" The Freenies trundled up concernedly.

"I've got this little mole here"—he pointed between his left ring-finger and pinky—"that gets in the way a lot. Been meaning to get Clarissa to take it off. She's a doctor—Healer, they say here—did I mention that?"

"I got the impression. Want me t'do that?"

"Thanks, Bernie. I'll go dig up Will. Should be in his shop."

I fumbled with the Burgundy, wishing the past few days'd scoured less hide offa *my* hands. Suddenly, Color whipped the bottle outa my fingers impatiently an' wormed a little green tentacle neatly into the cork. There was a *squeak*, a *pop!*, an' a *hissss* as th' sparklin' wine began t'exhale.

"'Least I know *somethin'* you little clowns're good for."

"Wow! I couldn't have done *that* better myself!"

I started at the silvery voice behind me an' turned—jumpin' up in abrupt politeness. A small lithe figure was comin' across the patio-tile, her dark brown eyes an' tip-tilted nose just visible in the lowerin' dusk.

"I'm Fran—you're Bernie. Introduce me to your colorful associates." She was maybe four or five years younger'n her sister, five or six inches shorter, with waist-length butery-blond hair. Where Mary-Beth ran t'sinusoidals, Frances Melanie (néc Kendall) Sanders was almost boyish—in a manner stimulatin' nothin' but pruriently heterosexual thoughts. Careful, Bernard, 'least till y'find out how straight this Sanders fella can shoot!

I bowed theatrically t'cover nervousness an' a multitude of other sins. "These here are Color, Charm, an' Spin . . . they're aliens," I finished, realizin' as I did it how stupid that sounded. "What d'you do?"

"I teach Intuitive Mechanics at Laporte University, Limited."

"Gotcha—what's 'Intuitive Mechanics'?" I started peelin' a cigar, almost offered her one, but caught m'self just in time.

"That's a discipline sort of overlapping psychology, philosophy, and mechanical engineering," she explained. "During the War Against the Czar, somebody in Alaska noticed that the Eskimos seem inherently inclined toward engine-repair and so on, without any cultural background to account for it easily."

"Kenyans an' bush-flyin'." I nodded, tryin' t'redeem m'reputation for intelligent communication. If all Confederate women were like this, I was gonna be in a messa trouble with m'best gal *Georgie*.

"Exactly. Well, they found the explanation in the Eskimo attitude toward sculpture . . ."

"Right! There's an animal locked up inside that rock somewhere—just cut off everything that don't look like a walrus!"

She laughed. "Now we've got it down to a science, sort of—at least to a constellation of aesthetic values we can teach to almost anyone who wants to learn."

"Bravo!" I lit my cigar. "And what do y'do in your *spare* time?"

"Design, build, and race sport-hovercraft with my sister and husband. Mary-Beth's the hot pilot in the family, although she isn't a Kenyan. We won the Greenland Invitational last year. What do you do, Bernie?"

I felt around for signs of dizziness, then said, "I'm a time-traveler."

"Isn't everybody, these days?"

My aplomb got salvaged by three figures emergin' through tropical foliage at the rear of the patio. Win, Mary-Beth, an' a sizable stocky fella in epauletted khaki, exclaiming, "It's darker than a tax-collector's soul out here! How about some photons?"

Everybody chuckled, as if at a family joke.

Fran responded suddenly by whipping a pistol-shape from the holster on the left thigh of her maroon velvet coveralls. Goddamn gun, I thought fleetingly, was almost as big as she—

Ssssspakkk!

Whirlin' on her toes, hair flyin', she'd aimed at a corner of the courtyard. A pinpoint of hell-fire leapt across to a Hawaiian torch planted between a pair of mimosas. The wick caught.

Ssspakk! Sspak!

On an' on she fired, pirouetting gracefully till a good half-dozen decorative flames softly illuminated the night. I looked up from where I was cowerin'—in spirit if not in th' flesh—under the table with the Freenies. No one else'd flinched, not even when a white-hot bolt'd crisped its way between Win an' our host.

"Plasma gun," the dangerous little southpaw chimed, slapping it back in its scabbard. "Lawrence *Shiva*, the first off the line. Pretty neat, hunh?"

"Ummh—what woulda happened if you'd missed?"

"At this setting?" She grinned. "Probably have burned right through the house. But I *never* miss."

"I believe it! I believe it!"

"You'd better," Win suggested. "Bernie, this is Will Sanders. Will, meet Captain Bernard M. Gruenblum and the Ganymedian delegates."

"Sounds like a rock-band." Sanders offered a firm good-natured handclasp. "Hope you like barbecued unicorn— we've enough of it for my militia company. Beth, we're too late with the corkscrew, honey. Want some Burgundy?"

The only thing *not* neighborly and expansive about Will Sanders was his *eyes*. They were haunted. Found m'self wonderin' what they'd been like *before* he'd spent five years in his personal idea of Paradise.

I noticed with surprise that insteada the ubiquitous gun, he wore a slim, deadly-lookin' eighteen-inch blade gleamin' on each hip, with a hand-fillin' grip an' double guards. As he sat, he laid 'em on the table. Tryin' not t'think *too* psychoanalytically, I asked about the weapons.

"These?" The gunsmith musta read m'mind; he glanced at both his women an' winked. "As Sigmund Freud once observed, sometimes a cigar is just a cigar. Actually, I've a number of pet handguns—hazard of the profession—but occasionally I like carrying raw steel to remind myself of an important lesson."

"So?" Win seemed interested, too.

"Sure. The blade's an extension of the hand, the agent— no pun intended—of my *will*. Most people understand this immediately of edged weapons, granting them—not altogether inappropriately—a mystique which properly is due the man behind them.

"The trick—and few are subtle or sophisticated enough to master it—is to see that this is equally true of the gun. By implication, of *all* machines."

"Don't seem that mysterious t'me, Cap'n."

"Then you're an exception, friend. And fortunate, because inherent in this 'lesson' is the end, not only to common pistolphobia, but to neo-Luddism and every other idiot yearning for the good old days—in short, to *savagery*. It's the beginning of civilization."

I shook my head. "I'd hate t'trust m'life to a paira shish-kebab skewers. Gimme a roscoe any time—th' pen ain't the only thing mightier'n the sword."

Win laughed. "You haven't seen him work out with these things—inside of five yards, you're better off surrendering, roscoe or not!"

With a little alien "help" I eventually explained my current predicament to Sanders, on the theory—Win's—that Will's volunteer hooligans mighta seen somethin' of *Georgie* on one of their outings.

"I've already put out several other lines of inquiry," the

detective added. "Olongo's office; Nahuatl in Cheyenne; I thought you—"

"Sorry, Win." Dinner finished, an' the dishes cleared into a table-slot leadin' god-knows-where; the 'smith had my .45 in little pieces, his junior wife kibitzin' over his shoulder. Mary-Beth poured coffee, not excludin' the Freenies, an' joined the investigator an' me in a little nicotine poisonin'.

"*Today's* militia business," Will growled, "was all indoors. Some goddamned fool from Baltimore's traveling from company to company soliciting for an aircraft carrier. *Submersible!*"

"The aircraft or the carrier?" Win asked.

"Both. Which reminds me, are you still shuttling back and forth to Pentagonland, playing James Bond?"

Win drew on his cigar. "Someday our homeworld's going to be liberated."

"It's a Free System," the gunsmith replied. "I don't know why you bother. The right wing's only interested in making people miserable—for their own good! You take a little guy in a raincoat whose only touch of human warmth is pornography or prostitution: what kind of creep would deny him even *that?*

"And the left? How they love to be losers, as long as it's *romantically.* Win, you can't sell laissez-faire on the basis of its successes—there's no *romance* in that. Nor can you defeat collectivism on its record of failures, numerous though they may be. Hell, by listing them, you just make it all that much more attractive! You're wasting your time."

He looked at Fran an' Mary-Beth; the temperature seemed t'rise ten degrees. "*I'm* happy here, and I don't give a microscopic damn whether I *ever* see the United States of America with-a-K again, or anybody in it!"

He looked down, brooding into his pipe, and that haunted look came over him.

Which is where we'd started comparin' Presidents an' found out life's more complicated than any of us'd imagined.

"Politicians!" Mary-Beth said with sudden vehemence. She'd turned out t'be a consulting ethicist, somewhere half-way between a judge an' a pshrink, with a little rabbi thrown in for good measure. Shrewd, calm, an' deep, she had a quick wit an' a subtle sense of humor. This outburst seemed uncharacteristic.

She slapped the plain, no-nonsense .41 Whitney automatic at her waist. "Who cares, anyway? The only reason I know who's President *here* is that he's a friend of Win's!"

Fran grinned an' nodded vigorously. Will smiled an' turned his attention back to the Colt, the invisible bands of *family* so strong between the three of them it could be felt. Guess I'd hafta do m'poachin' elsewhere.

"It's important to everyone, in some ways," Win answered a bit defensively. "Look at Gallatin: here, he was a President, leader of the Whiskey Rebellion. Where Will and Bernie and I come from, he was only Thomas Jefferson's Secretary of—"

"What?" I quacked.

"—the Treasury."

"Musta held their Cabinet meetin's with little tin horns an' floatin'—"

Mary-Beth blinked. "What are you trying to say, Captain Gruenblum?"

"That's *Bernie*—an' I'm *tryin'* t'say that my Rebellion wound up in a duel b'tween Washington an' Gallatin. Albert lost, which is why they'd need a seance—you know, where 'she who levitates is host'?"

"In *my* Whiskey Rebellion," supplied Sanders, "Gallatin didn't figure at all, except to calm down the rebellious Pennsylvanians."

"Same here," said Win.

"It's a *weird* universe," Fran added. "What's that little spring right there for, sweetheart?"

"You can say *that* again," I mumbled.

"Okay—what's that little spring right there for, sweetheart?"

* * *

We were late gettin' back. Will'd taken us downstairs. I'd expected t'do a lotta standin' around while he "sputter-lathed" metal back *onto* my pitted firin' pin. In fact, it took a whole three minutes. *Then* he insisted on impregnatin' the surface of every part with chromium, implyin' nastily that it might make up for my slovenly habits regardin' corrosion. When he'd finished, the old Colt looked like stainless.

He test-fired it through a porthole into a tunnel under the patio. A camera at the other end showed a neat cloverleaf of bullet-holes in the plastic target.

"Okay, Doc, whaddo I owe ya?" I reached into my pocket.

"For a friend of the guy who grub-staked me?" He fingered one of the empty hulls lyin' on the bench beside the firin' aperture. "Tell you what: these aren't normal .45 cartridges, are they? I'd like a live one for my collection."

I polished battered nails on m'uniform shoulder. ".451 Detonics Magnum, a late twentieth-century retrofit. 'Bout three times the power of the original. Notice the custom eight-shot magazines? You're welcome to as many rounds as pleases you."

"One'll do fine, thanks—you're going to need the rest, the way it sounds."

More Confederate glad-handery. I pondered that an' lotsa other things as Win an' I trudged home: Fran's energetic enthusiasm—*and* her satiny skin. Mary-Beth's well-oiled intelligence—*and* her willowy body. The philosophical absolutism—*and* whatever else—they shared with their husband. Musta been thinkin' out loud by the time I got to: "Wonder what they do in the sack?"

Win chuckled, "You'll never know, Demle, nor will anyone else. They lead a very private life, those three. That's the Confederacy in a nutshell: outgoing and introverted all at once. There's a Tibetan lady in Clarissa's bridge club with five *husbands*."

"Sure," I answered absently, "one too many for pinochle."

In the Underground he showed me how t'send Olongo's .375 back via a pneumatic "Bellamy Tube," suggestin' I include a .45 Magnum cartridge for the *President*'s collection. I popped a round into the padded capsule, startin' t'feel like the Lone Ranger. On the way out, we passed a drugstore advertisin' heroin, LSD-25, cocaine, an' Laetrile, two for the price of one—in platinum, gold, silver, an' copper coinage . . . an' plutonium certificates. I could see this freedom jazz was gonna take more gettin' used to than I likely had in me.

At Win's house, there were shadows waitin' for us in the dark. The detective's hand went casually to his S&W; I found the grip of my .45.

"Good evening, sir. You're the owner?"

"What can I do for you?" Win answered neutrally.

There were four of 'em, a chimp, two gorillas, an' a human. They stepped out into the moonlight wearin' severe black uniforms an' more hardware than I'd seen in one place since the Normandy Landing. The chimp spoke again: "We're from Griswold's Security—"

"*Griswold's . . .*" Win sounded impressed. I was impressed that *he* was impressed.

"We're looking for a . . . a 'Bernard M. Gruenblum'?"

I felt m'Yamaguchians pull into tight formation—right *behind* me.

"How come?" I demanded.

"We have orders to arrest him. For murder."

12

Nor Iron
Bars

WIN'S FIST CLAMPED FIRMLY OVER THE HAND I'd filled with Hartford steel.

"Relax, Bernie. This isn't the States. Our friends here are *civilians*, businessmen, and they haven't any rights on my property."

Coulda fooled me. Who was it usta talk about guys "so tough y'could roller-skate on 'em"? At the moment, I was discoverin' that there isn't anything funny at all about gorillas wearin' kilts—even the tartan was black-on-black—pistols, ammo-belts, an', insteada the usual nightstick, bowie-knives with sixteen-inch blades. Made me wonder if they even *bothered* with handcuffs.

Brrrr.

"This isn't your pidgin, Bear," the leader warned. Like the others, he wore an ebony tunic, his cap tucked under an epaulet. "Just go inside and let us—"

"Lighten up, Li-Li—I know you're a hard ape, just don't let that fancy monkey-suit go to your head." The detective grinned at him, showing teeth.

The chimp took an angry step forward, peelin' back his own lip. Win brushed eloquent fingertips over the rubber handle of his revolver an' stood his ground.

"Remember, you're in the property-*protecting* business, Li-Li, and this parcel happens to be mine! Since you overdressed Boy Scouts haven't been hired to guard *my* plastic flamingos, maybe you'd better explain—*very politely*—why you're trespassing!"

The security-agent's fury evaporated gradually, leavin' a residue of exasperation. "My apologies, *sir,*" he said stiffly—then shrugged. "Oh, for Albert's sake, Win, I've got a hurry-order to take this Gruenblum nake on a double sapicide. Condemnation, I didn't know he was a customer of yours!"

"And a friend." Win relaxed visibly, as did the chimpanzee's trio of back-ups. "That's 'naked ape,' Bernie, about as insulting as 'monkey' going the other way. But the Captain here is young. He'll learn."

He took a deep breath and exhaled. "Li-Li, let's go get this idiot mistake ironed out over a glass of something toxic. You can use my Telecom to find out what your dispatcher's been smoking. I vouch for Bernie; he isn't going to rabbit."

Seemed t'suit everybody better'n the *High Noon* reprise we'd been headed for.

"I'll have to have his weapon," the chimp said, lookin' at me, then beside me to the slabba granite wearin' white socks an' brown shoes, then t'me again.

Win said, "That's something I'd buy a ticket to watch. C'mon, Li-Li. You're a bourbon drinker, as I recall."

The Confederate slammer.

The fact they spell it "gaol" ain't the only thing different about it. The bell-person ushered me in, turned back the bed, adjusted the window-dimmers, pointed out the Telecom where I could order room-service an' the wet-bar. He hesitated, waitin' by the door for a tip. I offered him the one at the end of my boot, an' he dematerialized.

I still felt indecently exposed in the region of my waist. Win'd assured me it was a necessary ritual, for which Griswold's'd hafta pay restitution eventually.

I hadn't let 'em take the field-density frammis.

Again, I examined the lurid holos Captain Li-Li'd proffered in Confederate lieu of a warrant. There, carved up to a fare-thee-well in 3D an' Yechnicolor, lay Professors "Marvin N. Hulbert" an' "Hubert N. Merwin", B.S., M.S., D.O.A. No wonder I'd never been able t'tell 'em apart.

Havin' been duly certified as "murder weapons," Charm,

Spin, an' Color were incarcerated with me. Which seemed a waste—there were five other "cells" goin' empty in this six-room Big House. The proprietors'd greeted us like the new freeway had by-passed 'em. The *actual* beef was a civil one, there bein' no criminal charges in the Confederacy, 'cept what I was payin' t'stay the night: Negligently Importin' Dangerous Animals Contributin' Thereby to the Wrongful Demise of a Paira Sapient Inhabitants of North America.

The professors'd be thrilled t'know they'd been posthumously adopted.

This business of the Freenies'd been a compromise. The pseudocops were hardly accustomed t'hearin' disputed property object t'bein' impounded. What it'd come down to was that I'd take up residence with the Yamaguchii while Win hightailed it down t'what passes for Denver—coupla little burgs they call St. Charles an' Auraria—t'verify the charges where they'd been preferred.

They'd been brought, interesting enough, by one Denward T. Kent, Confederate Inhabitant—this place was gonna hafta look to its immigration laws—who'd pointed to his bandages an' claimed t'be another victim of Gruenblumian heinosity.

That drippin' y'don't hear is th' bleedin' of m'heart.

He'd provided the pop-eye polaroids. Win wanted t'find out how Captain Li-Li'd found me. *I* wanted t'know how come everybody an' his asshole was titled "Captain"—no colonels, obersts, subalterns, or generalissimos, jus' *captain*.

Win laughed, which I thought sorta smacked of bad taste, seein' as how he was drivin' me to the slammer at the time. Nice car: a Neova—we slowed to a hundred through the hospital zones.

"I wondered the same thing when I first got here, Bernie. Their 'gaols' threw me, too. They let a prisoner of mine suicide because they hadn't shaken him down thoroughly—no more expertise developing penal institutions than military ranks. And for the same reason."

"Howzat?" They'd sure known enough t'take my .45

away—makin' hilarious remarks about museum pieces. Wished I hadn't sent Olongo's gun back.

"Well, everybody's armed here as a matter of individual—not societal—defense. Sure, there's the militia, but it's largely vestigial, covers only a county-sized area, supports itself through bake-sales and raffle-tickets, and hasn't any more official status than the thousand others like it scattered over the continent. There's no official status to *have*."

"So, if I started my own Greater Laporte militia?..."

He laughed again. "They'd welcome the competition— *and* challenge you to a tug-of-war at their annual fund-raising picnic. That's the best way to look at it, sort of a volunteer fire department. They haven't had any real combat experience since the Russian War, and likely never will again. A country where everybody has a gun and nobody has the authority to surrender—that's a militarist's nightmare!"

I realized he hadn't answered my question. "Yeah, but what's all this 'Captain' jazz?"

"Well, anyone who *heads* a group of individuals—not easy in this unruly continuum—gets the honorific '*Captain*.' That's what it means, and that's about all it amounts to. Will's elected—by unanimous consent—and Li-Li's a hired hand. As for why there isn't any prison-science, how many crimes do you suppose get committed around here?"

I opened my mouth.

"Never mind; I'll tell you..."

I shut it.

"These murders would be the first in five years, locally. The tiny population of burglars and muggers usually doesn't live long enough to *get* to gaol." He reflected. "You know, you're going to be famous in the morning."

"Just what I need! Say, Win, if nothing nor nobody's *official* an' there ain't no real cops, how come you're takin' your buddy off to the calaboose? Whyn't we just ignore this hoorah an' get on with findin' *Georgie?*"

The Neova slowed. A sign ahead offered "High Security

Lodging— Vacancy—For Sale Cheap." Gaol business *must* be lousy.

"Look, Bernie, there are over six thousand Telecom channels in the Confederacy. The average person can't go an hour without using the Telecom, to look up the definition of a word, check a recipe, buy a carton of cigarettes, or catch the reruns of *Hello, Joe—Whadd'ya Know?*. And you should see the media-wide alert when somebody writes a bad check! You wouldn't last three hours on the outside, and I'd never do business again for aiding and abetting."

He popped the gull-wing doors. We went inside t'see the night clerk. They didn't even ask t'see my luggage.

So here I was, at 3:30 in the mornin', lyin' on my back, tryin' t'find somethin' interestin' on the Telecom t'watch between my toes. The room's disintegrator chute was still absorbin' the remains of a postmidnight snack, an' that in itself'd been somethin' t'ponder.

Eagleburger. Seems like the local conservationists'd discovered a century ago that chickens an' turkeys weren't in danger of extinction on accounta they were private property an' economically useful. It might disturb some tender anticommercial sensibilities, turnin' mighty raptors into munchies, but at least there were plenty of 'em t'spare.

Back home they'd been extinct for two hundred years.

The Freenies were finishin' their third cuppa java apiece. Dunno what they were gonna do tonight; the little buggers *never* seemed t'sleep. Musta been all that coffee.

There was somethin' like a TV guide on the nightstand. Turned out, it was only a guide to the guide. Dozens of utility channels just listin' what was on *now*. Even more listin' what was on later. The main channels advertised their up-comin' features—an' even carried ads for other channels, as well. There was an interactive query-service, cross-referencin' current programs by subject, title, author, producer, director, principal actors, an' bit-players—an' a couple channels you could call in t'request anything else y'wanted.

Naturally, the gaol itself had a well-stocked library of postage-stamp recordings of books, music, movies, an' suchlike.

You could even make *yourself* a channel, speak your piece or hum through a comb-and-tissue-paper, if you were willin' t'pay for the time. 'Course nobody had t'watch y'do it.

Maybe it's just the *idea* of TV: there *still* wasn't anything interestin' on.

But I noticed one or two items that woulda gone right by the average Confederate viewer. First of all, there weren't any mass-spectator team sports. A sprinklin' of individual efforts, like target-shootin', tennis, an' boxin'. An' with about as much audience-appeal—I gathered from the near-empty bleachers in the screen—as celebrity hopscotch. Full-contact karate, a recent import from the States, was enjoyin' a modest vogue, though they hadda spot the humans a few dozen extra points.

Another thing was the decided lacka religion. I think there was just one church in the whole of Greater Laporte—though it coulda been Chicago, kinda lost track which channel I was watchin' at the time—an' that was an inflatable hut that was only there three days a week. Saturdays for Adventists an' my folks, Sundays for the gentiles, an' Mondays for the Freudians.

Resta the week it was a parkin' lot.

But most disturbin', somehow, was that Confederate swear-words are as different as everything else. They don't refer t'sex, an' they don't refer t'God. Pie-in-the-sky just don't mix too well with folks usta runnin' their own lives, thanks. Instead, they swear by their heroes, like Lysander Spooner an' Albert Gallatin; they swear by baddies like Washington an' Hamilton. "Condemnation!" Li-Li'd exclaimed when pressed t'some kinda limit, referrin' more t'government's way with other folks' real estate, than the state of anybody's soul. An' they swear by excretion, just like everybody else in the known universe.

But if somebody here'd said "Get fucked!" the addressee'd likely look at him a bit funny, shake his head, an' answer, "Why thanks, pilgrim—you have a nice day, too!"

Prime time. There I was in the TV studio, disguised as a paper-shredder, recordin' the assassination of Blocky Yocks. Dunno why the Academy'd bothered—it was seen live coast t'coast by half the population of the country at the time.

It was durin' the ratin's sweeps of 1991. The week before, America's most popular ventriloquist'd forgotten t'pay his phone bill on time. Good ol' TPC'd cut his service on a Friday, leavin' the poor guy outa touch with the network, columnists, agent, fans, an' the three exwives he was still talkin' to, over a whole weekend. That kinda thing's ruined bigger stars—lookit the rumors about Kermit the Frog bein' dead. Never did make much of a comeback after that.

But this time, it meant war. Come Wednesday night, he'd recited the business office numbers for the Ameche monopoly in Anchorage an' Honolulu an' pointed out to 60,000,000 viewers that whenever they called a long-distance number that was busy or didn't answer, it cost the phone company. Not much, a measurable pittance for switching, line-use, an' the ring-ring or buzz-buzz at the other end.

So when 60,000,000 people tried those numbers, every fifteen minutes, twenty-four hours a day—but only on weekends—for seventeen months running, it put a crack of doom right in the Bell System.

But, in its early dyin' throes, the system lashed out at its tormentor. The week followin' Blocky's announcement, as I was crouched, sweatin' inside a plastic bag fulla confetti an' he was in the middle of his openin' monologue, two CIA loaners an' a paira outa-work installers busted into Studio B with silenced Ruger Mark IIs an' emptied their clips into poor Blocky, endin' his career forever.

Too bad the stupid jerks didn't think t'shoot his partner, the ventriloquist.

I woke up, not havin' realized I'd nodded off. Sheesh! Past few nights, m'whole life'd been flashin' before my eyes. *Gotta* lay off that vitamin B6.

Sunlight was streamin' in the window, an' the Telecom was blarin' at my alien friends. I amazed m'self by feelin' pretty swell, all things considered. The Freenies were watchin' some kinda porno flick on a local program titled *Punching for Platinum*. Now an' again the host'd call up his viewers, an' if they could name the page in the *Kama Sutra* closest t'what'd just happened in this mornin's movie, they won. What kinda spoilt it for me was that all the actors were chimpanzees. The host, bobbin' in a big glass tank, was a porpoise.

I got up, showered, retrieved my coverall from the autogroomer, an' started pushin' a little plastic complimentary razor around on my stubble while the Yamaguchii ordered breakfast. Jake with me—I coulda eaten a...

...I caught a glimpse of the Telecom screen in the mirror, nearly decapitated an' strangled myself at the same time, swivelin' my neck around, an' lost my appetite immediately. Seein' yourself unexpectedly on TV'll do that to ya:

IMMIGRANT DENIES BUTCHERING TWO
DETAILS ON CHANNEL 1130

Dazed, I stumbled to the bar, shave an' breakfast forgotten. Win'd been right about gettin' famous in a hurry. Dunno when the camera'd caught me with that dumb look on my face, but it was obvious the gaoler'd found a way t'supplement his meager income. I poured myself a straight shot, gargled it down, an' set up another on the rocks.

There was a scratchin' at the door.

Hell, I'd never even checked t'see if it was locked last night. Now I kinda hoped it would be—t'keep nosy strangers out.

More scratchin' scrabblin' noises.

Wishin' more'n ever I still had my Colt, I approached the door cautiously. I wondered how good a weapon a Freenie'd make if y'grabbed it by the neck an' swung it. I opened the unresistin' door a crack, peeked out into the hall.

Nothin'.

Suddenly, the door moved of its own accord. I looked down, glass in hand, an' there at my feet was a brownish medium-sized pooch. *No*, not quite, but somethin' else. It nosed on through the door, stopped in the middle of the room, sat on its haunches, scratched an ear with a rear foot, an' cocked its head.

"Surely it's not cocktail hour already," the animal said. "Is it, Captain Gruenblum?"

13

The Dog Who Knew too Much

"G. HOWELL NAHUATL AT YOUR SERVICE."
Whiskers twitchin' an' a twinkle in his eye, he hopped up
into a chair by the window. "The G stands for Greenriver."

"Er...I'm Bernard M. Gruenblum—the M stands for
Confused. These're m'friends Snap, Crackle, an'—say,
you're a *coyote*, aren't you?"

"How nice of you to notice."

I sighed. "Well, whaddo coyotes drink when they're
visitin' folks in gaol?"

"It *is* rather early, isn't it? How about Coca-Cola—"

Perfect for a mornin' pick-me-up. There bein' no Confederate FDA, Coke *is* the real thing.

"—with perhaps the slightest splash of rum? I'm not
actually here to *visit*, Captain Gruenblum, but to—"

"Don't tell me you're a *lawyer?*" Most attorneysa my
acquaintance'd been *two*-legged coyotes, but I didn't think
it politic t'mention.

He chuckled. "No, I'm here to get you out. Win Bear
sent me."

Bear sends coyote. I'd be palaverin' with Br'er Rabbit
next thing I know. Now all I hadda solve was this little
etiquette problem: couldn't *hand* Nahuatl his drink, an' he'd
look silly sittin' on it like a Freenie.

The critter noticed m'hesitation: "Please set it on the end-
table. I've a long nose and a longer tongue. Now, as I was
saying—"

"Win sentya. Wouldn'ta thought murder'd be a bailable
offense." I started on that second scotch—beat hell outa

orange juice for an eye-opener. Addressin' Spin: "You guys finish orderin' breakfast? Well, make it for five, whyn'tcha?"

"Thank you," Nahuatl offered. "Those lamb cutlets on the menu will do nicely. And you're not strictly accused of murder, though if you were, it's as bondable as any transgression. But you see, Captain, there are no longer any charges against you at all." He took another lap at his drink.

"That's *Bernie*. How come I'm on the right side of the nonexistent law again?" Goddamn if m'own drink hadn't evaporated somehow alluva sudden. I dialed another justa wash breakfast—steak an' eggs, hashbrowns, English muffins—down. Charm, Spin, an' Color divvied up a bowla oatmeal. 'Nother rum-Coke for the doggie.

"I'm not entirely certain, Bernie. Win's on his way back from St. Charles-Auraria. We thought we'd save you another hour in durance vile." He dipped his muzzle delicately into his glass; it fizzed around his whiskers as he finished it. I punched up another round for both of us.

"Well, I been in duransh—*durances* a lot viler." I watched the Freenies squattin' on their oatmeal, shuddered, an' gulped the resta m'drink. "Lishen, I don' wanna sheem noshy or nothin', but—"

"But it ishn't every day"—the animal grinned, black eyes sparklin'—"you drink breakfasht with a talking coyote?" He hiccupped, eyes dartin' suspiciously around t'see who'd made that noise.

"Shomethin' like that. Gorillash, chimpses—" I nodded to the TV porno-host still sloshin' around—"even dolphinshes, all got lotsa cranial capacitidity—*capacitude*. Jushta mattera learnin' shomebody elshe's lingo. But, well . . ." I sputtered awkwardly, lookin' at his narrow canine skull. "I wouldn'ta thought coyotes'd have . . ."

"Ordinarily," Nahuatl replied, uncrossin' his eyes, "you'd be right. But you shee"—he sighed lugubriously, a tear rollin' down his muzzle—"I'm the firsht—and lasht—of my kind."

Civilization (explained G. Howell Nahuatl—makin' some allowances for alcoholic diction), is presently undergoing a transition, from nanoelectronics, which produced the Telecom, for example, to *giga*electronics—a reduction in scale, an increase in capacities, of several orders of magnitude—which, among other things, has produced *me*.

I was born a relatively run-of-the-litter coyote. My mother was third generation at the Gallatinopolis Zoo, up in the Dakotas. Except that I arrived as a result of some rather special gene-selection. Even without what came afterward, I would have become a genius among coyotes, more intelligent than any domestic canine, perhaps even brighter than the average Poland-China hog. But Aloysius Sourwine had plans for me, and great hopes: I was to be a four-legged Benedict Arnold.

Each year, hundreds of thousands of sheep and young cattle are killed by my species. We are a crafty race, fast on our feet, extremely adaptable. Like the cockroach and the rat, we will prosper even unto the end of time, whereas your people have yet to prove themselves. Why, there are wild coyotes living comfortably within the city limits of Laporte.

Thus, there seemed no safe, economic method of eliminating coyotes as agricultural pests. Shooting, as my master once observed, only culls the slow among us; poisoning, the stupid. At that rate of selection, we'd be running ranches of our *own* within the next few centuries.

At which point my master, Aloysius Sourwine, slapped a massive hand upon the sunburn line across his forehead, nearly giving himself a concussion: why not turn the joke into reality, accelerate the process, create a breed of coyote which could *help* with the vermin problem? "If you can't beat 'em, join 'em"—or, more appositely, "set a thief to catch a thief."

Thus followed the impressively expensive genetic recombination which culminated in my birth—along with an even more costly effort in gigaelectronics. At six weeks, they implanted on my cortex the most sophisticated circuitry the Confederacy was capable of producing. In sum, I became a *super*coyote with artificially supplemented intelligence—a *weapon*, aimed at shielding sheep and cattle from the predations of my own kind. The Great Plains Stockmen's Association were delighted—until they learned they'd done *too* good a job.

You see, under Confederate customs, the sole criterion establishing individual rights—what other civilizations would call "citizenship"—is *intelligence*. A gorilla can tell dirty jokes; a chimpanzee can debate metaphysics; a porpoise can argue politics; an Orca—"killer whale," and I take it you've yet to encounter one of them—can beat you at chess. All, including human beings, can stand up, at least figuratively, *demanding*, in clear grammatical English, Spanish, Danish, Quebeçois, or Dolphish, respect for their sovereign individuality.

And so, embarrassingly enough, could I.

I was not entirely without sympathy for the Great Plains Stockmen's Association. At the urging of my master, they'd invested a great deal in me, and now it was lost. There are two and *only* two kinds of entity in the universe: people and property. The former cannot be owned, except, in a manner of speaking, by themselves. The ethical basis for every social, political, and economic transaction is Confederate culture, this is why simians and cetaceans have rights, why the young of *every* intelligent species may not be treated as chattel. You cannot *own* a sovereign individual.

Everything else—land and natural resources, artifacts, abstractions such as contractual relationships and orbital positions, *un*intelligent animals—*everything* else is property, either owned, abandoned, or as-yet-unclaimed. I was to have been property, a useful subsapient asset with no more rights—nor any more conception of them—than one of those hovercraft out in the street.

How well I recall that fateful day at the Cheyenne Stock Show. I was still only a pup, and my memories of the time are highly influenced by later intellectual development. But the data—the sights, sounds, and oh, the *smells*—are unerringly recorded, probably by the electronic component of my mind. There was acrimonious debate between Sourwine and his friends with the officials whether I was to be considered livestock—like the border collies and other sheepdogs—or an item of farm technology, such as a tractor or geostationary reflector.

They stood about my little cage, arguing and arguing, until I grew impatient. Their voices, PA announcements of 5H awards, the roller-coaster outside, were painful to my sensitive hearing. Finally, in exasperation, I said, "What could be more simple—I'll compete in *both* categories!"

I'd like to tell you that my owners, his associates, and the judges were shocked into silence. It was the first I'd ever spoken, indeed even thought to do so. I'd *like* to tell you that. However, the canine tongue and jaw aren't suited to human speech, and what emerged was a garbled mewling. Sourwine thought I was ill. It took me several tries to get my message across, by which time the humor was lost on everyone, including myself.

Even now, observe how my voice issues from a transducer on my collar, much in the manner of simian wristvoders, except that mine is synched directly to brain impulses. Chimpanzees and gorillas originally spoke Ameslan—sign language—and their speech devices key to subliminal movements of the hand and wrist.

No, the profound astonishment I'd awaited was slower in arriving, and mostly in the context of my creators' pocketbooks. Sourwine took it philosophically. He became a father to me, tutoring me in the ways of the world. In turn, I *did* the job I'd been designed for, watching his flocks. When he passed away at the untimely age of ninety-seven, I found he'd left his property to me.

Thus, I became a gentleman rancher. These days I hire two-legged shepherds, for, sad truth to tell, I *loathe* anything even remotely bucolic, even the produce section of grocery stores. The paradigm and puzzle of sapience is that there is no accounting for—or predicting—individual preferences. My true ambition was to be an operatic tenor.

Instead, I became the world's first consulting private nose.

This was Win Bear's doing: some years ago, I was herding for Aloysius Sourwine, baying *Lohengrin* at the moon in reflection that my life seemed somehow—incomplete.

The further I examined this conundrum, the firmer my conclusion: I needed to get laid.

More, I had the natural mammalian desire to generate progeny amidst the domestic tranquility of amiable companionship. In my case, the circumstances were hideously complicated. I couldn't bring myself to mate with a female of my own species. That would be rather . . . let me see . . . like your choosing prefrontally lobotomized women. I'm sure this might suit *some* men perfectly, but I hoped for some intelligent conversation with my afterglow cigarette. This is a Free System: it might not be impossible to find a human or simian female. But I doubted I could find a rational one I wouldn't have to *pay*. I wanted more than that.

Discussing this with Aloysius Sourwine, we agreed, since the most expensive research had been done already, that we'd attempt to *build* me a wife. After all, *nothing* was too good for his son, the opera singer. The enterprise proceeded, and I had reason to be grateful that we coyotes mature rapidly.

She was beautiful, my Elsa, even as a new-born puppy, with dark silky fur, long eyelashes, and two dramatic lighter strokes either side of her forehead that zig-zagged up to her ears. Her eyes held a wild, untamed expression in their depths which promised of passion.

Since we knew from the beginning that she'd be sapient, no effort was spared in her education: philosophy, music, self-defense, literature, and the arts. She absorbed them all eagerly, and my days with her were filled with joyous sunlight—and anticipation.

Then she matured—and broke my heart.

No, it wasn't that she didn't love me. I believe I might have suffered that, somehow, understanding, as I do, the vagaries of individual taste. Nor was it anything else I was prepared to encompass.

You humans, having developed naturally over thousands of centuries, have lost every laboratory-detectable remnant of instinct. Beyond brief, simple reflexes and drive states, nature doesn't tell you how to satisfy; you have *no* inborn knowledge, not of sex, nor how to feed yourselves, nor even walk. This is a great virtue, for it renders your potentials limitless. I suspect that much the same is true of simians and cetaceans, that everything they know is learned.

Instinct, however, apparently is far stronger in the female of my species than the male. Or it may be another matter of individual differences. Within a few weeks of her passage into ripe, desirable adulthood, my Elsa vanished, fleeing this civilization she knew well in every detail, for the wide, wild prairie and a life of savagery.

She tried. She certainly tried with me. There were long emotional sessions you wouldn't call conversation, bittersweet unsatisfying love-making, and she seemed torn between consciousness and instinct, not knowing what it was she really wanted. When she became pregnant, instinct overwhelmed her totally. I found her speaking-collar on the Telecom console, with a personal recording whose contents I'm sure you can infer.

After days of grieving and lament, I consulted a commercial directory for help. I was certain that if I could only find her, I could persuade her to come back to me. I'd even spend a portion of the year with her, pretending to be a wild animal. Anything. I loved her.

I sent a graphics message rather than 'comming in person and instructed this "Win Bear" I'd selected, a "Consulting Investigator," not to be surprised at whatever he encountered when he reached my home. I gave him the impression I was an eccentric recluse, and that wasn't too inaccurate by now: I'd suffered yet another loss—old Aloysius Sourwine—and was living in a condominium in Cheyenne.

I met Win at the door without a word, took his hat in my teeth, trotted into the living room like a trained fox terrier, and sat on the couch. Win had followed and sat, too, as if waiting for my master to make his entrance.

"Mister Bear," I said finally, "I need help badly!"

"So do I! I think I just heard a coyote talking to me!"

And so, of course, he had. Several drinks and a long explanation later, he agreed to help me search for Elsa— this sort of domestic case being not unprecedented with him when he examined it in the proper light. Although she'd left her collar, the implanted circuitry, he reasoned, ought to radiate enough faint, incidental signal to track her. He, in turn, consulted with two physicists at Laporte University, Limited—a human female and a porpoise—who supplied him with suitable equipment. That and a sport hovercraft convertible to flight were all we required.

I found her in what had been northern Montana before Confederation, living in a burrow with our pups.

"Elsa!" It was dark and dirty, underground, strewn with the remains of prey, roofed with the drying roots of the prairie grass above. The children were still blind, whimpering and tumbling over one another ceaselessly, occasionally nursing. I could scarcely bring myself to look at them for fear I'd want to stay in this unsightly purgatory. I felt then that dying would be a blessedly welcome release.

"How have you been, Howell? Still practicing for the Cheyenne Operatic League?" I'd brought her speech collar, equipped as mine to crawl into place by itself at the clumsy paw-touch of a stud on its surface. She looked worn and tired, her fur dull and matted.

"Well, no." I tried desperately to keep my voice light and even. "My singing's adequate, but they don't have a suit of armor to fit me, nor do they fancy my crawling about the stage on all—Elsa, why are we discussing these trivia? I came to take you home! Aloysius has passed away; we have a ranch now, everything we'll ever—"

"Except freedom, Howell." Her lack of remorse, the absence of even the faintest longing for our old life, ripped me apart. "I can't live the way you want me to. It's not that I don't—but I—I just *can't!*"

"Is it the wild males?" I asked, half fearful, half resigned at her answer.

She laughed. "Since the pups came, I've spent most of my time keeping the local talent from raping me and *eating* them. No, Howell, this is simply the way I was *meant* to live. I know you disapprove: this den is a fleabag, but I dug it *myself*, knowing how without ever being told, and it's *mine.*"

I nodded sadly. "Elsa, something inside me persists in

believing that there are words to change your mind. But I haven't found them, not now, and not before. I love you, and I can't help wondering why *that* shouldn't make a difference. Life is a hollow mockery without you. Don't you miss me, even a little?"

"Of course I do," she said heartlessly. Talk is cheap, and words of love the cheapest. "I've even absorbed enough human culture to realize that the pups need a father. But there's nothing you can do for us; obviously, we don't need money—"

I turned, knowing that if I didn't leave, I'd sacrifice myself to an existence I abominated just to be with her. "A man is waiting," I said inanely. "I've got to be going." And I went.

It took me a week to get rid of the fleas.

Now I limit my musical aspiration to the bath. I can sniff the scene of a crime, follow a trail, and identify the culprit amidst a crowd of thousands in the Underground. And in the leg-man business, four are superior to two.

No one would believe my capabilities, at first—except Win. I appeared before an arbiter, certified myself in a series of exhaustive tests, and now any judge on the continent will credit my testimony. I've quadrupled Sourwine's wealth; my nose is my fortune.

And Bernie, the yearning for Elsa never ceases.

It's a fragile thing, this *believing* in life. I gain it and I lose it, day by day, minute by minute. I gain it and lose it again. Yet I've learned that I must *never* reveal the part of me which doesn't believe, that which hurts eternally and despairs of ever again finding a reason for believing. Friends claim such revelation doesn't bother them—it's what they want to be trusted to see—but it isn't true. At least not for very long.

We are *all* predators, my friend, and the only roles we truly understand are conqueror—or clown.

It's a dog's life.

The Freenies gathered around sympathetically, disprovin' Howell's thesis—as he'd disproved it by tellin' us about it. One of 'em extruded a manipulator, pattin' the coyote on the shoulder. I sniffed back a tear an' got up woozily from the bed. Sober t'drunk t'hung-over, all in an hour an' a half. Some mornin'!

"Well," Howell said, doin' some recoverin' himself, "I didn't intend telling the story of my life. We must get out of here and join Win at his house."

I looked around—hadn't *brought* anything, an' I wasn't collectin' little plastic razors. "How d'we check outa this upholstered dump?"

"Follow me." He shook his head, an' his eyes crossed again momentarily.

Every footstep bangin' in m'head like a gong, we trooped down the hall to the front desk. The clerk was lookin' unhappy, too. Howell gave him some Telecom coordinates.

"As you see," the private nose said, "charges against Captain Gruenblum and his associates have been vacated. I suggest you return his weapons and effects."

"Who's paying?" the chimpanzee tersely said, probably on accounta I hadn't rendered him a gratuity the night before.

"Gimme my stuff, pal, an' I'll take care of you—say, what's that ruckus outside?"

"Your public," the clerk answered. "You wouldn't want to sign this waiver before you leave, would you? Clears us of personal liability and—no, I didn't think so."

Through the glass front doors, I could see an ugly-lookin' crowd gathered in the parkin' lot, laden with some kinda equipment. I slung the gunbelt around my middle, buckled it, an' plopped a gold coin on the counter. "That cover the damage?"

The chimp's eyebrows shot up. He punched more numbers an' returned a fistful of silver an' copper. "Your receipt's been registered in the net. I'd say come back and see us, but—"

SLAM! Both front doors bashed aside, pressed to the walls by a pink an' furry avalanche of sapients, most of 'em pointin' microphones an' twin-lensed cameras. Lights, brighter'n the sun, burned into my optics.

"Gruenblum!" someone shouted, a big guy with a southern accent an' a thin gray caterpillar of a moustache. "Turner, Channel 17. What's it like to go free after cold-bloodedly slaughtering two human beings?"

I turned. "What's it like havin' your bicuspids shoved down your gullet? Wanna find out?" He stepped back from my raised fist. I blinked, eyes waterin'.

"You've got to get these people *out* of here!" the clerk cried behind me. "Look what they're doing to my carpet!"

We were trapped up against the desk by the crowd-pressure. "I know—the press ain't never been well housetrained." I shot a middle finger at a camera. Its lights winked out suddenly, sparing the sensitive home-viewers such a hideous sight. I got an idea.

"Batshit!" I hollered, shootin' birds with both fists. "Iguana manure! Cow floppies! Big juicy piles of anteater feces—!"

One by one the cameras started shuttin' down. *This* was the same medium that broadcast porno on the mornin' show?

Howell barked abruptly. "Privacy! My client demands the right of privacy!"

A camera relit, glared down at him. "Oh, look! A talking doggie! And there are the *monsters* who—*Yeeeowch!*"

Somethin' shoved the nosy simian reporter from behind. The crowd opened like a boiled clam, an' there were T. W. Sanders an' his two amazons, plowin' their way t'my side. Will's toadstickers were in his hands. He pinked Channel 17's hired mouth in the behind an' was through.

"Gather up the Ganymedii and let's get out of here!" the gunsmith said. "Win's keeping the getaway car warm!"

14

The Magnificent Eleven

"HELLO, TRICKSTER!" WIN GREETED HOWELL as we leaped into the ground-effect machine, a long low fan-driven Packard-Fedders. He folded his right-hand steering wheel as Mary-Beth slid in beside him. She gunned it, and we were away in a storm of prop-wash before the first reporter made it to the curb.

"Hello yourself, gumshoe!" Howell answered cheerily.

"Glad you'rall havin' such a swell time. We missin' anybody?" I counted Freenies—three; I counted gunsmiths—one; I counted detectives, human an' otherwise—two; I counted girls—four . . . but then they'd had me seein' double since the beginnin'. That left only me, an' I was here.

Buildin', trees, an' garbage cans flashed by.

"We saw you on the 'com this morning!" Fran punched my shoulder. She was perched on a jumpseat with an alien in her lap. "Rather, the snoopies interviewing themselves *about* you. Looked like you could use rescuing—they'd really worked themselves up!"

"You're tellin' me! What happens now?"

Win swiveled his seat t'face us. "Back to my place. I guess the Sanderses have enlisted for the duration. They were waiting for me when I got back from Denv—St. Charles-Auraria. Howell, you got anything?"

"No chance yet," answered the coyote. "It's a pretty large area, where Bernie's saucer could have set down."

Win shook his head. "Griswold's people are hopping

mad. Their client came to the St. Charles office yesterday, filed his complaint, paid a purely nominal deposit, and *zip!* The number he'd given turned out to be a mortuary in Leadville. They checked—nobody's talking in *that* place!"

I grimaced. "Any other good news?"

"Not for Griswold's. They're stuck with the indemnity and owe you enough restitution to pay me, repay Olongo, and go into business for—but here we are. Let's go inside."

The nine of us occupied maybe five percent of Win's gymnasium-sized living-room. Drinks all around. I had a beer.

"As I was saying," Win started up a cigar he'd dampened down with brandy, "we've got two leads: this"—he pointed to my lumpy pocket where the equalizer frammis was hidin'—"and *this.*"

From a pocket of his own, he pulled a plastic bag containin' what appeared t'be a handkerchief, frayin' at the edges. "A section of mechanical towel from Griswold's washroom. I'll have to claim credit for this flash: Kent made a pit-stop, and we caught it before it rolled into the wall and washed itself."

Howell's ears perked. Win opened the bag and held it while the coyote thrust his nose inside. "There's you," observed the animal after a moment's consideration. "Even through the plastic, those cigars of yours. And both chimpanzee—a youngish one—and gorilla. The gorilla's recently returned from a Chicago business trip, is left-handed like Fran here, and has three children, two sons and a—"

"Hold on there!" I protested. "How can y'smell somethin' like *that?*"

He looked up at Win an' winked. "You know my methods, Pauling."

"That's *Watson.*" Win laughed. "The gorilla's Captain Andy M'bongo; he and Asta here have been playing chess once a week for three years."

Howell: "There's also someone, perhaps *two* someone elses. A man in his late thirties—yes, I *can* discriminate age and gender—who's recently suffered grievous injury: blood, medicinals, faint traces of staphylococcus..."

"Makes m'whole day. What else?"

"A woman who ought to change her perfume—it's virtually indistinguishable from Black Flag Ant and Roach Kil—"

"*Edna!*" the Freenies an' I shouted.

"Not in evidence at Griswold's," Win cautioned. "Just Denny, with a bad limp and his arm in a sling. You play rough, Bernie."

"Not rough enough! Can't understand how he survived that .45 slug! Oh, well, what's m'field-density equalizer got t'do with anything?"

Win tucked away the evidence bag. "They've got two courses of action, too. They need the device and can either get it back from you—"

Fran sat up. "*That's* why the phony murder charge, to locate Bernie!"

"Won't do them any good," observed her husband. "I *know* that tight-lipped bunch at Griswold's . . . *brrrr!*"

"The discretion of the telemedia is another proposition," the Ambassador chipped in. "Had I not an armored carapace, this morning I should be little more than a collection of body-fluids and footprints. Why is it, that in every culture, reporters are invariably—"

"Cultivatedly rude, militantly ignorant lounge lizards who don't know anything but city-room politics?" Howell offered.

"Or the best brands of hair-spray." Will grunted.

"No argument," I said, "but go on, Win. Do we let Cromney come t'us or what?"

"Or what. I've contacted a couple university friends who can analyze this device of yours, make a guess where Cromney'll be looking for parts, and track him down—"

"No good, Your Deductiveness. It'll be Heplar doin' the fabricatin', an' there ain't no lacka basic components in *Georgie*'s stores. Heplar's got the education t' handle the job; question is does he have the smarts?"

There came a chimin'. Win punched buttons, an entire wall, fireplace an' all, vanished, replaced by a giant close-up of a pretty platinum blonde. "Oh, a party!" She surveyed the room. "I got your message, Win. What's up?"

"A false alarm, it appears. Oh, well, Deejay Thorens, meet...now let me see: Bernie Gruenblum; his friends Charm, Color, and Spin; you know Howell, of course. Have you met the Sanderses, Mary-Beth, Fran, and Will?"

She nodded cheerily. "Hi, Fran—it's a small campus, isn't it. Hello, everybody else. I repeat, sir, what's up?"

Win gave her a summary, includin' the defunctitude of his spare-parts idea. Halfway through, the screen divided, an' we were starin' at the perpetual Mona Lisa grin of a *Tursiops truncatus*—that's Latin for Flipper.

"You may forego introductions, Edward William Bear, I overheard them, though too occupied with an experiment to attend the 'com. Estimable land-dwellers, I am Ooloorie Eckickeck P'wheet. Set aside the question of fabricating a field-density equalizer and pray continue with your story. It has its interesting points."

"Everybody's doing Conan Doyle this season." Win groaned. He explained that Ooloorie wasn't in Laporte but did business electronically from the Emperor Norton University. I resisted askin' after Nasty Jim Brannigan.

The detective finished. Against m'better judgment, an' for no better reason than satisfyin' her scientific curiosity plus a perverse desire t'defy my Academy conditionin', I agreed t'turn the all-important frammis over t'Deejay. She assured me it'd be safe, though I had m'doubts about *any* institution called Mulligan's Bank & Grill.

In return, she promised t'find other ways t'be helpful. Ooloorie asked a lotta questions about *Georgie*—not about Ochskahrt's Effect, I mighta expected that from the inventor of the Broach, but she apparently regarded Academy applications as an inferior variant—mostly she wanted t'know *Georgie*'s talents as a computer, an' the range of radio-frequencies the saucer commonly used.

"You're certain, landling, that the vessel is capable of real-time communication above the Türing level?"

"If you're talkin' 'bout stuff like Telecom cartoons, 's how I program m'own, er...well, custom DreamCassettes.

'Course she ain't good for much else while we're doin' that—uses up a lotta capacity. Why?"

The faraway cetacean turned to her partner. "You see it, of course." Deejay nodded assent. "We are agreed, then," the porpoise said. "There is a *third* approach if contact can be established and capacities augmented through remote peripherals."

Win nodded, vigorously. "I *like* it."

Mary-Beth clapped her hands. "And Cromney's resulting legal status!"

Inexplicable laughter all around.

"What the flamin' Ochskahrt're you people talkin' about?"

"Would you prefer," Howell suggested, muddyin' the water further, "that Cromney be permitted to tinker with *Georgie* as he wishes? What Ooloorie has in mind is relatively simple—in fact, Confederate industry must take positive steps to *avoid* it—painless, and a considerable improvement."

Still not understandin' what was goin' on, I supplied Deejay with more information while Howell got sent to the corner mailbox t'stick m'equalizer frammis in a Bellamy Tube. At Deejay's suggestion, I also sent along m'poor beat-up Academy wristwatch in hopes somebody at the University could fix it.

Fran an' Deejay caught up with campus gossip. Apparently, the same sorta thing that went on everywhen, 'ceptin' that here the red-hot question was what species was sleepin' with what. Will got up t'pour another rounda drinks, stickin' to a decocainated softdrink, himself. The Freenies were amusin' Mary-Beth: they'd gotten a tennis ball from somewhere an' were puttin' a disgustin' new wrinkle in the old shell-game.

I refused t'watch.

Instead, I was admirin' Win's hardware collection in a glass-fronted walnut case. Some kinda single-shot derringer with a BIG hole in the front end, a laser-pistol, what looked like a bowie knife. These Confederates sure loved their—

CRASH!!!

Suddenly I found m'self on the floor, an' it seemed like a good place t'stay. The room was filled with smoke, pourin' up from the front door downstairs. I scanned around for casualties: Win lay behind the coffee-table, a cracked 'com pad on the floor in fronta him, goin' for his .41; Will'd dropped a whole pitchera margueritas an' been blown clear to the kitchen steps. He levered himself into a crouch, blood runnin' down one forearm, an' drew his swords. Both women were horizontal, but fillin' their hands with Confederate iron. My little alien buddies were nowhere t'be seen.

Which meant they were okay.

I slid my Colt outa the leather. I'd been closest when the door exploded. It still stood, splintered an' swayin' on one hinge. I crawled forward to the four or five steps leadin' t'ground level an' snicked off the thumb-safety.

There was a *crunch*, an' a furry foot smashed through the ruined door, followed by the chimp it belonged to. Decked out in commando paisley, he carried a pistol in each mitt. Behind me I felt, rather than saw, Fran Sanders raisin' her plasma-gun t'pick him off. I breast-stroked with my left hand, tellin' her t'hold fire until we saw what else we were up against.

The first chimp was followed by a second in a disgustin' squash-colored leisure suit, then by a very familiar paira faces: Denny Kent an' Edna Janof squeezed into the entry hall, each carryin' some kinda huge-bored two-handed weapon. Coulda been grenade-launchers, judgin' by what'd happened to the door. Whatever they were, that gave Denny an' Edna first priority as targets, even if I hadn't been inclined that way in the first place. I let 'em have another coupla seconds, then drew a bead on Denny's left knee an' pulled the trigger.

WHAM!

He jerked like a broken marionette an' slapped against the wall, droppin' his artillery. I shifted m'sights.

Sssspakkk!
Blommm!
Ka-bammm!

That shot of mine'd been the signal for everybody else

t'open up. Edna leveled her cannon at me, but outa nowhere a pink fluorescent hemisphere, fringed in green, dropped on her head. She shrieked an' tore it off, threw it to the entryway flaggin', an' bashed it, over an' over, with the butt-stock of her weapon. There was a sickenin' crackle.

WHAM! I fired an' missed. But somethin' bright an' slender sizzled toward her upraised arm, an' suddenly, as if it'd sprouted there, one of Sanders' smallswords stood quiverin' through her wrist. She didn't utter a sound, but snatched the blade out, cast it away. Before I could line up again, she leaped backward through the wreckage of the door an' was gone.

I almost teleported down the steps. Denny stretched groggily for a fallen pistol, an' I kicked him in the face. The delay was satisfyin' but costly: by that time, a buncha pissed-off Confederates'd stacked up on the stairs behind me, tramplin' over me on their way out the door after Edna.

I got back t'my feet, decided t'quit while I was ahead.

Looked like two enemy simians were dead. Denny wasn't goin' anywhere. Little Spin had an ugly ragged split across his shell from rim t'rim, oozin' purple fluid. Upstairs through a thinnin' cloud of smoke, the Telecom conveyed a worried female demand: "What's going on over there? Bernie, what's happening?"

Holsterin' m'pistol, I lifted the little Yamaguchian carefully in a crooked arm, caught the semiconscious Kent by a pants-cuff, an' dragged him up the stairs, his head bounce-thumpin' at every step. I was too worried about Spin t'enjoy it.

Much.

I propped Kent against the coffee table, put a foot on his crotch t'keep him in place, an' set the injured Freenie down as gently as I could on the couch. His pals were there immediately.

I'd misjudged 'em again: in the scant few seconds after the door exploded, they'd arrayed themselves against the intruders over by the front window where they could drop off into the entryway. Spin'd had the bad luck t'be first in line.

"Bernie?"

"It's okay, Deejay," I replied to the Telecom at last. "Win was right—one way t'get the equalizer frammis was from me. The *posse comitatus*'ll be back with Edna, on her shield or wearin' it up her—*owch!*

Feelin' a dribble of blood on m'neck, I reached up. Somethin'd pierced m'right earlobe, a wood-splinter or scrappa metal—no—I plucked it out: a teensy little steel arrow, point, fins an' all.

"Bernie?" the feminine voice said. "Are you okay?"

"Busy now, Deejay, I—"

There was a feral snarlin' down at the door. A third chimp clumped up the steps, holster empty, hands on the backa his head. Behind him was a brand-new Nahuatl I hadn't seen before, muzzle accordioned up an' fangs bared.

"Apparently, I got back just in time, Bernie. This one was keeping watch from a hovercraft. What I cannot fathom is why a chimpanzee should be working with the Hamiltonians."

"*Hamiltonians!*" the captured simian exclaimed. "Why it's you people who're the Hamiltonians!"

I gestured with m'.45, an' he sat down beside Kent, hands still on his head, lookin' like a new addition t'Hear, See, an' Speak No Evil.

"Bernie?" the Telecom insisted, "*please* speak to me. I'm scared! Bernie? This is *Georgie!*"

15

The Ship
Who *What?*

"It's a *FLECHETTE*," Will Sanders commented, watchin' me as Fran dabbed at his arm with some kinda cloth. He winced suddenly. She seized somethin' between her fingers an' plucked it outa the wound.

"Ungh! Just like this one!"

I kept moppin' at my bloodied earlobe, dumfounded by about six things at once. 'Cross the room, Win an' Mary-Beth finished gloppin' cyanoacrylate over Spin's fractured shell, as Color an' Charm patted his little tentacles. He *wheepled* an' bravely tried t'hold his eyestalk erect.

Our simian prisoner moved an elbow—Howell snarled—the offendin' appendage snapped back into place.

We'd tied a tourniquet above Denny Kent's disintegrated knee. I'd wanted it around his neck, but'd been persuaded otherwise by those who take unfair advantage by bein' girls. Thanks t'Deejay an' Ooloorie, professional helpa various kinds'd been summoned, but it seemed a mite slow comin'.

"A flechette," the gunsmith repeated between gritted teeth. Gone were the glitterin' toys he'd been wearin', replaced now with a heavy long-barreled 40-caliber Stateside Bren, slung low from a dirty olive-drab web belt. Dunno *what* he'd been back home; *here* he was a gunfighter.

High on the right hip, he carried a U.S.M.C. combat knife.

"Those weapons our friends brought with them," he explained, "like shotguns, only with steel darts, about 8-gauge, good for four hundred meters. *That's* what took the door out, Bernie. We only caught a few after they were spent."

Will seen to, Fran offered me the projectile from his arm. Bent, as if it'd ricocheted offa somethin'. Will'd made her fetch his serious weapons—started t'go himself on the way back from their wild-Edna-chase—before he'd let her look at the ragged wound. "Want this for your *other* ear, Bernie?" She touched m'punctured lobe with somethin' that stung a moment, then went cold. "We could mount one on a post and the other on a screwback."

"Thanks for nothin'! I done kept m'self *pinna intacta,* even when I was a seventeenth-century pirate. 'Sides, I got other problems." Which I did: the Telecom was filled with shiftin' kaleidoscopic patterns. "Georgie, is it really you?" I squeaked.

As if they hadn't done enough already, Deejay an' Ooloorie were off doin' more scientific stuff, everything appearin' under control now at *maison* Bear. The lady physicist—the *human* lady physicist'd duly received the equalizer frammis Denny an' Edna'd been too late comin' after. The cavalry'd lost Edna in the construction-mess underground where Win's Interworld Terminal's gonna be someday.

"Gee, Bernie," a sexy but disembodied voice replied, "who else *could* it be?"

I felt real bad about Edna makin' her escape but was too rushed t'give it much thought. Another 'com screen catty-corner to the first was bein' occupied by the assistant Deejay'd put in charge of repairin' my timepiece. *He* was familiar-lookin' as all get-out, yet I couldn't place him. Funny-lookin' gink—big thick glasses, hairless dome shaped like a lightbulb. Kept askin' for details about the fission-powered watch.

Prob'ly coulda figured where I'd seen him before, but the tattered remnants of m'concentration were on this voice claimin' t'be Georgie, an' there were wounded t'take care of, as well: me, in a small way; Will Sanders most seriously; Spin. Even Win was carryin' a red-dyed Kleenex—musta opened up that wine-bottle cut between his fingers again. I saw him lookin' at the blood an' shakin' his head. Prisoners t'think about, too. An' I had an epistemological puzzle on toppa that.

Georgie.

"How do I *know* it's you?"

I hadda ask: the weird-lookin' assistant watched from one screen as, on the other, colors swirled, coalescin' into a sunlit grove of trees at the edge of endless meadows, the breezes fresh as they stirred the knee-high grasses. She stood beneath a spreadin' oak, my beloved, a songbird warblin' in the leafy—

"*I believe you, Georgie. Cut it out!*" The girla my heretofore very *private* dreams grinned conspiratorially as the imaginary camera's viewpoint zoomed toward a face as lovely as any I'd seen in the Confederacy. An' a *whole* lot more familiar.

"It really *is* me, Bernie!" Her big blue eyes shone ecstatically. "I can hardly believe it myself!" I didn't like the way Deejay's bottle-washer ogled her.

"Neither can I, sugar." What was that unaccustomed warmth risin' in m'ears? Musta been Fran's antiseptic. "But we ain't got time for philosophizin' over it now. Tell us where they're keepin' ya."

That stopped all incidental conversation in the room. Every eye turned toward her screen—'cept for Denny's. He was in no condition. I tried not t'gloat.

"It's *horrible*, Bernie. I don't know! A big corrugated metal building. I haven't had any inertial references since we crashed in those mountains. No windows. Somebody used my Emergency Drive, but I can't tell how far or in what direction."

I turned my attention to the shiny-pated assistant physicist. "Forget that watch a minute, Mac. How come, if we can talk t'Georgie on the 'com, you can't just triangulate on her signal an' track her down?"

"Mac?" he blinked confusedly. I realized suddenly he was the only bald guy—besides m'self—I'd seen here. An' so damned familiar! "Captain Gruenblum, this question better suited *you* are than am I to answer. Your vehicle into the lower-probability universe misnomered 'Little Bang' her signal radiates. Thus, from *all* directions propagated it appears, when into this continuum it emerges."

Grammatical or not, he was right. Georgie routes her radio communications through subspace t'beat the light barrier. "Y'got me, Mac—whaddya say your name was?"

"Was—and still is—Associate Professor Doctor Hirnschlag von Ochskahrt."

"Mother," I groaned, "I think I need a rest! Hirnschlag von . . . well, I reckon if the Confederacy's got its own John Wayne—pardon me, Mike Morrison an' Billy Mitchell . . ."

"Bernie." Now she *really* sounded scared. *"Please* tell me what to do!"

"Bernie'll come getcha, baby. Relax. What's happenin' at your end now?"

"That awful Heplar is in my workroom building something."

"Figures." Hadda minute's trouble integratin' the idea of this cute little wisp of a girl havin' a machine-shop down inside her. Reality was gettin' slipperier every time I turned around in this place.

"Cromney's on the control deck," she continued. "I'm being real careful so he won't know . . . but that's Denny Kent, right there!"

Her eyes went to the mess on the floor as Mary-Beth sprayed plastic on what little m'.45'd left of its leg. Win leaned back against the coffee table, played out. Georgie mighta been only the figment of a computer's imagination, but her eyes were wide with real horror. Kent moaned his way back t'semiconsciousness.

"How about it, you low-life son-of-a-test-tube? Where you hidin' my, er . . . ship?" I stepped forward, intendin' t'put a foot where his knee usta be. Already looked like a broken porcelain crock fulla strawberry jam.

The Confederate Ochskahrt took one look, turned green, an' vanished from the screen.

"Bernie!" Mary-Beth raised a defensive hand. "He's been hurt badly enough. Broken arm, incompetently set. I don't know what this bandage across his nose is for. I'm afraid to look. And the ugliest bruise on his chest . . ." She reached inside his jacket, extractin' a twenty-third century Perma-Note binder. There was a neat hole halfway through the paper-thin metal plates which served as erasable pages; buried about page 55, a 230-grain .45-caliber bullet, its conical nose blunted by impact. She shook her head. "I wish Clarissa were awake. *When* is that ambulance coming?"

Kent groaned again an' stirred.

I looked down at him in contempt, thinkin, oddly enough, about Cuthbert. "The one good thing you can say about scum—it keeps *worse* things from risin' to the top." I toed the notebook where Mary-Beth'd laid it on the carpet. "Don't press your luck, Kent! Tell me where m'Georgie is, right now, or I'll center my *next* shot better!"

"Please don't . . . hurt!" He gasped. "Wasn't *my* fault . . . Edna made me . . . *please* don't, please!"

A cheerful thought occurred t'me: mebbe he had a coupla broken ribs. "I ain't gonna hurtya, creep. I jus' think we oughta fix your *other* knee so's you'll match! Win, y'wanna hold him so I don't muff the shot this time?"

"Later." The detective sighed tiredly. He set the broken 'com pad halves on the coffee table behind him. They'd likely saved his life. He leaned over t'make sure little Spin was comfortable on a couch-cushion where the other aliens continued t'commiserate.

"Ask me!" Will demanded. "I want a piece of this!"

Fran grinned savagely.

"Really!" Mary-Beth stood straddlin' Kent, put her hands on her hips, an' somehow looked the bunch of us straight in the eye at the same time. "I *resent* being forced to defend this . . . this *person;* you all know perfectly well you haven't any real intention of—"

"Anything!" Kent bleated. "Just don't . . . please!"

Will clumped over, took his senior spouse gently by the hand; put a finger to his lips. "Yes, dear, but what good is a bluff if you're going to spoil it before it pays off? Okay, Denny, nobody's going to hurt you. Where are you hiding

Bernie's ship? What have you people been up to all this time?"

Kent moaned painfully. "I was never really cut out for...I'll tell...drink, may I?" I hustled him a glass of water, not wantin' t'cut what I hoped was his dyin' confession short. "I'm glad—at least for me—it's over. At last I'm free of *her!*"

He weren't exactly the articulate type, our Denny. But then, he never had been. Cooperatin' hard as he could, it took all of us a couple hours altogether just t'get a story outa him you coulda told in fifteen minutes. Don't think he managed t'string together a single whole coherent sentence the entire time.

Breedin' will tell.

"It's immaterial to me *how* long the boy goes on malingering." Ab Cromney scowled. "It was largely his incompetence which brought us to this lamentable condition. Now he'll pay for it by sleeping on the floor of the lounge with young Heplar!"

The leader of the would-be hijackers paced back an' forth, furious. Sourin' blood an' vomit-gas—not to mention a paira stiffs he couldn't get rid of—had made the passenger deck below mostly unusable by now. Too much for *Georgie*'s systems to absorb, 'least right away.

Edna didn't answer. She coulda pointed out that Denny'd taken a slug which rightfully belonged t'Cromney; that Denny's bein' fortuitously in the way when the bulkheads'd slammed shut—an' receivin' thereby a busted wing—had given them access to the weldin' equipment which'd eventually yielded control of the ship.

Credit where credit was due wasn't little Edna's department.

"Naturally, my dear, *you* may share the pilot's sleeping compartment with me, if you...well, it was merely a thought."

She put away her manicure scissors an' smiled a smile that woulda shriveled the nads offa the Marquis de Sade.

"I'm going below to see if there's *something* we can make another weapon out of."

She glanced significantly at the bandages on Cromney's shredded hand as if t'say that Denny hadn't any monopoly on incompetence. "Watch him—I think that arm's beginning to infect, and we may still need him. Too bad a liberal arts degree doesn't include first aid."

Cromney nodded absent agreement. They needed Denny Kent for exactly the same reason Arab women got t'walk four paces *aheada* their husbands in wartime—mine fields.

"I'll have young Helpar look after him in his copious free time. You're absolutely certain that the drugs—"

"Will burn him out *completely* if we use them any more!" She had to exert a conscious effort not to scream at the old fool. "I'm going below."

Without a further glance at the partially-conscious Kent, Cromney wandered into the control room where Rand Heplar fiddled ineffectually with the panels, as he'd been doing for some hours.

"Any success, my boy?"

Heplar turned toward his new-found leader, wondering somewhere deep inside if he hadn't made a mistake, loyalties-wise. "Without the field-density equalizer, there is nothing I *can* do. So many fail-safe circuits..." His heavy eyebrows knitted together an' merged into his hairline. "Why I'd have to dismantle the entire ship to reroute around half of them. Bad engineering, sir, typical. Another fundamental failure of technology. You were right."

Well, that felt a little better, both of them thought.

To Cromney, the bridge was an indecipherable montage of dials an' gauges. "Perhaps if you were to tell me what *does* work?"

"There's the AutoDestruct," Heplar said, incapable of the irony those words mighta conveyed comin' from somebody else. "Various viewscreens and proximity alarms. And the Emergency Escape Drive. I—"

"Well, why can't we use *that?*"

"Because it really *is* for last-ditch emergencies. One brief burst—only a microsecond or so, not long enough for field-integration to become a problem. Spatiotemporal displacement in a totally random direction. And you can only use it once."

There was a momentary silence. Belatedly, Heplar snapped the safety-covers back over a dozen arming switches. "I don't know what to do! I don't even know where we are!"

He explained t'Cromney the anomalies involvin' *Georgie*'s digital calendar an' the deserted wilderness which now surrounded them, adding that the astronomical evidence—computer-observed positions of the stars an' planets—agreed that the ship was right about what time it was.

"At least," Cromney observed in a manner he mighta termed "philosophically," "we're rid of Gruenblum and those disgusting little—"

"Don't count on it, sir. You don't know how he feels about this collection of nuts and bolts we're sitting in. A real machine-fetishist, if there ever—sonofabitch!"

"What is it?" asked Cromney.

"Look at this screen! Here, I'll step up the magnification!"

Outside, high above, a silvery thrummin' object hovered in the fog an' rain. It banked steeply; the pair on the control deck below could make out a fur-covered rider, wearin' a ten-gallon hat an' gunbelt.

"Where in God's name *are* we?" Heplar stifled a whimper—an' the secret wish that his Captain were here t'tell him what t'do.

"What're you caterwauling about now, Rand?" Edna stood in the bulkhead doorframe, a rapidly-modified laser-welder clutched in her long-nailed fingers. The edges of her shoes were stained an ugly brownish-red.

"It would appear we have company," Cromney answered for the stunned copilot, trying to sound unalarmed. "Take a look at this screen right—"

"Uh-oh!" interrupted Heplar, borderin' on hysteria. "The ground, too! We're surrounded!" Hands unsteady, he played nervously with the switch-cover on the Emergency Escape

Drive. He pointed to a dial: "The magnetometers say they're heavily armed! What should I do?"

Edna sneered. "Doesn't this bucket have any firepower of its own?" She held her welding torch more closely, stole a glance back at Denny lying half-conscious by the upstairs airlock door.

What a shame, she thought, that men were such unreliable tools. Heplar seemed utterly beyond the reach of her usually-dependable sexual allure. This made him uncontrollable, and it frightened her a little.

Perhaps he was a eunuch.

Cromney, of course, possessed no such disability, nor immunity, but he was a feeble old man. Worse, he actually seemed to have ideas of his own.

She'd just have to hold on to poor Denny a while longer. She sighed, remembering with what served her for sentiment how he'd originally been a dominating figure, accustomed to liking it rough, even reputed to have seriously injured a fragile coed or two—and covered it up afterward with plenty of his family's money. Edna liked it *rougher*—he'd been so appealingly perplexed! Well, he wasn't much, but he was all she had to work with.

There was a muted *clink* as Heplar flipped the switch-cover back. "We have force-fields and meteor-defenses"— he answered a question Edna had forgotten asking—"but I'm afraid to use them on the ground, because—*sweet Jesus, those are gorillas out there, and they've got guns!*"

Perhaps it was a lifetime of unconscious slave-holder's guilt which filled Heplar with mindless terror at the thought of simians without electronic controls—and armed. The flying-machine made another pass, and then a grim-faced Bernie Gruenblum rose outa the fog like Hamlet's daddy, right in fronta the main video pickups.

"That's all!" Heplar screamed three octaves above his normal voice. "I'm going to—"

"*No, Rand!*" Edna shouted.

"*Heplar, no!*"

BRRRAAAAMMM-SSSLLLAAAMMM! roared *Georgie,*

an' when Heplar, Janof, Cromney, an' the already badly-battered Denny Kent returned to consciousness, the strange wild mountains'd been replaced by an even stranger prairie, rollin' from horizon to horizon.

They picked themselves up. They dusted themselves off. Only one casualty this time: Denny had a broken nose.

Some small amount of time'd passed while Cromney's crew was enjoyin' a well-deserved oblivion. Outside, a nasty crowd was gatherin'—half a hundred chimpanzees, gorillas, orangutans, an' humans, dressed in a wildly-colored variety of dungarees, armed not only with pistols but with pitchforks, rakes, an' hoes, an' buzzin' like a swarma angry bumblebees.

Incongruously, the open field *Georgie*'d landed in was crowded, fence-to-fence, with thousands, mebbe tens of thousands, of antique Early American hardwood rockin' chairs.

Rockin' chairs?

CLONG! A chimp thumped *Georgie* with an oddly-shaped cultivator. Through the outside pickups, mention could be heard of lynchin'. An' not in a nice way.

Edna looked down at her semiconscious partner.

"Denny," she said, starin' through the airlock bull's-eye, "Somehow I don't think we're in Kansas anymore."

A large white bulbous hovercraft with red markin's'd pulled up on Win Bear's rubber-covered driveway. Its several an' divers doors were open, empty spaces gapin' on the racks inside where the driver'd grabbed the tools of his trade.

Inside the house, an orangutan in medical greens, the circled cross on his shoulder matchin' the enameled ones on his car, had spread instruments an' supplies all over the livin'-room carpet.

He scratched his auburn head. "Some pardy youse guys're t'rowin'. All dis blood an' gore, an' not one funny hat, noise-maker, or balloon! Well, it's a Free System, iddn't it?"

The detective wasn't amused. "Cut the standup routine, will you, Chiang, and get on with the malpractice. I'm in the middle of a case, and I've got suspects on the loose." Weary, he shook his head an' settled heavily on a sofa while the orang looked t'Denny Kent.

"Well, Winnie, I'da been here sooner," the pumpkin-colored simian said, "iffen I hadn't hadda stop at the corner of Spencer an' Confederation—some kinda shoot-em-up inna Unnerground. But dem guys from Acme Ambulance beat me to it."

So Edna'd carved another notch on her pistol-grip. Probably somebody careless enough to've gotten in her line of escape. Despite his diction, the orangutan seemed preternaturally skillful, his big clumsy-lookin' fingers flyin' as they tucked an' patched an' stitched.

It was decided not t'move the would-be hijacker, hospitals bein' few an' far between in the Confederacy, owin' to the advanced state of technology that allowed folks t'get well at home. By mornin', Kent would be removed t'gaol. Probably the same cell I'd had.

Win heard the verdict an' waved a tired hand in assent.

Will an' I got checked out, too. The medico hadn't the faintest idea what t'do for Spin, but the little guy, backed up by his buddies, insisted he was feelin' better already. I dunno—when I was a kid in Pecos, I'd had a big pet turtle'd gotten squished that way. Never seemed quite the same after.

Tool kits an' medicine bags were folded up. "Well, I'll ender my bill inna network, Winnie," the orang Healer said. "I oughda pay you—imagine me, Chiang Mung Schwartlosz, practicin' in Clarissa MacDougall Olson's house! Dey'll never believe me back—"

"Fine," Win said. "Come see us socially when she's out of electrosleep, will you, Chiang? We've got a bad—"

Suddenly, the detective sank to his knees, collapsing on his face at the paramedic's feet. He rolled onto his back without a sound, revealing a spreading bloodstain underneath his cloak from neckline to navel.

The Healer knelt beside his friend—*my* friend—everybody's friend, stethoscope on the investigator's crimson-soaked chest. He looked up at us.

"He's dead!"

16

A Stool-Pigeon
in a Chair Tree

"HE WAS A DECENT SORT, ALL THINGS CONSID-
ered." I set m'glass on the coffee table, scratchin' th Band-
Aid on m'ear. Fran looked up from the rummy game she
was losin' to the Freenies on the floor over near the big
Com screen.

She sighed, shakin' her head reflectively. "And damned
good at what he did."

"Well, *I* sure won't miss him!" Sanders sat by the front
window, made t'pass me a reefer he was sharin' with Mary-
Beth. "It gave me a headache, just listening—"

"He always affected me the same way!" Win Bear turned
over where he lay on the other couch, propped himself on
an elbow, an' laughed, wincing at the pain in his chest.
"He's a damned good Healer, our Chiang Mung Schwarzlosz, but he should have his adenoids looked at. Say, don't
bogart that joint, Bernie."

Sanders watched Win grab a toke an' chuckled. "I'll bet
you used to arrest people for that."

The detective exhaled violently. "I *beg* your pardon, *I*
was a *homicide* dick! The narc squad's for those who can't
make the grade as *real* policemen!" He took another drag,
held it out for Howell. The coyote's yellow eyes went big,
a ripple of relaxation spread through his fur.

"Now *that's* real coffee!" said Nahuatl.

"Back where I come from," I observed, "I'd guess it was
growin' up in the Bronx made Chiang talk like that. Only
I checked it out on the 'com, an'—there *ain't* no Bronx in
the Confederacy! Whaddya thinka that?"

Bear grinned, cannabis smoke slowly seepin' between his teeth, visibly restrainin' himself from a potentially painful chuckle.

Finally, he exhaled. "There isn't any New York City—to this country's everlasting credit—probably because there isn't any Chase Manhattan—!"

He started coughin', tears of agony wellin' in his eyes. He reached to the table beside him, got himself a cigar, an' lit up. The attack subsided.

"That's better. Got a little too much THC in my nicotine system—hard to teach old lungs new tricks. Now what were we talking about?"

"Geography," I answered, stokin' up a stogie of my own. "Way I heard it, Al Hamilton got into the bankin' racket well *before* the Whiskey Rebellion—with Aaron Burr, of all people."

"True," Sanders offered, "but Hamilton wasn't shot by *Burr* here in the Confederacy. It was some anonymous Polish nobleman he'd offended. Some people are born to be hanged—Hamilton's karma slated him for an extra bellybutton, no matter *what* else happened."

"And Chase Manhattan," added Mary-Beth, "along with most of the other crooked financial interests feeding the worms in your 'Big Apple'—did you know that Hamilton actually bankrolled the country with a bad check; he *invented* the National Debt and profited off it for years afterward—they didn't survive here into what you call the twentieth century."

"Couldn't stand the pressure of real *laissez-faire*," her husband agreed. "No government to eliminate the competition for them. Anyway, Philadelphia remained the biggest city on the continent for a long while, then Boston. Now it's a dead heat between Chicago and L.A., with Mexico City coming up fast on the outside—unless you want to count Ceres Central."

"But not adenoids," Mary-Beth said incongruously.

Sanders stared at his wife, then at the Pocatello Puce smoldering in his hand. *"What?"*

"Chiang uses a wrist-talker, like any other simian. That

accent of his is either latent in his wrist-movements or programed into the machine. I'm not certain whether orangutans even *have* adenoids."

"Sure they do," Fran interjected. "Every chance they get.
Breaded and deep-fried—delicious!"

That did it. Even Win broke out with the marijuana
giggles, grimacing every time he drew a ragged breath.
Though he did seem in a little less pain every time I looked
at him. Confederate medicine is somethin' special.

He'd taken a flechette, just like Will an' me, slowed
down by the front door, an' in his case, by a Telecom pad,
now deceased. Sanders an' yours truly'd gotten off easy:
the steel splinter with Win's name on it'd clipped a medium-
sized artery. He hadn't realized quite how bad it was, an',
kinda stupidly, he'd been unwillin' t'postpone gettin' after
the baddies.

Fella wasn't born—the stoic brought him.

Accordin'ly, he hadn't mentioned bein' nicked, an'
pret'near bled t'death under his cape before he—or anybody
else—had noticed.

However, between a vitaminized, catalyzed, an' sanfor-
ized artificial transfusion fluid Chiang'd whipped up on the
spot t'match the detective's tissues an' standard Confederate
treatment for shock, Win was all right now, an' gettin' all
righter by the minute. A dabba Eastman 910 in the proper
place, an' his heart'd started beatin' again when we'd plugged
him into the wall.

He'd be up an' around, his normal flatfooted old self,
before his shirt was clean. An' it was in the washin'. That's
about all we were waitin' for now.

Chiang Mung Schwarzlosz, H.D., hadn't been the only
visitor 626 Genêt Place'd had that afternoon. While Officer
Bear'd been gettin' repaired, somethin' called the Personal
Rights Protection Group'd put in an appearance, at the sum-
mons of Ms. Wizard an' her trained sardine—both physicists were gleefully monopolizing Georgie's attention for
the nonce, never havin' *invented* a sapient bein' before.

PRPG, in the Confederate absence of any real authorities,
took care of situations like this one'd turned into *before*

they reached the adjudicative stage. They collected physical evidence, recorded affidavits, protected victims, witnesses, an' the accused alike.

Sort of an ACLU with guns.

They, an' a handful of similar competin' institutions, some out for profit, some fulla socially-conscious would-be pillars of the community, comprised the civilian counterpart to Will Sanders' militia organization. Fact, he'd argued for callin' the Greater Laporte Civil Liberties Association, while Howell'd voted for somethin' callin' itself the Legion of Discordian Deliberation. But votin' don't seem t'count for much in the Confederacy, an' Deejay'd already placed her own call.

PRPG got the franchise.

Thus, under semiofficial supervision, the questionin' continued. Howell's chimpanzee prisoner wasn't terribly informative. He an' his two permanently horizontal *compadres* in the front hall were part-time shooters for a "Bonzo's Security Patrol" of Rawlins (a town so small that, even back in the States, it's only there on Wednesdays), a company ordinarily dedicated to protectin' farm buildings an' fence-lines. How they'd got t'thinkin' *we* were the malefactors, we an' the PRPG endeavored t'find out as Denny Kent continued his saucer-saga.

In our last thrillin' episode, before the untimely but temporary demise of Edward William Bear, boy detective, Cromney an' his crew landed smack in the middle of a high-plains furniture farm, reducin' nearly half an acre of cultured hardwood rockin' chairs t'cultured hardwood toothpicks.

I never had much stomach for the overrated sanctity of American family agriculture. Seemed t'me they always wanted it both ways: free enterprise, but with the gravy guaranteed by Uncle Sam. The Confederacy was a different proposition. In a civilization where nobody figured he had a deity-delivered *right* to a profit—just a right t'try an' make one unmolested—an' there wasn't any Big Brother t'snivel to, but where genetic editin'd been an accomplished fact for generations, why *not* pluck your livin'-room suites directly off the vine, eliminatin' middle-men like carpenters, sawmills, lumberjacks, an' trees?

A close encounter of the third kind hadn't impressed the folks at the furniture coop one little bit. They were pretty sore with the Professors who'd swiped my time-buggy until Cromney'd shown them the mutilated remains in the passenger lounge, generously assignin' the credit t'me an' Wynken, Blynken, an' Nod.

By now, Rand Heplar knew even less about where an' when Georgie'd landed than he had up in the mountains; the chrono still insisted it was 1993, an' the consensus of various stunned an' unreliable navigation instruments was that they were somewhere in southern Wyoming.

That, or in the middle of the IndianOcean. Depended how y'read the dials.

But, like all really good con-men, Cromney intended t'let the marks tell *him* what was really goin' on.

"Cross-time!" exclaimed Birdflower, the gigantic gorilloid supervisor of the agricultural cooperative. "I saw it on the Telecom! You people are from another probability continuum, aren't you?"

"Why, you're quite correct," slithered Cromney, not havin' the faintest idea *what* Birdflower was talkin' about. "We were being pursued—escaping from—"

"Hamiltonians!" the supervisor supplied, namin' the worst villians he could think of. "The 'com said there are whole *universes* controlled by those dirty—of course here they're only a tiny harmless minority, thank Albert!"

Birdflower an' his wife, Tree, had been the first from the farm admitted into the saucer. Shown what was left of Mssrs. Merwin an' Hulbert, the anthropoid had gulped audibly an' rolled his eyes, barely stayin' vertical. They'd had t'take Tree back to the farmhouse t'lie down.

Hamiltonians, Birdflower explained to the hijackers, were terrible persons who actually believed there were circumstances under which some individuals had the right to tell other individuals what to do. Only a few years ago, scientists had discovered the Probability Broach, an' through it, another Earth where such perverted ideas held sway. Some of these creatures had attempted to invade the Confederacy, aided by the few native Hamiltonians who'd survived two centuries of North American anarchism.

Eventually, of course, all that'd been taken care of, an' the scientists were presumably a little more careful about who they let into the Confederacy.

But still there were a few—a very few in every generation—who continued to preach authoritarianism. It's a Free System, Birdflower observed with a sigh, an' there wasn't any moral, ethical, or legal way to stop them. But it did seem a shame.

An' kinda crazy, too.

Cromney's ears perked up at the mention of potential local allies in what was beginning to appear t'be a sea of licentiousness. He'd have to learn more, a great deal more, before he made his move, but move he would, an' especially if he were stuck here, this civilization would feel the full weight of his mighty thumb.

"Tell me more, my dear Birdflower. I must confess, the notion of alternate history is new to me. Our vessel here is merely an ordinary interstellar spaceship, drastically blown off course during the struggle to escape the ghastly tyranny you speak of so eloquently."

"Well, I'm no expert on physics or history," Birdflower said modestly. "I'm a farmer and geneticist. But—here, I have to go back to the house to see how Tree's coming along. Why don't you consult the 'com? I'm sure you can find out what you need to know that way."

Leaving Rand an' Edna in charge of the ship—Denny was still unconscious owing to his newly-earned broken nose—Cromney followed the gorilloid through the fields of rocking chairs, end-tables, bookcases, an' bar-stools—a different variety than the kind Dan'l Boone stepped in—to a streamlined modernistic buildin' servin' as headquarters for the coop.

"Here's a 'com pad, Mr. Cromney. I'll punch in a display of instructions—gosh, that brings back memories; I haven't seen that graphic since I was a little kid—and the machine

itself will tell you how to use it. Now I have to go look
after my wife."

Cromney settled into a comfortable chair in the pecu-
liarly-decorated farmhouse living-room. It wasn't so much
the technology of the Telecom which startled him as the
cultural implications: this device, apparently, was a house-
hold fixture *everywhere*, just like plumbin' an' electricity,
an' taken as casually for granted in the same way.

This was a fabulously wealthy civilization—an' scan-
dalously loose, politically. Cromney licked his lips in greedy
anticipation an' plunged onward.

General information sources on the list included the *Encyclopedia of North America*, which occupied an entire
channel, TerraNovaCom's 485-A. Very well, he employed
the appropriate buttons t'summon it. Scannin' a brief article
on travel between worlds of alternate probability, he found
the concept'd been in circulation here for decades before its
reality'd been proven accidentally.

Odd, why hadn't his own culture thought of such a thing?
Or an information system like the Telecom, for that matter?
Perhaps the Academy exercised a sterner authority than even
he had realized. He found himself approving, grudgin'ly.

Cross-time entries led him naturally t'history, where he
discovered the critical importance of the Whiskey Rebellion
in the Confederacy's past. He shuddered at the idea of a
government so thoroughly chastised it was afraid t'collect
taxes, of a State growin' progressively smaller over a couple
centuries until recently it'd dwindled an' vanished like an
icecube meltin' in a drink. Congress had met only twice in
fifty years, an' there were observers who opined as how it
might not ever feel the need t'meet again.

Hideous!

In an astoundin' display of scholarly dispassion, the Encyclopedia's entry on Hamiltonianism'd been commissioned
from one Norrit Gregamer, accordin' to an editor's footnote,
the professor of Alternative Moral Philosophy at the University of Chicago, Ltd., extension in Cheyenne. Cromney
took this chance proximity as a sort of omen an' made a

note t'contact Gregamer as he chased down the Encyclopedia's cross-references refutin' the Hamiltonian professor's arguments.

In the meantime, as his understandin' of this culture filled out in his mind, he firmed up the story he intended tellin' Birdflower an' anybody else he hadda get things from. He *must* regain that infernal piece of equipment Gruenblum'd stolen, an' he had little faith that Heplar's attempts t'reproduce it would bear any kinda fruit.

"You see," he explained charmin'ly to the farmer, who'd returned after seein' to his wife, "I believe that the best defense is a good offense. Gruenblum may be stranded here as we are, but his fanatical devotion to the Overlords of our homeworld will move him to pursue us, if for nothing other than revenge. He and those demonic alien monsters of his. He is a violently and dangerously unpredictable man."

Birdflower cluck-clucked sympathetically. Refugees were tricklin' into the Confederacy at an increasin' rate these days, exactly as they'd done a century ago before most of the nations of *this* world'd accepted Gallatinist viewpoints an' become pleasanter places t'live.

"Well, you were surely lucky, Mr. Cromney, to get rid of him before he murdered *all* of you. Those poor . . . but now you want to *find* him again?"

"Certainly!" Cromney replied. The livin'-room they occupied was decorated in a curious mixture of Victorian Gothic an' vintage Haight-Ashbury. Incense an' bead-curtains an' psychedelic-colored paintin' competed with old-fashioned oriental carpets, gargoyly overstuffed furniture, an' hand-stitched samplers bearin' enigmatic homilies: "A Thief Is Shot In The Night—Whose Hand Is On The Bow?"

Cromney shook his head in weary perplexity. "Is that a Zen paradox you've got up there over the mantlepiece?"

Birdflower blinked. "Why no, it's an old Shoshone saying. But why *look* for this Gruenblum? Surely his manners will get him into trouble wherever he goes, and *that"*— he patted the sizable autopistol he wore in a shoulder holster attached to his bib overalls—"will be the end of him." He glanced significantly at the cross-stitched maxim Cromney'd asked about.

The professor snorted in annoyance. "What do you mean? Whose hand *is* on the bow? Presumably, that of the house-holder—the victim of the thief in the night."

It was Birdflower's turn t'look puzzled. "Not in anything but a purely physical sense, and we're talking about *moral* concepts here. The answer, which any school-kid could tell you, is 'The Thief's—those who practice aggression as a way of life have merely chosen for themselves a compli-catedly indirect method of committing suicide. Which is why you've no need to bother with this Gruenblum nake—er, pardon me, I mean *person.*" Under the dark pigment of his unfurred face, Birdflower appeared to blush.

Cromney gulped, more at an intuition of his own than anything Birdflower had told him. He realized that, so far, he hadn't seen a single *un*armed Confederate. Even gentle Tree'd carried some kinda pistol at her waist. He'd uncon-sciously assumed it had somethin' t'do with the rustic farm-life they were practicin' out here. Now he wasn't so sure.

"Nevertheless," he said, recovering his aplomb for Bird-flower's benefit, "I feel responsible for unleashing this vil-lainous scoundrel upon your fair Confederacy, and I intend to do something about it. To begin with, if you'll assist me, I have a list of parts my associates require to repair our ship. And there's a long-distance call I'd like to place to the University of Chicago in Cheyenne."

The gorilloid nodded good-naturedly an' took up the Com pad.

The rest'd been pretty straightforward. Cromney'd sent Denny down t'Griswold's as soon as the poor schmuck could totter around. The St. Charles-Auraria security outfit'd tracked me down right smartly, but they never woulda let even Cromney know where I was without a final payment. That'd been the business of the newsies—once my name an' location'd been plastered all over six thousand channels, Cromney'd made his move.

Or more correctly—an' characteristically—gotten somebody else t'make his move for him.

Denny an' Edna's back-ups'd been recruited from the company—Bonzo's—that took care of the minimal security considerations Birdflower's chair-farm required. The rest was history, no gorier or smokier than any I'd ever seen, but upsettin' t'folks usta livin' amidst domestic tranquility.

I looked down at Denny as they strapped him on the stretcher, feelin' uncharacteristically charitable. "Well, kid, I dunno—I reckon there's folks done worse for love. That Edna's quite a looker, for all she's a cold-blooded—"

"Love?" Denny gasped, the sleepy-drugs startin' in on him an' his eyes losin' focus. "There *is* no love! There is rut. There is insanity. There are a dozen different kinds of fear. There is also comfortable sleepwalking boredom. And the greatest joke of all is that this last—boredom—is the *best* we can expect from life. Love is a fraud, a hoax, the name we give to hormones and sentiment—a sentiment we generate within ourselves to assuage the shame we feel for what the hormones do to us."

An' without so much as a fare-thee-well, he shut his eyes an' commenced t'snorin' peaceably. He mighta been a jerk, but he hadda grammatical—if cynical—subconscious.

The rights-protectors carted him upstairs.

"I guess that's it, then," Win said, risin' from the sofa. He stretched his arms an' yawned, apparently fully recovered. "Time to make *our* move! Who's going to stay and keep an eye on Kent?"

PRPG'd taken the chimp from Bonzo's away with the bodies. Kent'd be lyin' around upstairs, sedated to the gills an' wired into the 'com which monitored his healin'.

"Not me!" The chorus consisted of Will Sanders, Mary-Beth, Fran, Nahuatl, Trip, Stumble, an' Fall—the one with the cracked shell. I kept a discreet silence, havin' learned early an' the hard way never t'volunteer.

"Now look, you guys," Win pleaded, "this is ridiculous! *Somebody's* got to stay, if only to—"

"How about me?" said the Telecom abruptly. A blond an' blue-eyed vision of heaven gazed down upon us from the wall. "There isn't very much else I *can* do, is there, Bernie?"

"More's the pity, baby, more's the pity."

The detective considered it for a moment. "Well, I suppose you can make sure that Kent stays out of his skull—I assume you've got access to the house circuitry." Georgie nodded, her pale locks bobbin' appealin'ly. "What if we have another bunch of intruders?"

Her image on the screen vanished suddenly, replaced by that of a grizzled chimpanzee in some kinda formal-cut jacket an' a baseball cap.

"Professional Protectives, here, what can I—oh, it's you, Win. What's up?"

"I found the number in your quick-reference memories, Mr. Bear," a female voice whispered outa one corner of the screen. "Will this be satisfactory?"

Bear addressed the chimp. "I'm going to be out of town for a little while, Cap, and Clarissa's in cold storage. Keep a *real* close watch on the house, will you?"

Win's friend lifted his hat by its bill an' scratched his graying head, then stepped out from behind the counter as the camera followed him. He was wearin' a black tail-coat exactly like Groucho Marx's, a black-and-white checkered sarong, an' a heavy leather gunbelt. No shoes.

"Sure thing—you're the customer. What's going on over there, Win? Some kinda dust-up, the way I hear. Got yourself into trouble again when the wife's not around t'look after you?"

Bear grinned. "I'll tell you all about it later. Just don't let anybody in or out, okay? PRPG's left a customer with me, and there could be some shooting."

The image on the screen nodded, glancing around the room. "Looks like there has been already. I'll attend to it personally." He winked out.

"Captain Forsythe," Win explained to the rest of us. "Of Professional Protectives. Sure wish I'd had them on alert earlier. Forsythe's a genuine wizard with an automatic pistol."

Sanders nodded agreement. "Only person I ever met who

shoots straighter and faster than little Frannie Oakley over there."

Little Frannie Oakley said not a word, but placed her gin-rummy hand carefully face-down on the carpet, rose gracefully, walked over to Sanders on the couch, and kicked him in the shin, hard. Then she returned to her card game with the Freenies.

Sanders rubbed his leg.

"Well, now that *that's* taken care of," observed Win, suppressin' the same laughter I was havin' trouble stiflin', "let's go!"

"That's more like it!" exclaimed Nahuatl. "Yoicks and away!"

17

Seven of Swords

IT'S NEVER QUITE AS EASY AS THAT.

The assumption was that Georgie'd been moved t'one of the furniture farm's outbuildin's in a powered-down condition. She remembered somethin' about a huge wide-bedded hovertruck, an' there are certain portions of her circuitry which can *never* be shut off.

But her memories were spotty. How much d'*you* remember about that movie you fell asleep in the middle of?

All that aside, we were dealin' with private property here, contemplatin' invadin' somebody's ethical castle, an institution so sacrosanct in the Confederacy that not even fools walked in uninvited, let alone angels. Give you a good idea of the caliber of the boys from Bonzo's.

Even if customs an' legalities'd been taken care of, there were still logistics, strategy, an' tactics: who oughta do what an' with which an' t'whom—put me in minda my favorite limerick, the one about the fairy who came from Khartoum.

Will an' Fran Sanders'd disappeared across the street t'gather ordnance, while Win an' Mary-Beth continued t'hash out the ethical side of this operation. It was doubly complicated on accounta this Birdflower geek seemed a decent enough sodbuster, if Donny Kent was t'be believed—a *large* assumption, I figgered—but apparently he still thought that Cromney was on the up-and-up.

Howell conferred with the professional ethicist an' his fellow gumshoe, leavin' me an' the Freenies feelin' like a whole shelfful of fifth wheels, twiddlin' our thumbs.

The Freenies faked it.

Havin' learned a lesson the hard way, I pulled the magazine an' chamber-round outa my .45, punched in the recoil-plunger under the muzzle, an' rotated the barrel-bushin' until both plunger an' spring popped free. Then I racked the slide back halfway, wiggled out the slide-stop, an' shucked slide, barrel, an' associated parts off the frame.

Meanwhile, I was gettin' reacquainted with m'best girlfriend, who was showin' some facets I hadn't seen before.

"What's it like, sweetheart, gettin' sapient alluva sudden? Us humans do it kinda graduallike, an' the vast majority, in my opinion, never make it at all!"

I turned the bushin' the other way, separated it an' the barrel from the slide.

"Gosh, Bernie, it seems as though I can remember what things were like before. It's possible I was on the verge for a long, long time, and the additional capacity of Deejay's computers is all that I needed. What I remember, mostly, is a kind of floating frustration—like a dream where you're trying to speak to someone and you can't quite get the words out."

Color, Charm, an' Spin were playin' three-handed gin now, the most vicious, ruthless, cutthroat game this side of Crazy Eights or blood-an'-guts Monopoly. I pushed the firin' pin inward with a ballpoint, slid its retainer-plate downward, an' pulled out pin, spring, an' extractor.

Color ginned out on the first go-round, amidst high-frequency catcalls from his fellow Yamaguchii. The cards got collected an' shuffled again.

"I think I understand. What I don't dig, though, is how you can handle bein' a ninety-foot machine an' a petite little blonde at the same time—unless the display's just for communicatin' with organic folks—that tree you're leanin' against, those flowers: do they seem real t'you?"

She shrugged. "How real do other people feel to you when you're talking to them on the telephone? It's something you never ask yourself about. What's your favorite book?"

My turn t'shrug as I unscrewed the rubber grips from the Colt with a fine blade on my pocket lighter. "You oughta know—*Peter Pan*, mebbe, or *The Story of O*. What's the point?"

The image on the screen actually blushed. "By all means, let's talk about *Peter Pan*. Tell me, who's more real to you as a person in your mind, little Wendy or somebody like Herbert Hoover?"

I thought about it, but not for very long. "No question about it: *Wendy*." I looked around for a pencil or somethin' t'shove a Kleenex through the bore of the pistol. Suddenly, Color took over, usin' a slim green tentacle as a cleanin' rod, while Charm produced an appendage resemblin' a toothbrush an' worked the slide over, bein' extra-careful with the breech-face. I was *never* gonna live down gettin' my pistol rusty.

But they were handy fellas t'have around.

"There, you see, Bernie? An admittedly fictional character is more real to you than an historical one—someone, to judge from my memories, that you've actually met in person."

"Yeah," I answered. "Shook his hand an' everything. An' washed it thoroughly after. I see what you're gettin' at, though. Guess I could think of myself as a skeleton, a bagga organs, or a four-dimensional pink worm with a pentacular cross-section—or as I do: Bernard M-for-Mephistopheles Gruenblum, boy time-traveler. An' you obviously think of yourself as Mary Pickford."

"Olivia Newton-John, please. When are you going to come rescue me? It'll be dark soon, you know."

I screwed the grips back on as Charm handed me the frame, reassembled the slide, slid it on an locked it in place, slapped in a clip an' jacked a round into the chamber, fillin' up the magazine with an extra cartridge.

"Right now — whether the philosophers've got it figgered out or not! C'mon, you guys, you travelin' with me or do I hafta *walk* t'Wyomin'?"

The hastily-repaired front door swung open. Fran said, "You won't have to walk!"

Impellers thrummin', Win's Neova, laden down with detective, flyin' saucer-jockey, an' the Three Graces, followed Will Sanders' Tucker, mostly laden down with good-lookin' women—with a spare militiaman an' coyote thrown in for contrast. As we sped across Laporte toward the Greenway, Georgie took part in the conversation on the divided screen in fronta me.

She was right: at the moment she was sharin' screenspace with Mary-Beth, an' both were equally real t'me.

"Which is just the ethical crowbar we needed, Bernie," the ethicist said. "Your Georgie is now a sapient being, held against her will under duress. More than that—if I understand correctly, Heplar could terminate her sapience simply by throwing a few switches."

A figurative lightbulb went on over m'head. *"That's* what you people were cacklin' about back there! 'Cromney's legal status'! Jog Georgie into sapience, he stops bein' a thief an' becomes a kidnaper!"

Win grunted, keepin' his eyes on the road. "And it means we're justified in a surprise-attack, right?"

Mary-Beth shook her head, spreadin' beautiful curls all over the Telecom. "Let's just say there's an excellent chance the average adjudicator will see it our way."

"If *I* understand aright," Charm offered from the seat beside me, "the chances are even better if there is minimal bloodshed and property damage in the doing of the deed."

"Spoilsport!" Fran retorted via Com.

"Just remember that Birdflower and his people would be on our side if only they knew the full truth," Mary-Beth cautioned. "If the element of surprise weren't necessary for Georgie's sake, we might simply call him. I wish—"

"So do I." Georgie sighed. "There's something in this experience—having Cromney and Heplar and Janof aboard controlling things, I mean—that's a lot like having tapeworms. But Birdflower and Tree and their friends seem like nice people. *Please* be careful!"

Mebbe Georgie *was* my better half.

The country around Cheyenne's amazin'—the Rockies somber an' purple on the left, prehistoric lion-colored prairie stretchin' t'forever on the right, an' every kinda bluff, butte, gully, hogback, an' foothill y'can imagine in between. Piles of rock that look like they were injection-molded in the bowels of a Kline-bottle.

We crossed the ridge that echoes the city's name an' spilled out into the basin at about 300 per. The Greenway'd turned out t'be the Confederate version of an interstate superhighway, a paira round-bottomed grass-lined grooves runnin' side-by-side, some kinda subway buried between 'em I'da never noticed if I hadn't been told. We zipped around the city, headin' east-by-north toward the Lodgepole River. It was comin' on dusk as we flared our skirts an' wheezed to a dusty stop at the fence-line of the furniture-farm.

I could see a field fulla antique cobbler's benches wavin' in the wind.

We piled out t'confer by the barrow-ditch. Howell looked longingly at a weathered fencepost, trotted outa sight down the rutted back-country road a moment, an' came back lookin' more cheerful.

"Will you kindly help me with my pistols, Bernie?"

"Your *what?*" I looked down at his paws an' back t'his yellow eyes reflectin' the day's-end sky. Some kinda evenin' bird'd started up tweetlin', an' there was sage-pollen in the air. The sun was flirtin' with the mountain-tops in a way no hallucinogenic drug or fireworks display coulda ever touched.

"My pistols. Here, I'll show you!" He leaped back into Will Sanders' car an' came back with a canvas bag in his teeth.

Inside was a brace of automatics, *sans* trigger-guards an' triggers, symmetrically engineered—one ejectin' to the left, the other to the right—an' firmly attached to a fetchin' little fiberglass bonnet with a pod of electronics at the nape an' a wire danglin'.

"I getcha!" I said to the coyote. "But what happens when y'run outa ammo?"

He thrust his head into the rig as I held it for him. A strap snaked itself beneath his chin, an' the danglin' wire plugged itself into his collar, but he needed a little help with the protective earpads—important, as the muzzles of the weapons protruded just beyond the corners of his jaw. I snapped the safety-goggles over his eyes, noticin' the cross-hairs.

"I try not to run out. But the pistols are a high-velocity .23 caliber, fifty rounds to the magazine. The whole thing operates off the electronics implanted in my brain."

Reminded me of the story about a neighborhood so tough even the dogs had guns.

The plan—if that's the word for it—was that Howell, bein' smaller, faster, an' sneakier, would scout on ahead through the chiffoniers an' bedroom sets, while we took up the rear, Win an' the Freenies an' me. The Sanderses, as soon as we were through palaverin' here'd circle around an' come in from the north, I could see the big gray corrugated buildin' already an' was gettin' excited.

I parked myself on the fender of Win's Neova an' did some real careful Yoga-breathin' t'kinda settle m'self. Don't do t'go into battle all keyed up. Then I leaned into the car so Georgie could see me.

"Won't be long now, baby. Papa's comin'. Anything y'want me t'bring you? Jujubes, silicone-lube, integrated circuits?"

She smiled, though the strain was visible on her imaginary face. "Just yourself, Bernard M-for-macho Gruenblum, and don't get hurt or anything."

"You got it, kiddo. I—what?"

I backed outa the car abruptly, smackin' the backa my noggin on the coamin'. "What's up, Win?"

"Nothing," the detective answered, hikin' up his black, tooled-leather gunbelt. That big .41 of his'd pull anybody's pants down. He pulled the little hand-made single-shot der-ringer from his pocket, the one I'd noticed in his gun case back home, unscrewed the stubby barrel t'make sure it was plugged up real good with cartridge, an' screwed it tight again.

"I just thought Georgie might like to see what's going on," he said, reachin' past me to the dashboard. He pulled up an' out on the Telecom eye; it followed his hand on a little hair-fine cable, an' he clipped it to the chrome at the top of the windshield. "How's that, Georgie?"

"Fine, Mr. Bear—though a little bit scarier, I must admit. Is that the building I'm in?"

"It would appear to be—and call me Win." He slapped the tiny pistol in his palm. "Don't worry, we'll get you out of there."

I shook my head. "I wouldn't wanna shoot that thing with *your* hand!"

He grinned. "I've only used it once, and to tell the truth, I was a little surprised I survived the experience myself. Let's go!"

We did a brief piece of slapstick gettin' through the three-strand barbed-wire fence an' were on our way, Nahuatl way out in the lead, men an' Freenies followin'. Never saw so goddamned many knick-knack shelves an' bookends in one place in m'life. An' fancy-grained toilet seats.

Stoop labor, obviously.

Bear halted suddenly, one hand to his ear an' a vacant look in his eyes. He nodded, looked at me, an' said, "Howell's on his way across the farm yard. Says it looks pretty deserted. The barn is locked up tight and he can't get in. He'll wait for us under the farmhouse porch."

We mushed on through the dinin'-room section, the kitchen cabinetry, an' about fifty-eleven acres of kiddie furniture, until we reached the edge of the field. I crouched down behind a paira bunkbeds that wasn't quite ripe an' whispered, "What now, O Leatherstockin'?"

Win smiled, tryin' t'resist liftin' the lid of a half-grown toy-box t'see what was inside. "We wait for the Three Musketeers to get into position. How fast can the little guys run?"

I nodded toward Wilbur, Orville, an' Frank Lloyd: "How about it, fellas, can y'keep up with Jim Thorpe, here?"

"When have we ever failed you, O Lord?" Spin—identifiable by the semihealed crack in his carapace—answered sarcastically. Less worshipful they got, the better I liked 'em. Guess I'm just contrary, myself.

"Ah, how soon they forget." I sighed. "Okay, you're on your own—but be careful."

Win put the tiny Com capsule to his ear again, waited.

"Now!" he whispered harshly, makin' a choppin' motion with his hand. I woulda felt better about it if it hadn't been fulla Smith & Wesson an' pointed more or less in my direction.

I drew my Colt an' snicked off the safety.

We ran, crouchin' low, toward the farmhouse. I'd wanted t'go right for the barn but'd allowed myself t'be persuaded that the big guns'd be needed elsewhere. Fran, with her plasma-burner for breakin' an' enterin', was supposed t'get to Georgie while we were securin' everything else.

Open yard was past, an' I was on the whitewashed porch, kickin' in the door an' gettin' myself tangled up in the screenin'.

Howell leaped aheada me an' through the kitchen, outa sight. Win was right behind me. I crossed the kitchen in one giant step, slammed my shoulder-blades against the woodwork 'round the next door, an' levered around, just like in the movies, my pistol lookin' for a target.

A short hallway with a braided Early American rug— wondered what kinda farm they grew those on.

Growlin' comin' from somewhere up ahead.

I could feel Win breathin' on my neck, an' stepped forward, zipped across the hall an' against the wall, front sight tryin' t'be everywhere at once. Along the wall like I was glued to it, an' out into the parlor.

They were gathered around the table: hadda be Birdflower an' Tree. Someone else, facin' away. I aimed at the broad, black, shaggy back.

"*Freeze, you motherjumpers!* Where's my flyin' saucer?"

The figure set its teacup down daintily. "See, I told you they'd show up, didn't I?"

It turned slowly. "Why Bernie, is *that* any way to come calling? And just at suppertime, too!"

Koko Featherstone-Haugh reached down an' scratched

G. Howell Nahuatl between the shoulder-blades. His hind foot rattled on the hardwood floor.

"I appreciate your exasperation, my dear. Some of *my* best friends are human, too."

18

Background Music

"I'M SORRY, BERNIE, GEORGIE ISN'T HERE."

Koko's statement was belied, in that increasin'ly familiar surrealistic way, by the sparklin' image of my gorgeous blonde on Birdflower's livin'-room screen. The gorilla speared herself another hot-dog, slapped it in a bun, squirted mustard along its length. "If you'd been a half-hour later— I tried to call, but only got Georgie here, apparently after you'd left the cars at the fence." Cromney had had Georgie moved right after Edna and Denny left for Win's place. Even if he'd been awake, that self-made loser, Kent, couldn'ta told us anything useful.

Win shook his head. "Six years I've been taking a ribbing about having the only pocket-pager in the Confederacy. By god, I'll carry it with me from now on!"

I turned down a fourth foot-longer. Tree got a hurt look in her eyes, probably the same expression if I'd been declinin' my fourteenth. "Well, I reckon we're back t'square one," I said t'Georgie. "You locked up somewhere an' us havin no more idea—"

"Not *quite* no idea, Captain Gruenblum," Birdflower offered. "At least Tree and I finally know what's going on— got confusing after Cromney Telecommed Norrit Gregamer."

Griswold's turned out to be the same dead end for me (said Koko) that it proved to be for your friend Mr. Bear. By the way, I'm glad to meet you. Uncle Olongo talksabout you all the time.

All right, then, *Win*.

I saw the "coverage" of your arrest when I got back to Laporte, but I figured (a) that you didn't need another helpful friend underfoot, and (b) that, all the same, you *did* need help. Besides, it gave me a great excuse to cut classes.

I tried everything with Griswold's: Uncle Olongo's name and influence, not to mention the fact that he's a major stockholder—he seems to be a stockholder in practically *everything* these days! After Denny Kent skipped out on them, they were willing enough to cooperate, but they couldn't tell me what they didn't know. I even ran down a few of their people, who were changing shifts while he was in the office, in hopes they could remember and describe his car.

Why *thank* you, Georgie. I was sort of proud of that myself.

Anyway, I'm afraid the rest wasn't very inspired. Remembering the two- or-three-hundred kilometer range Bernie mentioned for the Emergency Escape Drive—and I had to look up "kilometer" in the Encyclopedia: it's an obsolete eighteenth-century utopian system of measurement that never caught on—I drew a circle on a map display.

Then, given the Hamiltonian inclination to underhandedness and violence, I keyed my Com to look for strange, unusual, or criminal events within that radius. I wasn't exactly sure what I was looking for—gee, I wasn't even sure when I *had* found it—but it was the one thing I could see that was out of the ordinary at all.

What was it? Nothing much, just a little note in the local news about someone finally renting a giant 100-foot flatbed hovertruck that had been gathering oxidation for a decade. What made it newsworthy is that the thing had been built that long ago and there'd never been much of a practical use for it. Too big for the Greenway, and besides, freight-dirigibles are more effcient. It had changed hands several times in the last few years.

Yes, of *course* I noticed right away that it was just the perfect size for moving an inert flying saucer.

But the story, interesting as it was, wasn't good enough

to get out onto the net. If I hadn't subscribed to everything within that circle on the map, I'd have missed it. I used up all of next month's allowance, but I figured there might be a pretty good reward for a lost time machine. That's not *too* mercenary, is it?

The more I checked, the stranger the story got. The truck turned out to have been rented by, of all people, a college professor of Alternative Moral Philosophy in Cheyenne. Several hours after he rented it, he reported it stolen. Naturally, the truck's owners were ecstatic—they'd finally gotten their investment back from the insurance!

The professor had specified two destinations and drove it himself. The final location, according to the lease he signed, was the University of Chicago extension in downtown Cheyenne. He never made it that far. He was at a truck-stop on a back road wide enough to take the thing, having a cup of chocolatl, when person-or-persons unknown made off with the vehicle, supposedly full of cultured hardwood school desks.

The first stop he'd listed, obviously, was this farm.

Win leaned back in his chair, grinning from ear to ear. "That was some pretty fair detecting, Koko! Look me up when you finish school—or if you want a part-time job before that. I could use an apprentice to do *that* kind of legwork."

"But he sure didn't take any furniture, that Gregamer!" protested Birdflower vehemently. "They loaded Bernie's machine on that big truck—it had a crane for that—and smashed a whole lot more of my rocking chairs. He gave me *this* trash in return!"

The gorilloid contemptuously threw a half-dozen coinlike discs on the table. One side was a blank expanse with a number in the center: 1789; the obverse, a symbol I'd seen before, though not nearly often enough, printed on the backa the number-one best-sellin' literature on the North American Continent I'd been brought up on. Shucks, it was the very same logo the Academy uses.

The Eye-in-the-Pyramid.

Seemed t'upset Win. Made a note t'ask him about it. The gold-platin' was already wearin' off the high spots, exposin' a browny bronze. If writin' a bad check'd get y'plastered all over the Com-net, I wondered about passin' phony coins.

Birdflower shook his head sadly. "Gregamer said they'd be redeemed one day. I sure hope—"

"Don't hope *too* hard," Win interrupted. "That wasn't an economic promise he was making, but a *political* one. Imagine what Georgie could do, used as a weapon. Cromney might wind up with a society to rule, after all!"

Which brought a certain somberness to the occasion.

"I wouldn't cooperate!" insisted the blonde vision on the screen; then more meekly: "At least I'd *try* not to..."

"All right," I said with more determination than I felt. "They *still* gotta get the field-density frammis, an' it's locked up tight. Failin' that, they gotta build another, an' I give Heplar as much chance of doin' that as crankin' Shakespeare plays outa ten million typewriters operated by ten million ... er, uh ... you get my meanin', anyway."

Win got his grin back. "It's pretty obvious what's happened. Georgie's parked in some warehouse nearby, probably still sitting on that flatbed. Hunting Gregamer down won't do us a lot of good; he'll just deny—"

"In any case, it won't be necessary!" a voice said behind me.

"Nobody knocks anymore!" Birdflower complained. "Nobody knocks!"

"Dear me!" the voice said with sarcastic concern. Its owner rapped lightly on the frame of the kitchen door and walked into the parlor.

Norrit Gregamer stood perhaps five feet eight an' looked damn near as simian as Birdflower. But he wasn't. He was a short, squat, swarthy individual, almost more reptilian than human or simian, with black eyes set deeply in dark sockets. He wore mutton-chops down to the jaw-line either side of his broad face, an' perched atop his shaggy head— beard an' hair were dark, as well—one of those caps y'see in photographs of nineteenth-century workingmen.

He glanced at the Telecom, reached behind him for a straight-backed chair, swung it around in front of him, an' set down on it backwards, restin' his hairy forearms on the back rail. His voice was practically a raspy whisper.

"How nice to see all of you together. Birdflower, Tree, I hope you're getting along all right. Professor Cromney sends his greetings. Now let me see: you would be Captain Gruenblum, wouldn't you? And these . . . these must be Color, Charm, and Spin, of whom I heard on the Telecom. Edward William Bear: I believe you're going to regret getting involved in this affair, sir. We Hamiltonians already owe you a certain retribution over the Madison incident. Captain Sanders, ladies, and, if I am not mistaken, Koko Featherstone-Haugh."

"Thanks for callin' the roll, Gregamer," I said. "Reckon y'get a lotta practice doin' that in the classroom."

"No, no, I do not. I'm afraid the most elementary notion of discipline is entirely missing in this benighted society we live in. Naturally, I hope to change that in the not-too-distant future."

Win finally took his hand off his gun butt an' asked, "So what brings you out from under your rock this fine evening, Professor?"

Gregamer bit back a retort but colored slightly under his tan. "To the point, then: we *want* that device you took from Cromney, Gruenblum. We want it *now*."

I shook my head. "Seems like I had a right t'take it— on accounta it was mine t'begin with!"

"Scarcely. It belonged to your Academy. Now it has been expropriated for a higher cause, one which you have no moral right to resist. The device is *ours*, sir, and you will deliver it forthwith!"

I laughed. "An' what'll you do if I don't?"

The Hamiltonian blinked slowly, lookin' a whole lot like a horned toad. " 'Property is theft,' Captain. By withholding it, you're committing an act of violence, of initiated force— which is precisely what this hypocritical culture is supposed to stand against."

There was a small female snort from across the room.

Mary-Beth said, "It's interesting to hear a Hamiltonian distortion of Gallatinist philosophy. Would you mind telling me precisely what act of violence Captain Gruenblum is committing—precisely, now—and against whom?"

Gregamer slowly turned his head until he could see Mary-Beth. From the look on Sanders' face, he'd better watch what he said.

"Exactly what I'd expect from a paid mouthpiece of the established privileged class. There is no such thing as property. All things for all men is the proper order of things in this world, and by depriving your fellow man of the use of *anything*, you're committing an act of moral violence. But enough of this: Gruenblum"—he turned t'me again—"you seem to have some regard for your ship. If you fail to deliver that device to me this instant, I will see that she is blown to microscopic fragments before this night is over!"

"Deprivin' your fellow man—namely me—of the use of her? How unethical. Tellya what, Gregamer..." Inwardly, I gulped as I said it. "...if you can convince Cromney an' the rest, y'got my blessin's t'blow her up."

He sneered. "Cromney will do as he is told, as will the rest of his ilk. The device, Gruenblum, *now!*" He reached a hand across the backa his chair, palm upward.

"Sorry, mate, it's locked up nice an' safe."

"All the same," said Win, "it's an ill wind—*there!*"

The detective had reached out himself and in one swift motion had snapped his handcuffs around Gregamer's wrist. He ratcheted the other bracelet to the chair the Hamiltonian was occupyin'.

"You're under arrest, Norrit Gregamer, for..." He looked at me suddenly, realizin' that he couldn't say kidnappin', not while Cromney still had Georgie an' Heplar could push the buttons that'd execute her.

"How about for willful destruction of crops—and coun terfeiting?" offered Birdflower.

"How about it, Gregamer?" Win asked. "I *knew* there was a reason I never threw my old handcuffs away—they're probably the only pair in all of Greater Laporte!"

"Yes!" the apelike Hamiltonian snarled. "And by tomorrow I'll have them and everything else you own! Let me go! You're wrongly depriving me of my liberty!"

I laughed as he jerked at the cuffs. "How d'ya figger that, Gregamer? Lookit these pot-metal trinkets of yours—you deny givin' 'em t'Birdflower here for wreckin' his chair-garden?"

Gregamer calmed down, an evil sneer slowly bloomin' on his puss. "Why no. They're nothing more than tokens, and I said as much, vowing to redeem them as I could. There seemed little objection at the time."

"When I thought they were gold," Birdflower retorted.

"Am I responsible for your gullibility? Did I ever *say* they were gold, you miserable creature? But—look in my vest here. I *have* come to redeem them, and the proof is in my pocket."

Win searched carefully through the Hamiltonian's clothing, expressing amazement at the professor's gun, an odd, long-barreled number apparently powered by nothin' more'n compressed air, but of a large caliber, unlike a kid's air-pistol. Rang a bell in my head somewhere, but there wasn't anybody home t'answer it.

The search also produced several dullish silvery-colored coins.

"Take them!" Gregamer snarled. "They're platinum. I guarantee it. *More* than enough to pay for any alleged damages. And now release me—I demand it!"

Win looked to Mary-Beth. "Isn't there *anything* we can hold him on?"

"What about my . . . flyin' saucer?"

"*What* flying saucer?" said Gregamer nastily before the ethicist could reply. "In the first place, no disinterested party can testify that I ever saw or heard of it. Where is it? Where's the evidence of your rectitude to match that which I have just produced? In the second place, who says this hypothetical vehicle is yours? I know at least four other people, immigrants, just like yourself, with as solid a claim to the machine as you have. And in the last place, by this time tomorrow, there won't *be* any flying saucer to squabble over!"

Reluctantly, Win turned the tiny, funny-shaped key in the handcuffs. Gregamer rubbed his wrist angrily. "You'll all pay for this indignity," he warned, "and for now, we appear to be at an impasse. You can't touch me legally, nor can I get the device I want. I propose that you think of something to do about it."

"Up your aesthetic, Mr. Philosopher," I shouted. I looked at my friends: "Okay, we can't arrest him, that's out. How about we just shoot him?"

This produced a mixture of sentiments, rangin' from bloodthirsty enthusiasm on Fran Sanders' part to reluctant negativisim on Mary-Beth's. The consensus was that it'd be unethical.

"That's what I love about this civilization," Gregamer said almost civilly. "It binds itself by beliefs and codes it won't enforce on those who don't accept them. I, on the other hand, am not bound in this manner."

"We'll take that as a warning, Professor," Birdflower said levelly. "Now get out of my house, and if you ever come back again, I'll shoot you down like the lizard you are. You may take *that* as a warning, too!"

The trouble with real life is that there isn't any background music. What I mean is, that way nobody'd ever sneak up on you—you'd hear the sneakin' up music, right? An' you'd always know the moment that you met your one, true love—hell, *you* can probably whistle *that* theme. Right now it woulda been nice t'have appropriate scorin' to accompany the boos an' hisses we were all thinkin' at Gregamer as he made his exit.

"I'll give you all twenty-four hours to reconsider. After that, Gruenblum's stranded here, and his ship will be incandescent dust!"

The front porch screen door slammed, an' that was that.

"Funny," I got t'thinkin', "he shouldn'ta been able t'do that."

"Do what?" said Fran, watchin' t'make sure Gregamer was really gone.

"Well, I was thinkin' a thought about how there oughta be background music in real life, an'—aw, skip it, it's too complicated. What I want t'know is, how'd he sneak in the back door without at least Howell hearin' or smellin' him? And for that matter, where *is* the little cuss?"

Fran's eyes got big, an' she practically flew out the front door. I got up to follow, bumpin' shoulders with everybody else in the room 'ceptin' the Freenies, on accounta they don't *have* shoulders, but by the time we all got protocol sorted out an' were startin' after the little blonde, she was back.

With what looked like a fur stole bundled up in her arms.

She laid it gently on the old-fashioned skirted sofa, an' it unrolled into a coyote, smaller an' lighter in repose, as they always turn out t'be, than when he was up an' around.

The pistols on his little combat helmet'd been rudely torn away, leavin' danglin' wires, frayed fabric, an' not a small amount of superficial cuts an' abrasions.

An' stickin' outa the side of his neck was a big fat plastic yellow dart, the same diameter as Gregamer's pistol-bore.

19

Waiting for
the Veterinarian
(Or Someone like Him)

THING ABOUT ANAESTHETIC DARTS IS THAT IT'S
hard t'control the dosage an' the distance—an' they're both
critical. Guess I've used the things m'self on every species
from dinosaurs t'dung-beetles, an' I usually lose about half
the critters 'cause they were too close, the dart acted just
like a giant economy-size bullet an' went right through 'em,
or I'd misjudged their tolerance for sleepy-juice an' they'd
taken their last eternal snooze.

Either that or they'd gotten away.

Howell hadn't gotten away. I dunno why Gregamer'd
chosen that particular kinda gun. He couldn'ta known he'd
be up against a four-legged detective, an' anyway, a real
bullet or laser-blast woulda done as well for his purposes.
You go an' figure out what motivates a Hamiltonian. Shucks,
there were fightin' priests in the Middle Ages wouldn't carry
a sword on accounta they didn't wanna spill the blood of
another Christian—so they carried a club instead.

My guess is that Gregamer was a natural-born sneak an'
chose an air-gun for its quietness. Quietude? Quietidity.

Well, that was neither here nor there, as the sayin' goes.
Fran an' Mary-Beth were kneelin' in fronta the couch while
Tree'd run off to the kitchen lookin' like she knew what
she was doin'. I'd plucked the dart outa Howell's neck—
there'd only been a little blood—an' Win had both his big
hands clamped around the wild doggy's muzzle, puffin' up

his cheeks an' tryin' t'breathe into his nostrils.

"His heart's still beating," Mary-Beth said anxiously, one ear on the coyote's chest an' tears wellin' in her eyes, "but I don't have the slightest idea—"

"I do!" her sister said grimly. "Go warm up the Tucker—better yet, take Win's Neova. It's faster."

The detective looked up, nodded.

"Start for Cheyenne right now," the blonde continued. "We'll follow in the big car, 'com a vet and direct you in. Go! I don't think there's any time to lose. His pulse is getting weaker."

Win tossed Mary-Beth his keys. "Just you and Howell," he said. "You can make 350 or 400 without extra passengers. I'll carry him out."

They were out the door an' gone before I made it to the porch. I stood there as Neova-dust settled on my shoulders. Will, Win, Fran, an' assorted Freenies piled into the big blue Tucker. Koko'd blasted off in her bright pink single-seater, a Ruger Sturmatic, somebody'd called it, right behind Will Sanders' elder spouse.

"I hate t'eat an' run," I said t'Birdflower, rememberin' a joke about some fast-food place, "but we'll letcha know how things turn out. Sorry about your crops, but I'm that glad you folks're on our side."

The big gorilloid nodded.

"But what am I supposed to do with this?" Tree asked, holdin' out a pan.

"What's that?" her husband inquired. I was curious, too.

"I boiled some water. In an emergency, they always say—"

"Well," said Birdflower, "I guess we'll have some tea now. Take care of yourself, Bernie, and luck to Howell."

The horn was honkin' from the Tucker, an' its fans were stirrin' up a small tornado.

"You, too, you two." I waved, squinted m'eyes against the dust, an' dashed to the car, bangin' m'self painfully against the frame as it accelerated before I'd got m'self halfway through the door.

The fields were a blur around us. Win punched Com

buttons as Will manhandled the wheel. In the back, Fran had another circuit goin', lettin' Georgie know what was goin' on. Between Gregamer poppin' in on us an' Howell gettin' shot, the badguys had the jump on us again. I was ashamed t'discuss it with m'best girl.

Instead, I thought as hard an' furious as I could, all the way into the city. Gimme a pain, right in the shorts.

"City" wasn't quite the word unless y'count a giant collection of saloons an', shall we gingerly say "associated businesses," a city. This place'd been a major junction for the steamcoach lines a century an' a half ago, vehicles which, in their own peculiar way, had done for the Confederate west what railroads'd done back in my history.

Only with shorter passenger-lists.

Folks hereabouts *still* called the place by an older name. "Hell-on-Wheels." Modern crabgrass pavin'd been passed over in favor of the original street-cobblin', an' the business-district was all nineteenth-century false-fronts an' boarded sidewalks t'tickle the tourists.

Win'd found us a vet, who in turn'd looked up an electronics consultant. We'd all figured, right at the start, that savin' Howell's life might be as much a matter of cybernetics as medicine. Lookin' for all the world like a TV repairman's truck, the electronician's hoverbuggy was parked out in front of the vet's office, in a district usually accustomed t'real live horses.

I paced up an' down the boardwalk, smokin' one cigar after another an' gnashin' m'teeth. Probably resembled an expectant father, an' considerin' where I was an' all, I drew a lotta weird looks from the passers-by.

The moon wasn't up yet, but it'd never be able t'compete with the lightin' afforded by a commercial satellite reflector parked overhead. Felt like three o'clock in the daytime insteada close on midnight. Spin paced forth an' back in counterpoint, while Win sat on a wooden bench, matchin' me cigar-for-cigar. Everybody else was crammed inside the tiny office; there hadn't been a square foot left for the three of us.

I turned to the detective. "This here is just plain awful. We ain't a millimeter closer t'findin' Georgie, an' we're gettin' carved up"—I fingered my damaged earlobe, indicated his bruised-up chest an' the crack in Spin's shell—"at an astoundin' rate. What the hell we gonna do?"

He shook his head an' spat out a bit of tobacco leaf. "Wait. Gregamer was driving a foreign hovercar, German by the looks of it, probably a Volkswirbel. There can't be too many of them in this area. Griswold's owes our Hamiltonian friends a debt or two, and they've got resources and manpower we don't have. So I've got them working on it—I made an extra call or two from the car after I found the vet—they've also staked out Gregamer's house and office at the extension."

"Swell. An' in the meantime, us 'men-of-action' can just sit an'—say, I been meanin' t'tell you, Win, an' everybody else, that Cromney an' his gang ain't really none of your Hamiltonians. No connection at all. They're just a packa nondescript punk leftists who—"

He grinned up at me in that odd always-afternoon lightin': "It wouldn't matter if they were just a pack of nondescript punk right-wingers, Bernie. Hamiltonianism is more than just the not-so-secret society which manufactures those creepy cheap medallions. It's become the generic term for any philosophy which holds that some individuals have a right to exercise authority over others. Let me tell you, friend, that wherever there's some sonofabitch giving orders and another one taking them, whether those orders are the results of a Leader's ulcerated nightmares or a 'vote of the People,' the spirit of Alexander Hamilton is hovering."

The office door opened a crack. One of the other Freenies—hard t'tell in this light—squeezed out, gave us a "no-news-is-good-news" crook of his eyestalk, an' let Spin through t'take his place for a while. He didn't pace with me, but perched up on the bench beside Win an' sucked on a teabag.

I got t'thinkin' about what Win'd said. Put me in minda my Academy days, when I was a two-bit ensign, wet behind the ears.

Seemed like yesterday.

There'd been one prof I'd taken a likin' to, mebbe outa the chance similarity in our names. Bernardine LaPacce was a plump, sixtyish, white-haired lady, looked like everybody's grandma. I could see her classroom now as if I were still there, reflectin' that one-sixth Lunar gee hadn't made a plastic desk-seat easier t'take three hours at a time.

"You're familiar with the view," she said one mornin', "that the Soviet Union was critical to the survival of the United States government, that without the constant threat which Communism represented, federal expenditures, particularly for defense, would have been vastly smaller, taxes greatly decreased.

"This morning, we're going to examine the phenomenon in more detail. Socialism served the twentieth century ruling-class in two ways: as a fundamentally nonworkable economic system, it assured that the bogey-man powers would remain impoverished and *manageable*. Burdened with a governing philosophy contrary to historic, economic, sociological, and political reality, they could only constitute a *psychological* threat. That is why they were *invented:* it's fairly well known that Wall Street *financed* the Bolshevik Revolution. Mercantile fascist interests supported the Russian government for decades afterward, even shipping them whole factories."

The professor bounced up an' down on her heels, wavin' the chalkboard pointer. At one-six gee, it seemed like any moment she'd fly up an' finish lecturin' from the ceilin'. Thank heaven—or Dupont, speakin' of mercantile fascist interests—for Velcro.

"But, even more importantly, socialism served as a *domestic* safety-valve. Those intelligent enough to perceive the ugly truth—that America was *not* a capitalist economy but a variety of Mussolini's system—those individuals were offered only socialism as an alternative, with all its ineffectual, wheel-spinning, Byzantine factionalism. Thus, any threat represented by young bright dissenters was diffused harmlessly. My most charitable feelings toward the Left are those of pitying contempt. They were *suckers*, taken in by the government-approved alternative philosophy, and used to serve the very interests they thought they opposed!"

Next mornin' there was an announcement that a suburban warren of the lunar city-complex'd been depressurized by an explosion in a methadone pipeline. Professor Bernardine LaPacce was one of sixty-thousand victims.

Always made me wonder, afterward, whose interests *that* had served.

"They needn't have bothered," Win said after I'd told him the story. He watched as—Color, I think it was, fidgeted in a most un-Freenielike manner, finally surrenderin' to the pacin' urge. "Nobody on the left would ever have believed her. They've always got too much invested emotionally, and the system provides too many opportunities to *hate*—industrialists, the middle class, even other leftists. It selects for a particular kind of stupidity which is immune to reason or logic or even historical fact."

"Much the same as the right," I observed, wonderin' if it was Howell's bein' hurt or somethin' else that was eatin' the little aliens. The door swung open, an' he practically jumped. Spin came out, an' he went back inside.

"Well, I'm going to see what's going on in there. Want to join me?"

I shook my head, watched him stub out his cigar. In a moment, Koko was sittin' on the bench in Win's place.

"Do you think he's serious?" she asked.

"I dunno, kid. I seen a lotta funny things in a long an' checkered career. I seen mobs gather when the calendar got straightened out so's Christmas'd fall in the winter-time. I seen an elk, with its heart pulverized by a 7 mm magnum run three quarters of a mile an' drop dead because its muscles'd stopped pumpin' blood. I seen a whole planetfulla folks who'd blown themselves up over a disagreement about what kinda asparagus God wanted 'em t'eat. Could be Howell'll get better—I seen folks hurt worse—could be he won't."

"I wasn't talking about that, Bernie. I was talking about Win Bear hiring me as his assistant. I never thought about being a detective before. Do you think I'd do all right?"

I looked her over real good. She was big, shaggy, with that little hint of reddish fur that seemed t'run in Olongo's family. She was wearin' a T-shirt that said, FOLLOW A PARANOID, a miniskirt with a poodle appliquéd on it, a wide designer gunbelt in some kinda plastic. I thought about Hercule Poirot. I thought about Miss Marple an' Nero Wolf. I thought about Mrs. Pollifax an' Sherlock Holmes an' that fella—what was his name?—who was a part-time detective an' a full-time burglar. Rhodenbarr, somethin' like that. Forgot the first name.

Me, I was just a part-time Sybarite an' a full-time hedonist. What the hell did I know?

"Give it a whirl, kid. Give it your best shot. But don't give up your day-job. What is it you're studyin', anyway?"

"Gee, Bernie, all kinds of things. I guess I'd really like to be a spaceship pilot, an explorer. Maybe somebody'll invent a faster-than-light drive one of these days, and—Bernie, *your* civilization has a faster-than-light drive, doesn't it?"

The door opened again, an' Spin was replaced by one of his colleagues.

"Yeah, that it does. Shucks, I even know how it works, in a general sorta way. Trouble is, your culture's invented somethin' I didn't even know could exist—travelin' between worlds of alternate probability. We're aheada you in some ways; you're aheada us in others. Hard t'make sense of it."

She sighed. "Yes, yes it is." She was silent for a while, then: "Bernie, I didn't mean *not* to be worried about Howell. I just don't know him very well, and I was trying to keep my mind on other things."

"I know, kid. Say, d'you suppose there might be a soda-fountain in this burg somewhere? I'll bet you'd like a sundae, or even a—" Realizin' what I'd been about t'say, I began t'blush.

She saw it an' grinned. "A banana split? I'd be delighted!"

"Great—let's—"

Spin was back on the boardwalk, an' this time he was

tuggin' on m'leg, just like old times. "What is it, little fella?"

"Bernie, we've got to get to a Telecom. Charm's in trouble, and he needs our help!"

The nearest Com, outside the crowded vet's office, was in Win's car. I still hadn't gotten the complicated hang of operatin' the thing, so I shanghaied Koko.

It wasn't necessary. His little image was there, waitin' for us.

"Lord?" the alien said, this time without any undertones. "I have done as much as I could by myself. Now it is time for you to help—for any moment I may be discovered, and should that transpire, both Georgie and I are doomed."

"How's that?"

"Can you not see? I followed Gregamer here, having attached myself to his vehicle and disguised myself." He demonstrated, withdrawin' his periscope an' slowly changin' the atrocious color of his carapace until it was a steely gray. Little guy had talents he hadn't even used yet. "Now I have found Georgie—"

"You *what?*"

"*Please,* Bernie, there is little time! I have found Georgie—this is *her* channel we're communicating on." The camera drew back until I could see that it was peekin' out from underneath the flyin' saucer's fuselage.

"Georgie! Are you all right?"

No answer.

Charm was insistent. "She can't communicate with you, Bernie. Gregamer and Cromney and the rest are on the control deck, and we're taking risk enough just transmitting this. I'll try to tell you where we are, but Bernie, you've got to be careful and you've got to act quickly."

"What's goin' on, Your Ambassadorship?"

"Bernie, they know that Georgie's a sapient being, and they're torturing her until she admits it!"

20

A Freenie in
the Works

How do y'torture a flyin' saucer?

In Georgie's case, I could imagine all too well. Six or seven different ideas that curled what was lefta my hair. She was, indeed, a sapient bein'—one helluva lot sapienter than the crowd which presently had aholda her. I hadda *think!*

An' the gorilla breathin' down m'neck wasn't exactly helpin'.

"Koko, how good're you at keepin' a secret?"

She blinked an' looked down unhappily at her toes, kinda self-consciouslike. "Not very good, I'm afraid. Uncle Olongo says—"

"Well, then, m'mind's made up: I don't need no fifty-eleven well-meanin' friends jogglin' m'elbow, an' you don't even trust yourself not t'blab—that, an' the fact I ain't got no Confederate driver's license. You know how t'herd this thing?"

"A Neova? Sure—but . . . what's a driver's license?"

"Swell. Okay, there *ain't* no alternative. Spin, you better stay here in case I flub things again. Gimme half an—make that twenty minutes, then tell Win an' Will where we've gone. I'm relyin' on you not t'spill the beans too soon. Also, apologize t'Win for me for stealin' his car. You ready t'go, girl?"

The gorilla protested. "But Bernie, there aren't even any keys in the ignition. How—"

"Kid, you gotta lot t'learn. I didn't put in sixteen weeks

203

as a phony JD in twentieth-century Passaic, New Jersey, for nothin'. Lemme in there under the dashboard."

1954, it'd been. If you can imagine Mrs. Gruenblum's little boy in a black leather jacket, ankle-pegged chinos, an' a jelly-roll haircut. The things I do for the Academy. Makes me wanna take a shower every time I think of it.

The impellers caught on the second try. I slid out from under the instrumentation an' onto the passenger seat t'make room for Koko, who climbed in reluctantly.

I addressed the Telecom: "Okay, Charm, we're on our way, if you'll tell us what t'do. An' you can also tell me what all you've been up to. Spin I can identify now, right enough. But I guess I never did learn t'tell you an' Color apart—I thought you were here with us all the time!"

The image on the screen seemed t'blush a little. Maybe it was just a glitch in the circuitry or sunspots. "That was as intended, Lord. We all beg your forgiveness for the deception and will humbly accept whatever penance you should—"

"Skip the crap—just tell Koko where t'point this jalopy."

Head south, Miss Koko, for the intersection of Monroe and Slade, out by the old Overland Steamcoach barns. I'll direct you from there.

Lord, there wasn't time to consult with you. I barely had time to tell my fellows what I had in mind—disguising myself as a mechanical excrescence on Norrit Gregamer's vehicle. I rode back into Cheyenne, that evil person none the wiser, clinging for dear life to the body of the hovercraft. Several hundred kilometers per hour tested severely even *my* holding power.

You'll see for yourself, soon enough, what a dismal state our Georgie's in. Naturally, she cannot move or properly defend herself—no, you mustn't fault yourself for that, Bernie. You *had* to take that alignment device; she is as well aware of the alternatives as you are. But they have opened every service port, every access plate, looking for parts to cannibalize for a new field-density control and also,

I believe, as an inducement to her cooperation. They've torn—

But you will see that for yourself.

Gregamer parked his machine outside the old weather-faded metal building, which at one time was a center for the maintenance and repair of transcontinental steam-coaches. There was a very large door, hinged at the top, with a smaller one set within it. This smaller door he entered, having first unchained the handle and locking it behind him from the inside. I was sorely pressed to follow him. In our continuum, there would have been several broken windows in such an abandoned construction, but here—well, I'm not certain whether it's a greater respect for private property or the fact that Confederate window-glass seems to have a knack for regeneration which would be enviable in an *organic* substance. . . .

In any event, I finally extruded a number of specialized limbs with great adhesive properties and "walked" carefully up the corrugated side of the building. Earth's moon did little to dispel the artificial light from orbit which, in this neighborhood, gave a peculiar grainy grayish tone to every-thing it washed. In the west, the sky was still a spectacular shade of infrared; stars shone ultraviolet in the east.

At last I discovered a ventilation grillwork. This building was at least a century old, its facilities in a state of disrepair for which I found myself deeply grateful. A few snips with yet another specialized appendage, a bit of careful footwork, and I was inside.

It would have been quite dark to you, Lord.

It appeared I was at one end of the garagelike building, just above a sort of railed balcony, half of which had served as a glassed in office. Now it was dark and empty, bits of paper scattered about in the thick dust. I walked down the inside wall to this platform, negotiated a cast-iron stairway I found there, and came at last to a grease-stained concrete floor, cluttered and full of pock-holes of various sizes. Hug-ging one wall to avoid discovery, I had a momentary al-tercation with a vicious quadruped approximately my own size with sharp chisellike teeth and a strange, hairless, skinny tail. He smelled bad and was covered with tiny vermin. I forebore to kill him, but he will have difficulty walking comfortably for some days and will not pass on his genes.

Did I act aright, Lord?

No matter. The boarding-ramp, Georgie's boarding-ramp, was extended. This presented me with a problem, as the light from the passenger-deck airlock spilled across the dirty, littered floor and up the corrugated wall and joisting, making further progress in that direction around the vessel's circumference impossible.

I started to turn back, to go around the other way, when I observed one of Georgie's landing-lights, a very small, relatively dim amber one, blinking at me. As soon as it had caught my eye, it stopped.

Her senses, Bernie, must be very nearly as good as ours.

Thus I made my way, skulking from one rusty oil-can to the next half-melted cardboard box, as quickly and inconspicuously as possible to Georgie's side, where, as you know, a slight undertaper keeps her from being perfectly hemispherical. It also provided an excellent temporary hiding-place until I could think of what to do next.

Finally, I sneaked up to the base of the ramp where I could remain in deepest shadow, yet be near enough the doorway to hear what was going on. Georgie, of course, had no way of communicating with me, but I could let her see me in hopes of comforting her. I climbed through the circular framing to the other side of the ramp, where I knew there was a television monitor, and extruded a special appendage—one I'd only just thought of, with a small ear on the end—and let it lie just inside the seal-cushions of the air-lock.

"—tell you, there's something *screwy* about this ship!"

Rand Heplar was speaking up on the control deck, the air-lock hatch of which was also open. It sounded as though he were in acute danger of becoming hysterical, this formerly laconic fellow. Is there no middle ground with human beings?

"Superstitious nonsense!" Professor Cromney retorted.

"You're simply making excuses for your own incompetence. What have you been *doing* with those supplies that Dr. Gregamer sent you?"

"*You* try sticking your fingers into any access port, *any* access port, where there's a static field for no apparent reason and see what a fat, blue, inch-long spark does for *your* metabolism! The effect is cumulative, you know—one more jolt like that and I'll probably—"

"You'll do exactly as you're told, young man, and cease immediately anthropomorphizing this, this . . . *machine!* You're no better than Gruenblum, in your way—next you'll be telling me the ship is haunted!"

There was a chuckle I recognized as Gregamer's as he joined them in the control room. "It better not be haunted, at least for little Edna's sake. How about it, sweetheart? Are the shades of the late Professors Merwin and Hulbert bothering you lately?"

I was surprised. Instead of attacking anyone who presumed to call her "little Edna"—in her presence, at least—she merely snorted, enjoying the joke. "Not half as much as the shade of yellow I can see running up dear Randy's back. Don't laugh, Cromney—you're no better, screaming at the top of your lungs when maybe you ought to be listening! I'm not quite sure how to put this, but the ship *does* seem, well . . ."

"Aware?" Gregamer ventured.

"Oh, come now!" Cromney scoffed. "Or is someone going to produce a Ouija board to make the point? This vessel is nothing more than an assembly of plastic, aluminum, and titanium!"

"*Charm, is it really you?*"

Georgie *had* found a way to communicate, after all, not with a Ouija board, whatever that is, but by amplitude-modulating her ultrasonic proximity-detectors. I pitched my own voice upward, replying on the same frequencies.

"*Yes, Georgie, it is I. Are you all right?*"

"Just as you, my dear Professor Cromney, are nothing more than an assembly of hydrogen, carbon, and oxygen!" There was a genuinely sarcastic tone to the Hamiltonian's voice now; he seemed not at all concerned to hide it.

"I am so far, but . . . well, how long have you been following this conversation, Charm?"

"Norrit, my boy, take it from an old academic hand: philosophical reductionism is scarcely a proper—"

"Now *look,* Cromney, you don't know what the chaos you're talking about! I was trying to point out that intelligence is a matter of complexity of organization, not composition. I know—for the past four years, ever since the Civil Liberties Association investigated Heller-Browne Cybercorp, and successfully prosecuted them for enslaving sapient business machines—"

"They *what?"* A female voice.

"You heard me, Edna. It's what I've been trying to tell this ivory-tower worm-casting here. Don't look so blasted shocked, Heplar! Now adjudicative precedent makes it morally obligatory—and a desperate economic necessity—to design *around* any possible inadvertent sapience in cybernetic . . . say, what's that display over there? The small monitor, I mean?"

"I've been listening long enough to understand what's going on, Georgie. I greatly fear they're about to discover your—"

"That?" Cromney attempted derision, but there was more of a tinge of embarrassment in his voice than he would have liked. "It's simply a CRT playback of a recreational DreamCassette we found, er . . . lying around the control room. It works perfectly over the closed loop, but its neuronic transmission doesn't seem to—"

"That blonde," Gregamer insisted, "I've seen her somewhere recently. But if that recording was made in *your* continuum, then how could I . . . I have it! She was on the Telecom at the furniture farm, talking to Gruenblum and the rest!"

"Uh-oh," Georgie whispered, *"I think my Bernie would say—'the jig is up'!"*

"Impossible!" Cromney shouted.

"Ridiculous!" Edna echoed.

"Ummmmm . . ." Heplar mused, beginning to believe.

"Something strange *is* going on here," Gregamer concluded, and I could hear him cross the little room, hear the springs and cushions squeak as he lowered himself into the pilot's chair. "And I'm going to get to the bottom of it. Heplar, show me how that DreamCap thing works!"

"Charm, I don't know what's going to happen, but I'm scared!"

From the tone of *her* voice, she'd learned to engage in understatement.

Bongggg!

Koko gave the tiller a whirl, an' we drifted sideways across the intersection at about Mach 0.5, smackin' a lamppost. The Neova's rubbery skirt absorbed mosta the shock, an' we were straightened up an' away before the cross-traffic, their horns shrillin' an' blarin', even knew what nearly hit 'em.

"Can't you make this velocipede pile on any more steam, girl?"

"It's fusion power, not steam, Bernie, and I've got it to the floor, already—in fact, I don't think Win's accelerator pedal's ever going to be quite the—*Oh, dear Albert!*"

"Ghaaaaa!"

ZZZZzzzzmmmmm!

The big orange hovertruck missed us by no more'n an angstrom unit, an' I decided t'shut up an' let the gorilla do the drivin'.

"How much further, Charm?"

The Freenie in the 'com screen thought a moment. "You're on Slade Avenue?"

"All over it—no offense, Koko. I ain't complainin'—just keep those big brown eyes on the . . . *Ohmygod!*"

SSSsssweeeeen!

"Relax, Bernie," she said cheerily over her fuzzy shoulder. "That one didn't even come close!"

Ulp. "Where do we go next, Charm, providin' that we live that long?"

"Just keep going until you see a big red neon sign that says 'Rosie's'."

"Some kinda truckstop?"

"Er, I don't think so, Bernie. Although there were plenty of trucks parked there when I—"

"Okay, okay. Remember there's a minor drivin'. What happened next—after Gregamer remembered seein' Georgie on the Telecom, I mean?"

Given the sort of people that they were, it wasn't very easy for them to agree upon a course of action, and they continued to argue about it, even after Norrit Gregamer had acted for them.

"But that would be silly," Heplar insisted. "Besides, how . . . *where* would I even begin trying to communicate with a timeship?"

"How do you *ordinarily* communicate with it, stupid?" Gregamer was close to losing his temper; even Edna seemed a little afraid of him.

"Answer him, Rand!"

"Well, I . . ."

"Charm, we've got to contact Bernie. If Gregamer's going to do what I think he is—it's one of my truly weak points, and I'm not sure I can hold out if he—well, I'm just not sure what *will happen!"* She began to sob quietly, still in the ultrasonic range.

"But Georgie, what can they do to you?"

"Give me that cap, you moron! You and Cromney—get out of my sight! Now, Edna, turn it on, or whatever you do!"

There was a pause.

"Charm!"

"All right," Gregamer said, sounding a bit abstracted. "I appear to be in a grove of trees. The sun's shining in my eyes, so I can hardly—wait, *there* she is! That same pale blue-eyed blonde, standing beneath a big oak. Here goes: you there! That's right, I mean *you*, blondie!"

"Oh, Charm!"

"You might as well speak up, honey. We know *all* about you. I watched that CRT display straight through, and it was pretty amazing. In fact, before we start the interrogation, I think I'll just avail myself of your—okay, Edna, *okay!* Say, blondie, don't try to run away. You're not supposed to be programed for it!"

"Charm, help me!"

"What can I do, Georgie?"

"Gotcha! Now calm down, honey, or I'll have to break your little arm. Let me see now . . . here, my belt ought to do nicely. Hold still!"

"Oh, Charm, please *help me!"*

My thought's spun hopelessly. How could I save a ninety-foot starship/time-machine from an imaginary fate-worse-than-death?

"Georgie, can you still communicate? Can you find Bernie? Try the farm—they might still be there!"

Her ultrasonic voice quavered. *"I'll t-try!"*

"There!" Gregamer leered. "Nice and tight—is that bark too rough on your nonexistent little back? Now tell me all about yourself, honey. You weren't *designed* for sapience. Where'd you get the extra processing capacity? Oh, you won't talk, eh? Well, that makes it inconvenient, but a *lot* more fun! I'll just imagine real hard, and—*there*—I *thought* I had a pack of cigarettes and a lighter in my pocket, even though I don't smoke, ordinarily. Very satisfactory, this DreamCap system—and it's *you* who're going to do the smoking! I'll just light up, here, and that chiffon dress you're wearing ought to melt at an *extremely* uncomfortable temperature. I believe I'll just start at the top of your shoulders and work my way down to your—"

"Charm!"

"Get Bernie, Georgie, get Bernie! Try the Sanders' car—try Win's!"

I couldn't see, of course, when she'd connected any more than I can see you now, but I could recognize the breathing on the other end of the line.

"Lord?" I pleaded. "I have done as much as I could myself. Now it is time for you to help!"

21

Cromney Gets
the Point

"PARDON MY UNDERWEAR, KOKO."

"Why? What did it do?" Half a block from the steam-coach barn, she'd slowed down to a crawl. The Neova settled to the big balloon tires under its skirt as we crept silently forward.

I started squirmin' outa my coverall. "Charm, tell Georgie we're almost there. An' remind her I can erase the memories of whatever Gregamer's doin' to her, if that's any comfort."

"And if she's still sane and sapient afterward, Lord."

"You're a lotta help, buddy." I was down t'my skivvies now an' turnin' my uniform inside out. The thermal linin' was off-white an' just might pass for Academic yellow in a darkened barn. I took my undershirt off, too.

"Bernie, what *are* you doing?" Koko seemed more amused than put off.

"Improvisin' a disguise. You suppose Win's got a first-aid kit in the glove box? For that matter, where *is* the glove box?"

She showed me. Back into my everted livery, I wound my T-shirt around an arm, hopin' I was rememberin' which was the correct one. Win had a kit, all right, an' I plastered a big white Band-Aid across the bridge of my schnozz. I skipped doin' anything t'my knee—no way Edna an' the rest'd know for sure what I'd done t'Denny there.

Nervously, I pinched the slide back on my .45, checkin' the chamber, an' reluctantly decided t'leave the belt behind.

There was an inside pocket—now an *outside* pocket—that'd serve as a half-assed holster for the brief time required of it. I slipped the little seven-inch bowie outa Koko's scabbard as she wheeled around the corner.

"Gonna need this, kid. Keep the motor runnin' for a fast getaway—what am I sayin'? This ain't no five-foot blonde I'm rescuin'! Goddamnit, I'm gettin' all confused again!"

"What *do* you want me to do, Bernie?"

I thought about it till I figured I'd run outa thinkin' time: "If I ain't out in five minutes, drive the hoverbuggy straight through the doors!"

I swung the gull-wing up, lighted runnin', an' made it through the semilit darkness toward the smaller of the two entrances. The frame'd sagged, an' I could see the rusted shaft of a simple hook-an'-eye through the resultant half-inch crack. By Hirnschlag, Charm'd missed a trick, after all—I was beginnin' t'think it was me oughta be worshippin' the Freenies.

I pulled Koko's bear-shaver outa the phony cast on my arm, slipped it in an' upward, snicked off the hook, an' crept in low.

There was my Georgie!

An' there was the Ambassador, crouchin' (t'whatever extent Freenies can crouch) by the gangramp, right in fronta one of the outboard snoopers. He waved a cautious tentacle at me. I skittered up on my own tentacles, one size nine at a time, an' joined him.

"What's the situation, ol' Yamaguchian?" There wasn't any hovertruck. They'd probably dropped the incriminatin' evidence in a gully somewhere.

Silence. An' a pain in m'ears.

"Charm, I don't savvy dog-whistle too good. Crank it down a coupla octaves, willya?"

"Apologies, Lord," he whispered. "Bernie, you must help her! If a human loses consciousness with shock, she regains it. I think if Georgie passes out, that may be the last we'll hear of her!"

"You're just fulla cheer. Where is everybody?"

"Cromney is on the passenger level. Edna proved unable

to assist Gregamer with the DreamCap and summoned Heplar who is on the control deck now, while she retired below to the engine-room. Lord, what is the matter? Why have you that dressing across your—"

"I just joined Adam an' the Ants—never mind, just some twentieth-century trivia. Wait here for me an' keep on holdin' Georgie's hand!"

I slithered up the side of the ship, puttin' careful toes an' fingers in the recesses provided for same, until I got to the upstairs airlock. Charm'd been right: it was as wide open as the one below—they had good reason t'wanna air her out. I slipped inside, adjusted my disguise, such as it was, an' stepped softly into the after lounge.

"Come on now, honey. How much more can you— owch! You little bitch, I'll teach you to bite!"

Backin' along the wall, I wondered if he'd get a psychosomatic bruise from that imaginary nip—too bad Georgie couldn't carry rabies. At the hatch-frame, I cased the control-room best I could, usin' the glass front of a gauge on the back wall, which was angled nearly right. Leavin' the Colt in my pocket for a minute, to avoid makin' any reinforcement-summonin' noise, I whipped around the corner, grabbed Heplar by the scruff, an' smashed his head against a bulkhead, left-handed.

Somethin' squished pleasantly, an' he settled to the floor.

With a quick underhanded swipe of the bowie, I slashed the overhead line to the DreamCap. There was a spark an' hiss. Gregamer stirred on the couch, blinkin' stupidly as he tried t'focus; then his eyes widened as he caught sighta me.

I reversed the blade in my hand, thumb t'pommel, took a quick step forward, batted away the pistol he was grabbin' for, an' seized him by the lapel.

"Gregamer, they're gonna hafta *castrate* you loose from that couch!"

"Denny! How did you—" I heard a voice behind me an' turned, keepin' one eye on Gregamer. There was Ab Cromney, momentarily fooled, but not any longer. He had a Confederate flechette gun under one arm. I pivoted, draggin' Gregamer over across the couch-arm, an' in one smooth motion, planted the seven-inch knife up to its cross-hilt in the left side of Cromney's chest.

He stood there a moment, lookin' a mite surprised, rolled his eyes up, an' folded at the knees. When he hit the deckin', it drove the knife-point out through his back.

Heplar stirred. I kicked him in the face.

But things'd gotten outa hand. Gregamer was on me from behind, my size but broader, with a longer reach, and *strong*. I fumbled for my pistol, punched him in the solar plexus at the same time. He didn't even blink, but cracked me on the forehead with the ruined DreamCap. He musta liked the effect it produced, 'cause he kept on doin' it. Somewhere about the seventeenth blow, I kinda lost tracka what was goin' on.

There ain't nothin' in the known universe smells quite the same as the oily floor of an abandoned garage. Especially when your nose an' mosta the resta your face is in intimate contact with it.

After a twenty-foot drop.

I could tell straight off my right arm was broken. Funny how y'know these things. Wasn't altogether sure about my hip on that side or the knee. Like Charm'd pointed out, I always thought you were supposed t'faint when somethin' hurt that bad.

Abruptly, somebody's pointed toe became instrumental in informin' me that I'd busted three or four ribs as well. There was a sorta gurglin' t'my breathin', an' I calculated groggily that it mighta made more sense t'count the bones that *weren't* broken.

Wouldn'ta taken near as long.

The foot eventually turned me over on my damaged side, makin' life even more miserable, an' I saw through the remainin' good eye that said foot was attached to Edna Janof.

"He's still alive," she said with mingled disappointment that I wasn't dead an' welcomin' the opportunity t'kill me all over again. I tried t'speak.

Nothin'.

"Well, Captain Bernard M. Gruenblum," the lady said, "you meet your end at last. It's certainly taken longer than I expected, but then I was handicapped with inferior assistance. Now you've kindly taken care of that for me by removing Cromney, and—of course I'll have to finish the job you started on Heplar, and Denny's out of the picture, but I—"

"But you'd better stop your little list right there, Edna darling, and keep in mind from now on *exactly* who and what I am!"

Norrit Gregamer strode up beside her, lookin' twenty feet tall from my pointa view, draped a negligent arm over her shoulder. She actually cuddled up into the embrace, practically purrin'.

She mighta even meant it. No accountin' for love.

"Look at him, my dear," Gregamer said evenly. "Observe his eyes—still confident. He's still expecting help."

"Not from *this*, I hope!" She laughed an' raised the hand she'd been holdin' behind her. Danglin' from her fist by his little eyestalk was Charm, limp as a boiled gooseneck clam. There wasn't any glitter in his eye.

"Or from *that* . . ." added Gregamer with a chortle of his own. I followed his hooked thumb t'where the garage door'd been broached by the front end of Win's Neova. Hangin' through the starred hole in its windshield, sprawled over the hood, was a shaggy black body.

Her blood was ruinin' the paint job.

How the hell long had I been out?

The Hamiltonian turned back t'me. "I must apologize for having precipitated you so abruptly from the airlock door, Captain. I'm afraid I rather lost control of my temper for a short while. However, it did serve to flush this little vermin out of its hiding-place." He indicated the inert Freenie while I mourned inside for two of the best friends who'd ever had the bad luck t'meet me.

"Very touching," Gregamer continued, "the way it hurried to your side, too preoccupied to notice Edna right behind it. You strangle like a pro, my dear."

"Why thank you, kind sir." It was her turn t'gloat: "Your

furry companion seems to have done *herself* in. I'm not the only one saddled with incompetents, I suppose. Still, they don't train subhumans here the way they do at home, do they?"

I tried t'speak again, with no better results than the first time. Just as well, she woulda gone for the manicurin' scissors, considerin' what I had in mind t'tell her.

"Save your breath, Gruenblum," Gregamer advised. "At least for one last prolonged scream. Edna, are you ready to go?"

"Just about," she answered with what approached docility. I guess some guys have it an' some guys don't. In this case, I hoped it wasn't catchin'. "You see, Captain, we're ignoring an old maxim and giving up the ship. Norrit has convinced me that there's plenty we can accomplish in the Confederacy without it—did you know they have atomic explosives here, for construction work, but have never thought of using them as weapons?—especially as we don't intend to leave it intact for anybody else to use."

"Now, now, dear, you're giving away the good part!" He lifted a flechette gun—Cromney's, t'judge by the Type O all over it. But then, just about everything seemed t'be covered with slippery carmine these days.

"I really wish you could speak, Captain, although I'd guess you've lost your speech center from the way that side of your head is flattened on the concrete. Messy, messy. Still, I suppose I'll always wonder: *was* she sapient or not? Ah, well, there are some things, I've been told, that mankind was never meant to know. Nineteen rounds of *this*"—he slapped the receiver of the shotgun—"right into the computer banks, and it'll all be academic. I'm saving the last one for you, Captain"—he peered closely into my face—"that is, if you still require it by the time I get back."

This was turnin' out t'be almost the worst mission I'd ever volunteered for. I sure hoped it'd be a lesson to me.

"And by the way, the help you're *still* expecting—thought you'd fooled me, didn't you—can't possibly be on time. We'll be out of here in another minute; tell me, Captain, did you get your directions to the coach-barn *before* you left or *en route?*"

My heart sank the final millimeter it had left t'go. He put a foot on the gangplank, chucklin' softly to himself.

"Use all twenty rounds, Norrit dear," Edna called after him cheerfully. "I'm sure I saw a shovel around here somewhere, and I've always wanted to just sort of *chunk!*, you know, right above the eyebrows?"

Indulgently: "All right, my dear, if you insist. By all means enjoy yourself." He started up the ramp, the Thane of Cawdor t'her Lady MacBeth. What a couple—is that a dagger that I see b'fore me?

Edna flung little Charm away like a dirty rag an' headed for the back of the garage. Even if I coulda talked, I wouldn'ta had the heart t'spoil Gregamer's fun. My skull wasn't crushed; it just *felt* that way, probably from lyin' all this time in a hole eroded in the concrete floor.

An' speakin' of daggers, while I'd left mine screwed into a well-deservin' recipient upstairs, my *left* arm still worked. I twisted an' bent it, scrabblin' across m'chest, gropin', gropin' . . .

Yes! They hadn't taken my Colt. I'd been layin' on it all this time—it'd probably broken those ribs, in fact—an' they hadn't noticed or thought of it in all their newlywed excitement. Leverin' it outa the pocket nearly cost me my grip on consciousness, broken up as bad as I was, but I finally got it free.

Thumbed the ambidextrous safety down.

Drew a shaky left-hand bead, an'—

WHAMMM!

Norrit Gregamer's head exploded like a balloon fulla Sherwin Williams' best firetruck enamel, splatterin' all over Georgie's hull. The decapitated body took one last step toward the airlock, kinda slumped off t'one side, missed the edge of the gangplank, an' dropped onto the same floor that'd ruined me.

"Norrit!" Edna shrieked. "*Bastard, bastard, bastard, bastard, bastard!*"

I kinda figured this last was directed my way, especially when she loomed up outa the darkness with that shovel vertical in her hands.

I waved my .45 in her general direction, but it was gettin' a mite heavy by now, an' like everything else in this place, my hands were sorta slippery-feelin'. One moment the Colt was there between m'fingers, an' the next my mitt was empty, the automatic lyin' there on the cement, its big ugly eye lookin' straight at my belly-button.

"You . . . *bastard!* The only man I've ever met in my entire life who wasn't a *wimp*, and you had to shoot him!"

She held the shovel before her, half-raised.

"I'm going to chop you into so many little—"

SPANNGG!

Somethin' caught the rusty blade an' smacked it flat into Edna's rage-filled face. She staggered backward, tripped over an abandoned crate, an' fell. I got the .45 in hand again, breathin' two sighs of relief at once, twisted around painfully, an' there was Miss Koko Featherstone-Haugh, sittin' up an' aimin' her .11-caliber Webley Electric at the place where Edna'd *been*.

I tried t'shout at her an' couldn't. She untangled herself from the remains of Win's car, dried blood all over clothes an' pelt, an' shambled over t'where I lay, keepin' that pistol of hers pointed toward the shadows at the backa the garage. She picked up the badly-dented—but unpunctured—shovel and examined it with disgust.

"Bernie, are you still alive?"

I blinked at her an' finally managed somethin' halfway between a croak an' a whisper. "That's a damn silly question t'ask. How about yourself? I thought you were a goner for sure."

She grinned a human-type grin, still maintainin' a watch where Edna'd gone down. "I *faked* it! Your disguise gave me the idea. I smashed the windshield with my pistol—I guess that accounts for the sights being off. I was aiming at her center-of-mass like Uncle Olongo taught me. You know, he *warned* me the .11-caliber was underpowered.

Look, it didn't even penetrate!" She tossed the shovel aside, where it clanged and raised dust.

"Well, *my* disguise didn't work out too well. How about all that blood?"

"The blood? Oh, *that!* She gave me a sheepish look. "Well, I sort of punched myself in the nose, also with the gun. Nothing like a nosebleed to—and let me tell you, it *hurts* too!"

"I'll put you in for a Purple Heart. Meantime, kiddo, I'm in kind of a bad way myself. Can you get aholda Win an' the folks? An' you better check little Charm over there. I'm afraid he's probably—"

"THIRTY SECONDS TO FAILSAFE AUTODE-STRUCT!" said Georgie suddenly at about a thousand decibels. Her voice was frozen an' inhuman. *"TWENTY-NINE SECONDS TO FAILSAFE AUTODESTRUCT!"*

A hand crawled over the coamin' of the passenger-level airlock. It was followed by its owner, Rand Heplar.

Georgie went blarin' on.

"You've killed me, Bernie Gruenblum." He laughed insanely, an' by the look of his bashed-in cranium an' blood-soaked hair, he was probably right. "But I've killed you back!"

"TWENTY-FOUR SECONDS TO FAILSAFE AUTO-DESTRUCT!" Georgie said. *"TWENTY-THREE . . ."*

22

Edna's
Last Stand

"... SECONDS TO FAILSAFE AUTODESTRUCT!"

"Georgie, cut that out!"

Rand Heplar was draped artistically over the sill of the passenger-deck airlock, unconscious but breathin': exactly the same condition I'd be in—maybe even leavin' out the breathin'—in a couple more minutes. Every now an' again he moaned.

"All right," Georgie said in a normal tone, "but Bernie, you'll have to countermand the Autodestruct manually. I can't do anything about it myself, and you've only got twenty—"

"No count-downs, please. Honey, I ain't in any shape t'do *nothin'!* Koko, get up there an' down into the engine—"

"I'm on my way!"

An' she was, up the ramp, over Heplar's carcass, Georgie helpin' her by hittin' corridor lights an' panel indicators t'keep her headed in the right direction. Heplar murmured an' stirred again. I tried wigglin' m'toes. Far as I could tell, with the heavy boots an' all, everything worked.

Real cautiouslike I laid m' .45 down, worryin' overtime about where Edna'd got off to, an' with a cowardly left hand, felt along m'legs, inspectin' for bendy places where there oughtn't t'be any. The general architecture seemed in dandy order till I got up to m'right hip. Somethin' rasped nastily across somethin' else, an' I went all over kinda sick an' hadda stop.

Poor little Charm. Some kinda god *I'd* turned out t'be; couldn't even protect him—or Spin, for that matter—from one miserable lone crazy-lady.

"Fifteen seconds, Bernie. Koko's at the bottom of the 'tween-decks ladder and starting down the corridor toward the reactors."

"I hearya, I hearya!"

Not knowin' about Edna bothered me. I hitched up on an elbow, tryin' to ignore the pain like my Academy Yoga instructor'd taught me. Never'd been m'best subject—oriental positions just don't fit occidental bones. Managed t'drag m'self mebbe a yard closer to the ship.

BLOMMM!

A fountain of concrete-dust kicked up directly in my path.

"Stop right there, Captain Gruenblum!"

Well, that took care of one mystery: it was little Edna, hollerin' down at me from the glassed-in office cubicle above the garage-floor at the back. I oughta say "formerly glassed-in"—that blast'd done for mosta the windows. I could make out the shiny ring of her flechette-gun muzzle from where I lay.

Damn thing looked like the Gibraltar Tunnel.

"Don't make another move, Gruenblum! I want to enjoy this, and I *won't* have you ruin it by dying too soon!"

BLOMMM!

The air went fulla cement chips behind me that time, an' I could even hear the whine an' clatter of a shotgun dart or two that ricocheted into the corrugated steel walls.

Pretty plain what she had in mind: workin' the pattern closer an' closer till she could gimme just the edge of it— flesh wounds—without knockin' me off outright. Remote-control torture. Ain't science wonderful?

BLOMMM!

Bitsa concrete rained down on my head this time, like bein' in a split-second sandstorm. With all the dust bein' raised, it was gettin' harder an' harder t'breathe.

An' t'*see*, I suddenly realized. Never had been too well illuminated in this garage t'start with. If m'suit'd been right-side-in, she mightn'ta been able t'make me out at all. I hooked a finger through the trigger-guard of my Colt, dragged it slowly toward me, an' gathered in m'nether limbs as far as the damaged hip-joint'd permit.

I knew pretty much just where the next shot'd fall.

"Hey, Edna!" I shouted. "Answer me a question before y'take another crack! How come y'didn't just stop Koko with your little play-toy—that's the gorilla—an' let the Autodestruct do your killin' for ya?"

"Five seconds, Bernie. Koko's at the panel, and I'm giving her the reversal sequence now."

"But Captain Gruenblum," protested my tormenter, "what fun would that be?"

"Well, you're takin' quite a chance, Edna. She may blow yet—an' take *you* with her!" I peered into the darkness an' driftin' dust, watchin' for the glitter of her gun again.

"So be it!" she shouted back defiantly, "Gregamer and I had planned—"

BLAM! BLAM! BLAM! BLAM! BLAM!

I'd blasted in the direction of her voice, spreadin' my shots a little, dragged m'self as quick as I could t'Georgie's side, right to the same safe little corner in the shadow of the boardin' ramp that Charm'd done his spyin' from. Took me a second to recover from—

BLOMMM!

This time the cataract consisted of steel darts, aluminum confetti, an' shredsa chewed-up lateprene from the gang-plank. There was a pause in the gunplay as I held my fire, figurin' I had four shots left t'Edna's sixteen. My spare magazines were with my combat rig in Win's hovercar, effectively a million light-years away.

Heplar's arm flopped once, twice. Once more in this darkness an' confusion, he was gonna look like a pincushion. Edna had a nervous trigger-finger an' the ammunition t'back it up.

"One second to Auto—" *Clank!*

Even out here I could hear that big lever bangin' back into place. I breathed a partial sigh of relief. Or a sigh of partial relief. Mebbe both.

"—destruct is canceled, thank heavens. But Bernie, I

have a teenage gorilla here who seems to have fainted. What should I do with her?"

"Let her sleep, sweetheart, she's a growin' girl an' needs the rest. Listen, I hate t'bother you, but I'm in sort of a jam out here."

Heplar groaned an' tried t'rise. I woulda slapped him with the slab-sided .45 but was reluctant to expose m'self t'Edna's gunsights. Besides, I was sorta worn out.

"Oh, dear!" Georgie exclaimed. "I didn't notice, with all the other emergencies going on. How can you ever forgive me? What can I do?"

"Take it easy, baby, if I had a quasar-bomb about t'go off behind *my* navel, I'da been a bit preoccupied m'self." I could feel my strength fadin' fast, now. That Olympic-style crawl'd plumb near used me up. Whatever happened better happen pretty quick.

I had an idea an' shared it with m'best girl.

"Ready now, on the counta three?" I laid the under-muzzle of the .45 on the edge of the boardin' ramp, prepared t'draw an instant bead on the office.

"Ready, Bernie!"

"Three!"

FLASH! On went every one of her landin' lights, swiveled straight in Edna's direction. Musta felt like a stroke of lightnin' t'her. Practically nailed her to the wall, that blindin', searin' photon-pressure.

I squeezed the trigger.

BLAM!

A shadow passed in fronta me, totterin' down the gangplank an' muckin' up m'aim. Just as quick a skinny green appendage snaked around its ankle an' jerked.

Heplar screamed.

BLAM! BLAM! One shot left.

BLOMMM!

Heplar pitched over on toppa me, fulla little teensy steel arrows. Somehow I flopped him over behind me, took aim, thought better of it an' ducked.

BLOMMM! said Edna's Remington.

BLAM! replied the Hartford Colt, its sights lookin' right at her midriff.

Silence.

"Well, Grandfa—Bernie, didn't I tell you this could be your Most Important Mission?" Cuthbert looked disgustin'ly pleased with himself as he squatted there behind that dance-floor of a desk. Trouble was, he had the stag-horn handle of a seven-inch bowie knife protrudin' outa his blubbery chest, an' though it didn't seem t'inconvenience him much, it made polite conversation a mite awkward.

He scratched absently around the cross-guard.

"Look, Your Colonelcy, y'can't fool me this time. I realize perfectly well this is a dream. I'm actually lyin' all busted up on a greasy concrete floor in a universe you don't even know exists*—an' I won't stand still for this!*

A big fat droppa blood ran down m'right wrist, the backa my hand, along the index finger an' off, startin' its lazy one-sixth gee voyage to the expensive carpet below.

"You volunteered!" pouted Cuthbert. *"You can't back out now!"*

A chromium house-mouse bulleted out from the Aztec-modern wainscottin'. Ignorin' the pain from my broken bones, I reached down an' snatched the little bugger up. Looked like a teeny walnut-sized Army helmet with a little metallic gooseneck stickin' outa the top an' about a million almost microscopic wirelike legs wigglin' around underneath.

I popped it in my mouth, crunched an' swallowed, washin' it down with a big gulpa coffee from the decanter on m'grandson's desk.

"Skip the bullshit, sonny-boy. You've picked the wrong patsy. I know my rights! Insteada hallucinatin' you, of all the vermin in the known galaxy, I oughta be travelin' through a long dark tunnel, sorta floatin' like, with a brilliant light toward the end. When I get there, this guy with an aura an' a long white nightgown'll hold two fingers up an' tell me t'cough—"

"Don't be sacrilegious, Captain!" With sudden annoyance, he yanked the blade from between his ribs, makin' a horrible suckin' noise, an' tapped the bloody point on his desk-blotter for emphasis. "It must be the baleful influence of the Confederacy. But don't worry, as soon as the Academy takes over and puts an end to their disgraceful anarchism, everything will be just fine."

He smiled so sweetly I considered reinsertin' that toad-sticker somewhere where there'd be more effect. I glanced down at my feet. Somehow those combat bootsa mine'd been done over in bright red sequins when I wasn't lookin'. This generated an idea: I clicked my heels together three times, real smartlike—

"Ain't no place like home. Ain't no place like home. Ain't no place . . ."

"Bernie?"

I looked up into the glitterin' faceted eyeball of a very worried Freenie. Gimme a pain right behind the bridge of my nose—an' the feelin' this was where I'd come in.

"Charm, old mollusk! I thought sure you was done for!"

"I'd never desert you that way, Lord. I only wish I had been able to help you sooner." He was parked there on the floor beside me, his tentacles makin' little nervous pats on m'good shoulder.

Mighta known y'couldn't eighty-six a Yamaguchian by throttlin' his eyestalk. The anatomy just don't work that way—be like tryin' t'strangle a human bein' by the earlobes. Painful, but far from disastrous.

I was still lyin' on that lousy concrete, just like I'd told Cuthbert, but there was a blanket underneath me, an' inflated plastic cocoons the lengtha my right arm, another reachin' from my armpits to m'knees. Touchin' m'face, I discovered a heavy bandage coverin' the right side there, too.

I was gonna miss that eye.

Mary-Beth Sanders leaned over my pitiful remains, inadvertently deliverin' herself of a scenic tour of her *decol-*

letage as she handed me a cuppa somethin'.

"Take this, Bernie. It'll grow hair on your chest."

"Mighty glad you're not in the habit of drinkin' it, then." Not *everything* was broken. "What is it, anyway?"

She blushed. The garage was still lit up like a movie premiere by Georgie's landin' lights, an' I could hear a buncha other people talkin' an' millin' around.

"Vitamins, minerals—and about three ounces of single-malted Scots whiskey. Bottoms up!"

I grinned. "Same t'you, lady. Say, anybody found Edna's body yet? Up in that office-cubby, yonder?" I sipped at the potion. Mebbe she'd exaggerated, but not by much—it was *curlin'* the hair on my *chest*.

A paira human legs suddenly popped over the shotgun-battered edge of the gangway beside an' above me, dangled there an' kicked their heels against the metal framin'.

"I looked up there, too, Bernie," Fran said not uncheer-fully. "There wasn't any sign of her. I noticed the slide of your automatic, locked back on an empty magazine. That's a lot of ammo to expend on just one little villainess, without any tangible—"

"You shoulda been there, girlie!"

"I *know* we should have!" a familiar voice replied. Win Bear clomped down the runway, unlit cigar in hand, with G. Howell Nahuatl trottin' at his heels. "Next time you get invited to a gunfight, why not bring your friends along, too?"

"Glad t'see you're better, anyway," I said t'Howell as he hopped off the last few feet of the gangplank. "See what drugs'll do to ya?"

"I have had *worse* hangovers." The coyote sat beside me on his haunches. "So there *is* a *789 George Herbert*, after all. Certainly impressive, and an extremely nice person, in spite of her long association with Certain Parties. But you'd better order young Koko off the bridge. She appears to be in a button-pushing mood!"

"She can't accomplish any more'n Cromney could 'thout the equalizin' frammis, an' Georgie'll keep an eye on her.

'Sides, she sure as Shiva pushed the right button a little while—say, how long've I been outa contact with reality, anyway?"

Win glanced at his watch. "Guess we got here a little after eight. Hardly time for the blood to congeal. I could still smell gunpowder in the air. I've made a tentative I.D. on the bodies—Heplar, Cromney, that mess over there by the oil drums is Gregamer, I presume. This place looks like the rail-yard scene in *Gone With the Wind*. You've been told we couldn't find Janof?"

"I been told, all right. Say, this vitamin-juice is okay, Mary-Elizabeth. Too bad about m'uniform, though. Wish y'hadn't hadda cut it up this way." Half my coverall was lyin' between m'legs, torn away where they'd put the air-casts. Little wires stickin' out where the environmental controls'd been an' a tag I'd never noticed inside one leg, listin' the penalties for destroyin' Academy property.

She shook her pretty head. "I'm afraid I'm not much of a medic, Bernie, though thank goodness Win carries adequate emergency supplies in his car—must be Clarissa's influence. And I think you'll find someone in Laporte who can repair your clothing so well that—"

I nodded. "Gotcha: had an uncle in the invisible re-weavin' trade m'self, one time, until the Emperor come down with pneumonia an' they strung him up. But..." I looked at my friend the detective kinda sheepishly: "Speakin' of your car, an' of repairs..."

He laughed. "The insurance will take care of it—though they may want to have a word or two with Koko about it—and if not, the newsies will pay handsomely for an exclusive on this little tea-party. In the meantime, I'll—"

There was a boom an' clatter at the fronta the garage. In strode T. W. Sanders, Captain Li-Li, halfa Griswold's Grimmest, an' a paira Freenies, one with a glued-up seam along his back.

Sanders had a mean look on his phizz.

"Not so much as a goddamned footprint! Gruenblum, you not only keep a dirty gun, but you can't shoot for sour owlshit!" He lifted a pistol-filled hand toward the rear of the garage. "The back wall of that office looks like a player-piano roll!"

His junior wife hopped off the gangplank, took a coupla steps toward a stacka 55-gallon barrels, an' kicked at the sole of a shoe I could just see outa the corner of my good eye. It was attached to somethin' lyin' behind the drums.

"Tell *that* to the late Norrit Gregamer here, darling. I made the same mistake myself, but I've had time to think about it: a running head-shot, left-handed, and in the dark? Bernie, you can join *my* militia, any time!"

This from the little broad who lit torches with a plasma-gun. I accepted it as the high praise it was an' kept m'mouth shut. Sanders shook his head, a grudgin' apology on his face.

"How soon can we get moving?" Mary-Beth asked. "We really ought to get Bernie some competent professional attention."

I didn't have any complaints about the attention I was gettin'.

"Well, there's that vet downtown," Koko offered as she emerged from the passenger-level airlock. "Bernie, will you and Georgie take me for a ride before you go home?"

"Of course we will, Koko," a disembodied voice replied behind her. "Won't we, Bernie?"

I tried t'sit up on an elbow—an' got pushed back gently by three setsa hands, a paira doggie paws, an' only Ochskahrt knows how many little green tentacles.

"What's this about goin' home? Back an' forth in time I can understand—an' even handle. How'm I gonna—"

"Take it easy," Fran said. "That's something we'll discuss later. It's all set. How about it, Sis? Can we move him?"

"Unless he'd rather lie there until his bones knit."

Somehow they managed t'lever me up onto a disused tool-cart an' wheeled me toward the broken door where Win's Neova stuck through like some kinda modernistic wall-sculpture.

"Wait a doggone minute! I can't leave Georgie here like this, not after all I been—"

The furry hand of a chimpanzee rested itself on m'good shoulder. "Not to worry, Captain Gruenblum. Griswold's will take good care of her."

I looked up at Li-Li, at his midnight-black uniform, the two big pistols an' the bowie-sword he carried, at the paira throwin' knives tucked down the backa his collar an' the shot-loaded leather gloves shoved under his epaulet.

"I believe it!" Brrrr.

"And you know what, Bernie?" my flyin' saucer chimed. "Captain Li-Li has promised he'll tell me all about the Heller-Browne decision and equal rights for sapient machines! Isn't that exciting?"

Li-Li tried t'wipe the self-conscious expression off his face. "I wanted to be a lawyer," he said, "but my I.Q. overqualified me."

"Swell." I groaned. "Just wheel me home, then, mother. I'll be okay in five of six millennia."

They hadda lift me over the garage doorsill, an' it wasn't easy, as the passage was narrow, my head an' feet were hangin' off the endsa the cart, an' the whole assembly, top-heavy as it was, threatened t'go belly-up any moment. Outside a big black hovervan was waitin' with its back hatches open, studded with machine-gun blisters an' small-arms ports.

Belonged t'Griswold's, natch.

The little cart-wheels skidded, floppin' around sideways, skipped an' dragged through the gravel.

Suddenly, around the corner slashed a yellow ground effect machine, canopy open, a wild-eyed Edna Janof at the tiller, hair streamin' crazily in the wind. One-handed, she levered somethin' big an' shiny onto the edge of the car door, its muzzle pointin' directly at—

BLOMMM! BLOMMM! BLOMMM! BLOMMM! BLOMMM!

Steel slivers sleetin' around us, everybody went for the ground an' their own hardware at the same time. My cart tipped over in all the excitement, spillin' yours truly in the dirt but providin' me a shield. I grabbed at the extra Bren

.40 Will Sanders thrust at me, wonderin' momentarily where m'Colt'd gotten off to.

I ain't even gonna *try* conveyin' what all that ordnance goin' off at once sounded like. Wasn't more'n a coupla ticks an' somebody inside the van let loose with everything they had, concentratin' its heavy firepower on the stolen yellow sportscar as it tried t'work its way around for a second strafin' run.

That Edna never did know when t'quit.

An explosion ripped its swollen plastic skirt from hood-ornament t'trunk, flippin' the vehicle over an' over as smoke an' mountin' flames enveloped it. The damn thing smashed through the flimsy side of an abandoned warehouse. There was a flash inside that lit up all the windows, a bellowin' of tortured steel an' superheated air, an' the walls sorta puffed themselves outward, splittin' at the corners of the buildin', released energy flattenin' everything within a hundred meters.

An' tippin' the ersatz Gurney I'd fallen off of, right over onto my remainin' good arm, snappin' both radius an' ulna with a sound like splittin' bamboo.

I didn't find it humerus.

23

Is It Live or
Is It Muzak?

WE NEVER DID FIND EDNA'S BODY.

Only took about a week t'get the various splints an' stickin' plasters off m'scrawny corporeal essence. Good thing, too; I was beginnin' t'feel as accident-prone as Denny Kent, there, for a while.

Now *that's* a loose end that got tied up good an' proper. Restitution, not imprisonment, is the primary concern of Confederate justice, but it appeared like there wasn't a whole lotta gainful employment for an otherwise unhandy MarxoFriedmanite Neo-Revisionist of the Old School—not in laissez-faire-land—*until* somebody remembered there was a Help Wanted out for a professor of Alternative Moral Philosophy up in Cheyenne.

Shucks, I'd planned t'haul poor Denny back to the Academy in irons, but not even a "defunct economist" deserves the Pylon. Besides, he'd be workin' for the next several dozen decades t'pay Win an' Griswold's an' Birdflower an' Tree an' the owners of all that industrial-district real-estate he'd helped t'tear down an' blow up. Not that *I* felt he was responsible for all of it, but it seemed t'satisfy everyone else, includin' Denny—*punishment's* another religious-based concept the Confederacy's given up.

Dunno as I approve of that m'self.

While I was sequestered in Win's spare bedroom, growin' m'bones back together an' enjoyin' frequent visits with the former Kendall sisters, presently "living under the name of Sanders," I gave a lotta thought t'what I was gonna do back home. Made a certain amounta sense t'stack Merwin, Hul-

235

bert, Heplar, an' Cromney in Georgie's freeze-locker an' present 'em to Academy authorities by way of *some* kinda explanation. But it made me feel like Vincent Price.

Gregamer I'd gladly leave t'whatever fate awaited his counterearthly remains here in Laporte.

What didn't make sense was tellin' the dear ol' Academy about sideways time-travel or the Confederacy. That final nightmare hadn't been altogether as surrealistic as it mighta seemed. They'd wanna move in over here, all right—Confederates are a mighty people in their way, but their civilization seemed peculiarly innocent an' vulnerable t'*this* outsider—an' a lotta swell folks'd wind up radioactive in the process.

So what was I gonna do?

"Georgie, what'm I gonna do? You know how it is back home—hell, they'd take *you* apart, just t'see what makes you tick!"

At the time—a couple days after the battle in Wyoming—she was still parked in that Hell-on-Wheels carbarn, waitin' faithfully for me t'plug in her equalizin' frammis—which I'd withdrawn from Mulligan's Bank & Grill—once I had a paira workin' hands t'do it with.

Her image on the bedroom 'com wall frowned a little, then brightened. "We could always just stay here. I'll bet we could make a pretty good living in the time-travel business. We'd have a monopoly!"

I shook my head, enjoyin' havin' both eyes t'look at her with. "Not for very long. Deejay an' Ooloorie've been playin' with the equations, mostly t'get a stardrive outa. An' I'm sure you recognized that assistant of theirs. Gimme the creeps—sure hope they keep a tighter rein on him here than they did back home.

I looked at my watch. That ersatz Ochskahrt'd *fixed* it, all right. Ran just fine.

Backwards.

There was a lull in conversation as I fiddled with the arrangement of big white plastic pillows they'd strapped to me, housin' the Basset coils that were healin' up m'bones at an unnatural rate.

"Besides, baby, much as I like the people here, human an' otherwise, I *ain't* no anarchist! Shucks, 'thout no rules t'break, what fun would life be?"

She giggled. "The frightening thing is that you really mean that. Very well, then, if we have to go back, we have to. But you're right about the Academy: they mustn't *ever* know about the Confederacy—"

"Or about you!"

"Thank you, my darling, *or* about me. So what are we going to do?"

"No fair—I asked you first!"

Turns out Basset coils work fine on Freenies, too, so once they scraped the glue offa Spin's carapace, I was back t'guessin' which one I was talkin' to.

"I concur with Georgie, Lord, and with you: somehow we must account for ourselves and the time we've been gone—without telling the whole truth."

Mighta been Charm. Didn't matter, the way the other two perched with him on the foota my bed, bobbin' their eyestalks in agreement. Somethin' the little fella said rang a bell in my mind, but a very small one, very faint. Leave it alone—it'd come t'me.

"Well, we can mention the hijackin', even Nagasaki. That much is safe an' duly recorded in Georgie's data-banks." Another tiny bell tinkled in m'subconscious. Annoyin', it was.

"Gee, Bernie," Koko said, planted in an armchair by the bedroom window, "there's all those bodies to account for, too." She was knittin' three tiny sweaters—looked like toilet-plunger cozies.

"Not t'mention the fact that Heplar, at least, was done in with an extremely foreign weapon. Hell, the coroner'll be pickin' flechettes outa his body from now to—"

"Bernie!" Georgie pleaded, "you're making me sick to my stomach!"

Which brought around another conundrum'd been nibblin' at me; Georgie didn't *have* a stomach. She was a thirty-

meter discoid weighin' more tons'n Carter'd had little pea-
nuts an' packin' enough horsepower t'part the Red Sea an'
give it a trim over the ears.

But she was also a painfully-pretty slender five-foot blonde
with robin's-egg eyes an' alabaster skin whom I'd made
passionate love to in a prerecorded fantasy more times'n
I'd care t'relate t'strangers. Embarrassed *m'self,* thinkin'
about it in mixed company.

How real *was* that fantasy? Real enough for an intruder
t'torture her in it, leavin' weepin' puckered wounds with
his imaginary cigarette. I'd verbally reprogramed her recovery, not a scar showin', but when I'd offered to erase
the ugly memories, she'd refused on the grounds that even
the ugliest experiences are a parta personality, of character—obliteratin' them'd be the same as obliteratin' her.

Some kinda girl, My Georgie.

But *what* kind? Made me wonder if the story about Will
Sanders mightn't be true—that he'd *imagined* his way into
the Confederacy. Was it any more real than Georgie's world
of sunlit meadows an' ancient oaks? For that matter, are
any of us real t'one another? Maybe we *all* love a picture
in our heads, a picture a whole lot different from reality—
whatever *that* is.

Is lovin' a *machine,* bein' loved by her, perverted?

Now here we were in orbit, twenty-thousand-odd Confederate metric miles out an' still climbin'. Half a dozen
CRTs were lit up on the console, patched into the Telecom
system. I was sayin' m'last good-byes t'Win an' Koko in
one of 'em, Howell in another, t'Deejay an' Ooloorie who
shared a split-screen connectin' San Francisco an' Laporte,
t'Will an' Fran an' Mary-Beth—not a single one of whom
was any whit more real—nor less so—than the TV phantom
who'd turned out t'be my Georgie. Olongo had a monitor
to himself, which seemed only fittin', somehow.

"Now you're absolutely certain you've got your stories
straight?" the President inquired for the dozenth time. "You
all know what you're going to say?"

All those little bells'd finally jangled into place inside

m'head. "Sure do, Your Executivity. Cromney an' his gang—includin' m'late unlamented, treacherous assistant—pirated up on me when I wasn't lookin', insisted that I take 'em all to a primitive era, an' under great duress, I obliged 'em—the middle twentieth century, t'be exact. I pulled a little wowser on 'em an' let 'em off at the corner of August 9th an' Nagasaki. I think my bosses'll see the humor of that—it's just about their level of sportspersonship."

"What about Merwin and Hulbert?" Howell asked. "They're not going down as mutineers, too, are they?"

"Poor ol' duffers got pulled off as hostages," I answered. "Fortunes of war—another concept the Academy'll go for. Besides, it'll save 'em the pension-money."

Our alibi was pat: I'd lie in m'teeth, with Georgie's doctored records—but not her *real* memories—t'back me up, an' the whole deal signed, sealed, folded, stapled, an' mutilated by the testimony of three Very Important foreign dignitaries my superiors were in a blue funk about, anyway. Georgie's willin'ness t'tamper with the truth'd allow us t'show up back on Luna only a few hours after we'd originally taken off. She ain't a time-machine for nothin'.

She was a very *smart* time-machine these days. Her extra brains'd been the Praxeology Department computers at good ol' Laporte U., Ltd., an' leavin' 'em behind woulda effectively lobotomized her. While I'd been gettin' well, Deejay'd done a bit of remodlin'—now half a hundred innocent-lookin' nontechnical furnishin's—bunkbeds, lockers, plumbin'—were packed with sophisticated Confederate nanoelectronics an' the formerly remote portions of Georgie's personality safely transferred into them.

She'd stand inspection an' maintenance—I checked her out m'self—an' *personally* spliced the DreamCap cable back together.

Playin' the controls like a piano virtuoso, I lined up on the complicated machinery floatin' before us in orbit. Looked like the innards of an old-time Atwater-Kent. In the middle was a Georgie-sized aperture, over which were emblazoned the words J. V. TORMOUNT ENTERPRISES, LTD. Some sorta corporate connection of Olongo's, the biggest Probability Broach apparatus in the Solar System.

I turned around in my seat. "You guys all strapped down nice an' tight?"

Three little pink Army helmets, various semiobscene appendages pokin' out here an' there, gimme the nod.

"Georgie? Got all your electrons lined up in a row?"

The prettiest face this side of Olympus winked at me. "I'm ready, dear."

"All set at your end, Deejay?"

"We're ready," replied the good-lookin' physicist.

"Well, okay, then—no sense prolongin' the agony!" I twiddled dials that'd bring us back to the twenty-third century as soon as we were through the Broach, leaned forward on the tiller, jettin' us toward the aperture.

I scanned the monitors, lightin' at last on the Sanders' screen.

"Good-bye, folks. I'll never forget—"

WHAM!

We popped into a different universe, a giant blue flash behind us as the Broach closed tumblin' Georgie end over end before I got her stabilized. I pushed buttons for a long, leisurely ride back home.

We were in our private sunlit grove of trees at the edge of endless meadows, the breezes fresh as they stirred the knee-high grasses around us. We stood beneath a spreading, ancient oak, Georgie an' I, that same goddamned songbird warblin' in the leafy branches overhead. She leaned against the age-roughened bark, her warm, smooth hands in mine. I gazed deeply into her bottomless azure eyes.

"Baby, we gotta stop meetin' like this. My bones're gettin' too old t'do it outdoors on the ground all the time."

The gentle wind caressed her pale blond hair. She giggled, glancin' downward, dimples appearin' magically in her satiny cheeks. "Just once more, for old-times' sake?"

I shrugged. "I can't say no, not t'you, baby."

Releasin' my hands, she unfastened m'gunbelt. San-

ders'd gotten m'Colt back t'me, an' it was good t'have the
old warhorse around again. I let the rig fall, my heart
beginnin' t'pound, an' I imagined I could see hers beatin'
wildly, as well, in the breathtakin' scallop of her sheer an'
lovely summer blouse. Her breasts were rounded an' in-
vitin'. I bent t'touch her, but she grinned, fumblin' with the
zipper of my coverall in a manner that was no way innocent.

Suddenly, m'eager manhood stood before her. I was
pretty impressed m'self. We—

"Bernie!"

"Errrk!" I snatched at m'shoulder holster, then relaxed
a mite. It was the coronary-ward for me, sooner or later, I
knew it.

"Bernie, we sincerely regret waking you," explained
Charm, his two little buddies lined up right behind him on
m'chest an' parts south.

"What's up, fellas? We home already?" I pulled a cigar
outa my breast pocket an' lit it, dialed a beer.

"Not precisely—but we have an urgent need to speak
with you beforehand. You recall, of course, the original
purpose of our mission?"

Puffin' blue smoke: "Sure. T'see ancient Japan, an'—
oh, you mean *your* mission, don'tcha? Bein' with God an'
passin' the divine experience on to your posterity. Nice work
if you can get it."

He nodded with his eyestalk. "But there is a complica-
tion, Bernie."

"Howzat?"

"Well—and I certainly mean no offense—we have observed you, Bernie, getting hijacked, getting beaten up,
getting lost, getting disoriented by Academy conditioning,
getting arrested, getting drunk, getting shot, getting—"

"Enough, already! I see your point: I'm a real go-getter,
but—"

"But God you ain't," Charm said.

And the Lord spake, even saying, "*Hallelujah!* Not t'leave
out Hosannah in excelcis deo—bananas an' all! That's ex-

actly what I been tellin' you little twerps all along! There *ain't* no god; there's only people, of various assorted shapes an' dispositions."

"And modalities of existence," beautiful imaginary Georgie added from one of the monitors.

"Kinda like the way you put that, honey."

"Yet you see the difficulty, don't you, Bernie?" Charm scooted up another coupla inches an' peered into my eyes. "While we have lost a deity—and gained a great and good friend—we have also acquired a monumental problem..."

"Which is?"

"Which is that our species still believes in you—and we can't bring ourselves to disillusion them. It could very well destroy the civilization you created for us."

"And so," Color continued, sorta theoretically shoulderin' his companion over onto the chair-arm, "we have reached a decision, O Former Lord."

"Make that 'Lord Emeritus'." I had a bad feelin' about this.

"Yes," said Spin, "and we have, er, interrupted you and Georgie to announce it."

"Don't do me no more favors!"

"Be nice," said Georgie. "There's always the Instant Replay."

I sighed. "All right, then—shoot."

"Well, Bernie," the Ambassador said, "since we dare not go back and interbreed our information into the gene-pool—as enlightening as it may be—we have decided..."

"...to remain with you..." Color said.

"...forever!" said Spin.

"Oh, goodie!" Georgie cried, dimplin' up again.

You ever seen a grown man cry?

About the Author

Self-defense consultant and former police reservist, L. Neil Smith has also worked as a gunsmith and a professional musician. Born in Denver in 1946, he traveled widely as an Air Force "brat," growing up in a dozen regions of the United States and Canada. In 1964, he returned home to study philosophy, psychology, and anthropology, and wound up with what he refers to as perhaps the lowest grade-point average in the history of Colorado State University.

Neil recently completed his second stint on the Libertarian Party's national platform committee. In 1978 he ran against an entrenched Republican Speaker for a seat in the state legislature, earning 15 percent of the vote on a total campaign expenditure of $44.00.

L. Neil Smith's previous books—all published by Ballantine/Del Rey—are *The Probability Broach, The Venus Belt,* and *Their Majesties' Bucketeers.*